Murder
on the Lake

Paul Simonson

MURDER ON THE LAKE

ISBN: 978-1-7376308-4-5

Published by

RIVER PLACE PRESS

40274 Diamond Lake Street
Aitkin, MN 56431

218.851.4843

www.riverplacepress.com
chip@riverplace-mn.com

&

Harp Publishing LLC

To the memory of
Dick Johnson
1941-2019
A friend to the end

ACKNOWLEDGMENTS

This book would not have happened if I hadn't joined the writers' group at Mount Cavalry Lutheran Church in Eagan, Minnesota. Thank you to Rich, Mark, Karen and Cameron, and the other members of the group who, over a three-year period, read and provided constructive criticism of rough drafts of each chapter of this book, inspite of having to endure misspellings, bad punctuation, lack of contractions and other grammatical errors. Without their encouragement I would not have completed this effort.

Also special thanks to the people outside the writers' group who proofread the various edits and re-edits, as I moved the book to its final manuscript, and to those who read this work in progress and assured me that it was a project worth finishing.

PROLOGUE

"Revenge proves its own executioner"

John Ford "The Broken Heart"

The silence in the 10 by 20 foot fish house was in stark contrast to the noise inside the fisherman's head. He had come here directly from work since it was his main sanctuary from the storm that had been raging within him for over four years. Even though he had caught three nice walleyes in the three hours, he was having trouble finding the serenity he normally found in this, his one retreat from life. He glanced at his watch noting it was 11:37 p.m., and suddenly felt weary. He took one more drink from his bottle of Jack Daniel's and was surprised to see it was almost half empty. His drinking was one of the first issues he knew he had to confront to recover some normality in his life. He had been warned twice already about coming to work clearly hung over.

He spread his insulated sleeping bag on the single bed that lined one wall of the house, turned down his propane heater, opened a can of sardines and a box of crackers and started eating. He picked up his ice pick and began cleaning out his fishing hole so there would be less ice build-up in the morning.

That's when he heard the door open. He turned to see a large man wearing a ski mask, completely dressed in black. In the light of the kerosene lantern, he saw the flash of the switchblade knife.

Instinctively the fisherman threw his ice pick at the intruder, but in his half-drunk condition he threw it weakly. The intruder dropped his knife, caught the icepick in mid-air, and while yelling a profanity-laced tirade, lunged at the fisherman, burying the icepick into his forehead right above his eyes. The fisherman fell backwards onto his bed as the blood oozed out from the wound, covering his face and the icepick.

The intruder jumped back to avoid being hit by any blood, took off his bulky glove, picked up his knife, and pulled the door of the fish house shut as he left. In the cold moonless night, using a small flashlight, passing fish houses that appeared to be empty, the intruder walked a quarter mile to his car. He drove across the ice, avoiding any deep snow, to a road coming out from a private cabin which the intruder knew was unoccupied. He left the lake, got onto the highway and was gone.

CHAPTER 1

January 6, 1951

Gordon, Ronnie and Larry were on their way to a Saturday Night Dance at Parks Resort in Isle, Minnesota, a dance hall on the shore of Mille Lacs Lake. Larry, sitting in the passenger seat of Gordon's 1946 Ford coupe, said, "It's so cold out I bet we can pick up the Grand Ole Opry." After turning the dial a few turns, it hit.

Ralph Emery's voice blasted out of Gordon's radio. "This is WSM, a 50,000 watts clear channel station from Nashville, Tennessee. It's time for the live Saturday night broadcast from the Ryman Auditorium, brought to you by Martha White Flour. Here is our emcee for tonight, Red Foley."

"Thanks Ralph, great to be here in front of all these great fans, and hello to all you country/western fans out there in radioland. I know we cover a very large portion of the country. I had the honor of playing at the Flame Café in Minneapolis last week. Man, it was cold, but I survived. Had plenty of personal antifreeze in my dressing room. But every fan I talked to up there said they get a clear and loud signal from here, especially on these cold winter nights. Hello Minnesota! I don't get to emcee this show all that often, and I am excited." Red Foley's voice rang strong and clear over the radio.

"The reason I am so excited is we are starting this show with a big bang. Since he has to leave to catch a plane to Seattle as soon as his segment is over, we are having the hottest star in country music on as our first performer. That's right! Here he is, the Love-Sick Blues Boy himself, Hank Williams," Red said as he introduced Hank. "Well, Hank, you're hot!"

"Thank you, Red. Yes, 1950 has been a great year for me and, if the good Lord is willing, 1951 will be even better."

"O.K. Hank, enough talking. What will you start the show with?"

"I'm going to sing my latest release, which thanks to all you wonderful fans, has gone to number one. I think this may be my best song yet—'Cold, Cold Heart,'" Hank announced over the roar of the Ryman Auditorium crowd.

Listening and drinking, Ronnie said, "I'm glad we scored some of that personal antifreeze that Red was talking about. It is too fucking cold to drink beer tonight." Ronnie passed the brown bag holding the quart of Kessler Whiskey from the back seat up to Larry. "Wasn't sure Elmer would come through after he said he'd buy it."

"Easiest five bucks he's made for a while," Gordon answered.

"Hell, probably the only five bucks he has made for a while. Elmer doesn't work too hard," Larry laughed. "Gordon, it's damn cold tonight, may hit 25 below. Hope this wreck you bought keeps running and the heater keeps working."

"Don't knock my car. It cost me a hundred bucks which I earned by working my ass off cutting pulp for your brothers. I should charge a fare every time you ride with me," Gordon shot back at Larry.

"Hey man, we paid for the gas, didn't we? I can't believe you earned a hundred bucks working for my brothers; they must pay you more than me," Larry replied.

"Yaw, a big three bucks. Big deal, maybe they think that I work harder." Gordon kept the argument going.

"That 10 gallons, man, should take us almost 200 miles," Ronnie interjected. "Hope there are some hot babes at the dance on this cold night, maybe even Shannon Willis."

"Man, unless Shannon teaches you something you don't know now, you wouldn't know what to do if you got her out alone," Larry said.

"Yeah, I would be glad to have her teach me something, but at least she hasn't turned me down for a date because my fingers are too short, like she did to you," Ronnie jabbed at Larry.

"What're you talking about?" asked Larry, whose face was turning red as he took a swig from the brown bag. "Where did you hear something like that?"

When the great Casanova of Aitkin County gets turned down by the hottest girl in town, the word gets around," Ronnie said, enjoying the ribbing he was giving Larry.

Gordon, who was also laughing, said, "If either of you got it on with Shannon, and Jay Nyquist found out, you would probably find yourself face down in an ice fishing hole."

Anxious to get off the subject of his rejection by Shannon, Larry said,

"Hey, that's an idea. Let's take a quick spin out to Joey's fish house. On a Saturday night, there might be some action out there. It holds about twenty people."

Joey's fish house was on Mille Lacs Lake, which covers 207 square miles with three counties bordering its shore. It is one of the best walleye fishery in the world. It has a highly developed shoreline with small cabins and Mom-and-Pop resorts. In the summer the lake is a bee hive of activity with all water sports, but in the winter the lake is a city unto itself. For three months, the lake is covered with over 5,000 fish houses some just large enough to hold a single fisherman, to houses that could serve as a second home. Joey's house was out from Ole Johnson's resort a mile north of the Aitkin County line. Ole Johnson and his wife purchased the resort in the late twenties and managed to keep it open though the depression and the war, then enjoyed a boom in the post-war economy. By 1950 he had expanded to over 20 cabins that were fully rented during the summer's months, and had a full-service restaurant serving food from 5:00 a.m. to midnight.

Ole had a license to sell beer, known in Minnesota as 3.2 beer because it has less than 3.2 percent of alcohol content. He also has a license to sell set-ups, which allows his restaurant customers to bring in their own bottles of hard liquor, and then order 7-Up, Coke, tonic water or whatever they wanted to mix with their booze. These licenses allowed his resort to become a popular drinking spot along the lake. Given his location, on the southern edge of Aitkin County far from the county seat, he never worried too much about the age of his drinking customers, especially for the off-sale of beer.

Despite the good summer months, it was the ice fishing income that made the resort profitable. His resort had the best shoreline access for several miles up and down the east shore of the lake, so Ole maintained a virtual highway onto the lake for a distance of over three miles to an area of the lake called "the flats," known for outstanding fishing. Ole and his crew kept the road plowed, checked for ice cracks and assisted the fishermen in moving their houses when they felt the need to find a better location. For this service, he charged a minimum fee of $20 for moving a fish house out to the lake, and he charged cars a daily toll for using his road. That winter Ole had moved 798 houses onto the lake.

As Gordon was driving past the resort, Larry said, "Remember the night we first had enough nerve to try to buy beer by ourselves at this place?"

Larry, who was the youngest child in a family of twelve, had been told by many teachers and others that he had a high IQ. However, having grown up listening to his seven older brothers tell tales of their escapades and exploits, many of which involved alcohol, he had concentrated more on having fun than on his academic life. Standing only 5 foot 8, he was shorter than most of his friends, but was always a leader. With his fair Nordic features and a keen sense of humor he was popular with his classmates and a lot of girls from other schools in the area.

Ronnie yelled from the back seat, "Yaw, I remember. It was one of the first times you got to drive your dad's car. It was a hot Friday night in July between our freshman and sophomore years. Boy, I wish we had some of that heat tonight. My mom didn't want to let me go with you guys. Thought you both were delinquents. I told them we were just going to go watch a town team baseball game in McGrath. Dad then let me go."

Ronnie, was the oldest of two children from a family of German heritage living east of McGrath, about twelve miles east of Mille Lacs. Larry, Gordon and Ronnie were all seniors at McGrath High School. Ronnie was the most handsome of the three. He was 6 foot 2, blond hair and strong Germanic chin. He was also was the most laid back. He often said he just wanted three things in life, "Plenty of beer, fast cars and good-looking chicks."

"Larry, I really didn't think you would have the nerve to go in and ask to buy a case of beer. You were only fifteen but you walked right in like you owned the place." Gordon gave Larry a look of admiration.

Over four years ago Gordon's dad was washed overboard from an ore carrier into Lake Superior. Since Gordon was closer to his dad than his three siblings, the loss and despair that Gordon felt from his dad's death was greater. This grief was increased by the rumors that sprung up around McGrath that his dad hadn't been washed overboard but had jumped ship in Detroit or some other city abandoning his family. Gordon stood 6 foot 4 and weighed 245 pounds, although there was not any excess fat on his frame. Because of his bitterness over the rumors, he had developed an anti-social attitude and was the most likely of the three to do crazy, sometimes violent, sometimes destructive, things.

As Gordon, following Larry's directions, drove through the maze of fish houses all three of them noticed the red lights of the sheriffs' cars off to their right. "Hide the bottle," Larry said as he thrust the brown bag back to Ronnie. "We need to check this out."

A large number of fishermen were outside of their houses; in the cold, blocking the road to the location of the lights. Gordon rolled down his window. "What's happening man?" he said to the crowd in general.

Several responded in union, "There's been a murder on the lake!"

Sheriff Oscar Hewitt had served Aitkin County since 1932. At the age of 28, he had become politically active in support of FDR. Prior to that year, Aitkin County had been a staunchly Republican county, but with the FDR landslide, Oscar easily won his race for county sheriff. Aitkin County, Minnesota's third largest county, was over 50 miles from its southern to its northern border and was 25 miles across from east to west. However, in his 18 years as sheriff, Oscar had only investigated five murders. Two of them had been domestic murder-suicides, and the other three involved killers who knew their victims and had been easily identified.

As he finished his inspection of the murder scene, which happened in a cluster of about 100 houses a mile and a half off shore on Ole's road, he knew this case would be much more difficult. This was a murder of a fisherman, who appeared to have been fishing alone. His new Ford pick-up was still at the scene, and his wallet and fishing equipment seemed to be intact.

Based on what he had been told in a call from Ole, the murder likely happened two or three days ago. None of the few fishermen who had houses nearby, and whom the sheriff had been able to talk to, knew the victim nor had they noticed anything suspicious. As the sheriff finished securing the fish house and surrounding area, the boys drove up.

Larry, whose dad had been an Aitkin County Commissioner for 12 years and was a close friend of the sheriff, jumped out of the car and shook hands with him, as a cold wind caused small whirlwinds of snow to blow around them. "How are you doing out here, Oscar? Is it really true you have a murder on your hands?" By the time Larry finished his question,

Gordon and Ronnie joined Larry and the sheriff to see what had happened.

"That's right Larry. We have a lone fisherman, and someone slammed an icepick into his forehead with a lot of force." The sheriff was actually shaking from the cold. "Might be a tough one. If only it had happened a half-mile south; then it would be in Mille Lacs County, and I could be home sleeping."

"Sheriff, who was it? Someone local?" Larry asked, looking toward the fish house.

"No, he's from Eagan Township south of the Twins Cities. His name is Raymond Kelseltz."

Chapter 2

1936-1941

The best thing that could be said of Molly and Ray's relationship and marriage is that it had survived. Raymond Kelseltz was born in Buhl, Minnesota, on the Iron Range and grew up as a true ranger. Although he didn't subscribe to the theory that women should be kept barefoot, pregnant and in the kitchen, he did believe that a woman's main duty was to take care of the needs and wants of her male partner. However, thanks in part to a mother who was not afraid to talk to her son about sex, he learned that the best way for a man to obtain sexual satisfaction was to take care of his partners needs first. He also learned how to achieve that goal.

Molly Iverson was one of three daughters of the head minister of the second largest Lutheran Church in Minneapolis. Despite her dad's wish that she attend a good Lutheran college, she enrolled at the University of Minnesota and moved into an off-campus apartment with Janet, a high school classmate.

The relationship started on October 17, 1936, at a party in a spacious third-floor apartment in the same house where Molly and Janet had their basement apartment. The spacious room was full of students celebrating the win of the Little Brown Jug football game where the Golden Gophers had defeated the Michigan Wolverines, 26 to 0.

Molly, sipping on a drink Janet had made for her, was watching several couples do a jitter-bug dance to a hot Benny Goodman recording. Janet had called the drink a screwdriver, but, to Molly's surprise, it tasted just like her morning orange juice. It was her first-ever alcoholic drink. After a few sips she felt more in the party spirit.

"Hi, thinking of joining the wild ones on the dance floor?" Ray's question startled Molly.

"Oh, no, I have never danced like that." Molly was feeling flushed from her drink which by now was almost gone.

"Want me to get a refill?" Ray offered.

After a moment of hesitation Molly smiled. "Sure, I think it was called a screwdriver."

"I'm sure it was." Ray's all-knowing look sent a pleasant chill through Molly's whole body. Molly often had been told how her pure Swedish looks, with long blonde hair, full blue eyes and a perfect model's body, was a thing of beauty. However, she always considered herself to be very ordinary.

"Were you at the game?" Ray asked as he returned with her drink and a beer for himself.

"Yes, it was so exciting. Are you a football player?" Molly asked as she took a big gulp of her drink.

Ray chuckled, "You mean for the Gophers? No, I did play for my high school team, but it was a small school."

"Where? I bet you were good. You look like a football player to me."

Ray who was 6 foot 2 and weighed 210 pounds answered, "Buhl, it's up on the range."

As Molly looked a little confused, Ray added, "Iron Range, you know, up in northern Minnesota."

As a new record, Glenn Miller's *In the Mood* started to play, Ray took Molly by the hand and said, "Here is something we can dance to."

Molly, who had never danced except for her tap and ballet classes, started to object, but instead simply followed Ray's lead.

"You a student here?" Ray asked as he pulled Molly close.

"Yes, started five weeks ago, planning on going into nursing. How about you?"

"I'm a junior in the school of civil engineering." Ray, a smooth dancer, guided Molly around the floor. "Do you live on campus?"

"Actually, my roommate Janet and I live in the basement of this house. That's how we got invited to this party."

"Are you 18 yet?" Ray asked in an off-hand manner.

"Yes, had my birthday two weeks ago," Molly answered, not knowing the purpose of the question. Although she had a boyfriend most of her high school years, a member of her dad's church who was talking about becoming a minister, the excitement and feeling overtaking her whole body was a new experience. As Ray gently squeezed the back of her neck and moved her head closer to his face, she impulsively initiated a deep kiss squarely on Ray's lips. "Wow!" she whispered into Ray's ear. "What's happening to me? My whole body is pulsating internally."

Ray smiled, holding her even tighter as they finished the dance.

●●●●●●●●●●

"Good morning," Janet said as Molly came out of her bedroom headed to the bathroom. "Your dad called all ready to see which service you were attending. I told him you were still in bed and I was afraid that you might be coming down with the flu. You have to call him this afternoon."

"Well—" Janet said as Molly came out of the bathroom.

Molly looked at Janet who was watching her like a mother hen watching a new young chick. Then she started to both laugh and cry, saying, "it was so wonderful. I mean I—well, I don't know what to say. I certainly didn't think this would happen this way, and it was, it was so wonderful."

Janet smiled. She was two months younger than Molly and had grown up in a lower-income area of south Minneapolis. Their friendship had developed at Roosevelt High School and had always puzzled Janet. Molly's protective upbringing and her naiveté to a lot of facts of life was surprising to Janet, who had to grow up street smart. She valued the friendship and viewed it as one way to escape the trap of her background.

Now as Molly was expressing the apparent joy of her first sexual encounter, Janet recalled the loss of her virginity. Early in her junior year, she'd been on a double date and the foursome drove to a lover's lane on a cliff overlooking the Minnesota River. Her date was a boy from the neighborhood who she considered a nerd. They were in the backseat of her date's friend's car. They started doing some casual petting, but when she said "stop" and "don't" and "no" the nerd became more aggressive. Within minutes he stripped down her pants and underpants and was forcefully penetrating her. It was over almost as soon as it began. The date rolled off her onto the car floor and said something like, "There now you know what it's like to be with a man." Janet felt some blood trickle down her leg as she lay there recalling the pain of the penetration. She felt valueless and vowed never to be taken advantage of like that ever again.

"I am happy your introduction to sex was so good. What did Ray— that was his name wasn't it—say when he left? I heard him trying to sneak out about five." Janet was trying to hide her envy.

"Oh, he kissed me so tenderly. He's falling in love. He said he will call me this afternoon." Molly was trying hard to maintain her composure.

"Molly I don't want to ruin your dream, but sometimes men say things after they get what they want that they have no intention of carrying out. I don't want you to expect too much and then be hurt," Janet warned.

Before Molly could respond to the warning, there was a knock on the door. Janet pulled her robe tight and asked, "Yes, who is it?"

"It's me, Ray."

Upon opening the door, Janet saw Ray holding a large tray of homemade eggs and pancakes. A thermos of coffee and a bottle of orange juice sat at his feet.

"I thought you girls might be hungry. I'm sure Molly is," Ray said as he entered. "Janet, maybe you can take this into the kitchen and eat what you want. Molly and I have some unfinished business." He nodded toward Molly's bedroom.

From that morning on Ray and Molly were constant companions much to the chagrin of Molly's father. Three months prior to Ray's graduation in the spring of 1938 a mistake happened and Molly became pregnant. On the Monday after the graduation, Ray, Molly, Janet, Molly's parents and Ray's parents, who had been down from Buhl for the graduation, all drove down to Cedar Rapids, Iowa, where Ray and Molly were married by a minister friend of Reverend Iverson.

Ray was hired by Honeywell, Inc., a company benefiting from the increased military spending, at a salary that was substantial compared to the Depression year's wages. With this income, the couple bought a house on a twenty-acre piece of land in Eagan township directly south of the Twin Cities and were settled in their new home when their daughter, Holly, was born on Christmas Day, 1938. In October, 1940, a son, Ray, Jr., was born and Molly felt secure in a good marriage, with two healthy children and an ongoing rewarding love life

This changed on December 8, 1941, when Ray woke Molly up before going to work and said, "After listening to the President last night and hearing all the news, I didn't sleep much and have made a decision. I am going to enlist in the Army Air Corps. I have always wanted to learn to fly. I am going to tell my boss this morning."

"No!" Molly sat straight up in bed. "What about the kids and me? How are we going to survive?"

"Well, we have some money saved. I am going to talk to your dad and my dad, and hopefully they can help out. Everybody will need to be making sacrifices if we are going to win this war. Also, I read an article a couple of weeks ago, stating that if war came so many men may be needed that women will have to join the workforce in record numbers. You may need to get a job. It's good you have learned to drive." Ray had made up his mind.

"Honey, you're too old to be drafted. Why are doing this? What if you don't come back?"

"Life doesn't give any guarantees. You know that. This is something I have to do."

Molly started to cry. "What about, what about, you know, me? What am I going to do alone in bed every night?"

Ray laughed, "That will be the worst part. There are books on self-love. We will have to do it in our dreams."

Ray reported to Fort Leonard Wood on January 8, 1942.

Chapter 3

January 1951

Sheriff Hewitt pulled down his earflaps and pulled up the collar of his winter Mackinaw coat to better cover his face, as he talked to the boys. "How are you doing, Larry? How is your dad? Couldn't you boys find something better to do then be out here on a bitter night like this? Hope that's mouthwash I smell on your breath. You boys are a little young to be drinking anything stronger." The sheriff said as he looked at Gordon.

"We all had some cough medicine, Sheriff," Larry laughed.

"I know you, don't I," the sheriff said to Gordon.

"Yaw, you tried to put me in jail over those batteries Jake lost from his garage," Gordon said with bitterness.

"Damnedest thing I ever saw. Jake was sure it was you. You know he's been operating that garage for longer than I've been sheriff. He usually knows what's happening around it. Boy, how could someone be that dumb to steal five batteries from a garage and then come back three weeks later and try to sell them back to the same garage? What were their names?" the sheriff asked.

"Irving Moss, Virgil Larsen and Eddie Johansson." Gordon quickly provided the names.

"That's right. Jake was so happy to have all his batteries back he didn't press any charges. I wonder if those guys are committing so many crimes they can't remember who they've stolen from. Sorry I had to question you like that. Jake insisted." The sheriff shook Gordon's hand.

"Jake never liked me since I accused him of spreading lies about my dad." Gordon's bitterness switched to Jake.

The sheriff, feeling cold and hungry, had a plan. He knew Larry because of his strong relationship with Larry's dad, and he did not want to leave the crime unattended, so he said, "Can I trust you boys?"

"Sure," Larry responded.

"I really need to get out of this cold for a little while. But the main thing is I need to take a shit before I do it in my pants. So, I need to run into Ole's for a while. I don't want any of the people who are milling around here to come and contaminate the crime scene. While I'm there

I'm going to call the highway patrol and the Mille Lacs County Sheriff to see if I can get a little help watching this site for a few days. Also, I have to get the state boys to come and check the place for fingerprints and other evidence, and I have to call the Eagan police chief to notify the wife. We need to find out where she's been all week. It will be good to warm up a little. Might even have a bowl of Mrs. Johnson's homemade soup. I'm making all three of you deputies for the time I am gone. Keep everyone away from the house and the area I marked off. Of course, don't you look around, unless you want to become suspects too," the sheriff joked. "And don't drink too much of that cough syrup while I'm gone. Don't want to have to arrest my own deputies."

"Sure, we can do this, Sheriff. I always wanted to be a deputy sheriff like in the Westerns movies." Ronnie, who had been standing around listening to the others talk, spoke up.

"Think the wife did it?" Gordon asked.

"Unless she's a hell of a big woman, I don't think she actually did the act. Someone pretty strong buried an ice pick, probably his own, into the victim's forehead. Bloody mess," the sheriff said as he got into his car and drove past the few remaining onlookers.

As soon as the sheriff left, the trio of temporary deputies jumped back into Gordon's car to get out of the cold. "This is exciting," Larry said, "an actual murder happening here."

"That must be his pick-up truck sitting next to the fish house," Ronnie noted as he passed the brown bag up to Larry. "Must be a new '51 Ford."

"Won't do him any good now," Gordon said as he opened his car door. "Gotta piss."

As Gordon walked away from the car, a couple of the onlookers came to Larry's side of the car to talk. Larry told them what he knew and, with some authority, warned them to keep away from the roped off areas. After hearing what Larry could tell them, the group hurried back to their fish houses to escape the cold. As he watched them leave, Larry caught a glance of Gordon in the side view mirror, coming out of the fish house.

"What the hell were you doing?" Larry asked Gordon as he got back into the car. "I told the sheriff he could trust us."

"I couldn't resist. I guess it's morbid of me, but I had never seen a dead person before. Man, the sheriff was right. It's bloody in there, frozen though. Wonder when this happened." Gordon looked a little pale.

The sheriff returned after forty minutes and asked. "Any problems?" Gordon quickly said, "No."

Larry looked at him, thinking he would tell the sheriff about him looking into the fish house. When Gordon didn't say anything, Larry was going to but decided not to get his friend in trouble.

"How well do you boys know the three guys we were talking about earlier, Moss, Larsen and Johansson?" the sheriff asked.

"Not well," Larry said. "They're about five years older than us. Of course, we try to keep on the good side of them. They can be mean asses, especially Virgil Larsen. Why?"

"No real reason. Ole said they were in having a few beers last night, acting a little nervous, in Ole's opinion. You boys better take off. I would suggest you go home, as cold as it is. You should get out of here before the highway troopers I called get here. They may have better noses than mine." The sheriff winked at them.

Chapter 4
Fall 1943

Molly knew Rudy, her immediate supervisor, was approaching as she concentrated on filling her share of the machine gun bullets into the bullet harness as it moved down the assembly line. She had been working at the St. Paul arsenal plant for almost nine months. The plant which was a huge, stark warehouse, with walls painted peagreen, had one purpose. To produce the greatest amount of ammunition in the shortest amount of time possible. It was one of twenty-four buildings in the huge complex where over twenty thousand employees, half of which were women. worked to support the war effort.

Molly had managed to get by for over a year after Ray left, but it was hard. Then she saw the job ad at a wage she didn't think women could make, so she applied and was hired. Given their home was in a rural area of the metro, she had little contact with her neighbors, mostly older German farmers. The job was her first opportunity to have contact with other people outside of her family and a few of her friends, like Janet. These social opportunities had increased two months earlier, when Molly joined a group of 20 or so fellow workers, also working the 10 p.m. to 6 a.m. shift, at the Big Ten Restaurant across the highway from the Arsenal, for breakfast. She had an arrangement with her parents where she would bring Holly and Ray, Jr. to their house on her way to work. They'd keep them for the night and following day until Molly had enough sleep, then Molly would pick up the kids and have time with them until she had to go to work. It was not a good lifestyle, but everywhere you went there were signs with Uncle Sam asking, "Are you doing your part?"

Molly recognized Rudy's approach from the odor that preceded him. It was a mixture of both B.O. and bad breath. Molly expected he had a bottle hidden at the plant which he nipped on during the shift. She braced herself for the harassment.

"Hello Molly," Rudy said as he made contact with his full body against her side. "Have you been thinking about me? Remember last week when I told you that, given you are the best looking woman in this whole damn building, you should be working in the office, not on this fucking boring line." Rudy now had his hand under Molly's work apron and was slowly moving it up her leg on the inside of her thigh. "All you need to do is spend an hour or so with me in my car after work instead of going over to that breakfast for idiots, and I could make it happen."

Before Molly could make any kind of response, Rudy was being jerked away. As Molly turned, she saw him being lifted off the floor by his shirt collar by Tom, the section boss.

"Listen well, you son of a bitch, if I ever see you touching this woman or any other woman on this line again, I will cold-cock you and then send your sorry ass face down on the line. Then I'll tell the women they have permission to do to you whatever their dirtiest minds can think of. After that I'll have Mr. Phillips fire your ass for starting a riot," Tom said to Rudy.

Tom quickly stopped the line to prevent a major pileup, since all the women, after watching the sudden confrontation, were either laughing, clapping or cheering. This caused Rudy to leave the area as quickly as possible.

Molly, who had briefly talked to Tom a couple of times at the after-work breakfast, said, "Thanks, Tom, your breakfast is on me today."

"It's Tommy," he said. "That ain't necessary. Just doing my job. If we weren't so short of able-bodied men, Rudy would have been fired long ago. I've been trying to convince Mr. Phillips that he can make some of you women line supervisors, but he still doesn't believe women can be managers."

Without realizing it, Molly smiled a sensuous smile and said defiantly, "I'm buying."

The breakfast was a loud and happy celebration. Several of the patrons ordered tomato juice after getting the waitress to agree to spike it with vodka. The latest news had spread throughout the grapevine, just after the news about Tommy's actions had made the full rounds. Mr. Phillips, before he had been told about the incident with Rudy, Molly and Tommy, had walked by an open janitor's closet door, looked in and caught Rudy with his bottle in hand. Mr. Phillips fired him on the spot. Also, he had called Trudy Benedict, who most of the women agreed was the best worker on the line, into his office and promoted her to line supervisor. Most of the women either had advice for Molly as to what she should have done to Rudy when he first touched her or assertions, a lot of them rude or violent, as to what they would have done to Rudy; if, in fact he had been sent down the line by Tommy.

Tommy sat down at his usual place; at a different table than Molly. However, Molly bottom-holed the waitress to make sure she got his check so she could pay it. After the breakfast party was over Tommy caught up with Molly to thank her and, as they walked down the steps of the restaurant, he took a hold of her arm. This touch sent a chill through Molly's body that she hadn't felt since Ray left for the war.

As he walked her over to her car, Molly asked, "I know you said one time your home was about 100 miles north of here. You don't drive back and forth every day, do you?"

"No, I have a small sleeping room down on Selby Avenue in Saint Paul."

"I don't know if I should ask this, not knowing your situation with your wife and family, but I, well, I was thinking instead of coming here for breakfast, you could come down to my house for breakfast tomorrow. And if you are willing, we could spend a little time together. If you think it's a dumb—," Molly stopped talking mid-sentence as Tommy moved in front of her.

"Shhh, some of our co-workers are listening to us," Tommy whispered. "There's a gas station three blocks down Highway 10 to the right, and I need gas. Meet there."

During the three-block drive, Molly experienced a wave of excitement, a feeling of stupidity, a yearning for a yes, a fear of rejection, a sense of betrayal and guilt and, lastly the strongest feeling, a need that overtook her whole body.

Tommy, while he watched in his rear-view mirror to make sure Molly was following, pictured his wife Eleanor, at first angry and then very sad from the hurt. Then he recalled their latest fight, and how lonely he had been for the last four or more years, even when he was home, a loneliness based on a complete lack of physical, emotional or romantic contact with his wife.

As Tommy started to fill his tank, Molly pulled up beside his car and rolled down her window. Tom smiled and said, "You know your idea of breakfast tomorrow is a great idea, but that part about spending some time together...."

Molly took a deep breath. Tommy was about to reject the part of her proposal she needed most.

Tommy's smile got even bigger as he continued, "Don't know why we need to wait until tomorrow. Give me your address, in case we get separated, but I will try to follow you."

Molly reached for her purse but stopped. "Why don't you give me your address, and I will follow you. You can ride with me and I can drop you off at your apartment before I pick-up my kids." Molly was thinking ahead in case her dad made one of his infrequent visits. She didn't want to have to explain the second car in the driveway.

When Tommy got in Molly's car after parking his at his apartment building, he learned over and gave give Molly a quick kiss. She responded with a passion that had been building up for years, kissing him deep and long with a force that made both of their bodies quake.

"Wow! We need to get to your house," Tommy gasped when she let loose.

As Molly started driving Tommy said, "I think there is a drug store down the street just past Western Avenue. I should buy some condoms, right?"

"I'm glad you are still able to think." Molly reached over and placed her hand on Tommy's leg.

Tommy came out of the drug store with a bag in one hand and a single orchid in his other hand. "For the lady and for our relationship." He kissed her on the cheek.

For the next three weeks Tommy and Molly were together every Monday to Thursday, with Tommy going home after work on Friday mornings. After working out some details like what story each would used to explain why they no longer were at the after-work breakfast (Tommy said he had some problems at home and now had to drive the 200 miles round trip daily and Molly said she now had to pick-up her kids every day since her parents had to have a break), and how to avoid looking like they were in love while they were at work, the arrangement flourished. Some days they had breakfast first and then went to bed. Other days they didn't wait and went to bed as soon as they got to Molly's house eating later. One day during the first week Tommy suggested they stop at a liquor store where he purchased a case of beer. They drank a few bottles every day.

On the Thursday of the third week, after Tommy joined Molly in her car at his apartment, he said, "I'm really hungry today, but I don't want you to do any extra work. Isn't there a good restaurant down on Highway 13 by your house?"

"I think you mean the Valley Lounge. Ray—I mean—we used to go there on Saturday nights." Molly broke the unspoken rule of not mentioning their respective spouses.

After each of them had a Bloody Mary, a big breakfast and two beers they were both in the mood when they got to the house. Tommy introduced some new techniques into their foreplay resulting in the wildest and most tempestuous lovemaking yet. Afterwards Tommy fell soundly asleep, but Molly, who had reached a sexual high she never believed possible, could not sleep. The whole morning of being at the Valley Lounge, her mentioning Ray's name, and what had just happened with Tommy, caused her to think about when Ray would return. Would she ever be satisfied with Ray again? She tried to block it, but a thought raced through her mind. What if Ray didn't return? With this thought, guilt ragged in her head.

As she lay listening to Tommy breathing hard in his R.E.M. sleep, she recognized a loud car on the street as the sound was the local mailman. She slipped out of bed, dressed quickly and went out for her mail. Among a few pieces of junk mail there was a letter from Ray.

She opened the letter with a crescendo of guilt and anxiety. What if he somehow had found out about Tommy? She was crying even before she started to read.

ARMY-AIRFORCE
RAMFORD, ENGLAND   *Oct. 29, 1943*

Dear Molly, My Love,

Hope this finds you and the kids well. Were you able to do any-thing for Halloween? Of course, they are a little young for trick or treating. Maybe by next Halloween I will be home to take them out. If not, hope to be home for Xmas next year. You may get better reports on the news on what's happening. We don't get told much over here. Of course, the big question is when Old Ike will try to take a ride across the channel. When we go up for a run we can see the whole coastline of England, man you wouldn't believe the mass of ships, and tanks. Everywhere there seems to be troops drilling. More each time.

I do think the krauts are beginning to wear down. Each run seems to have less resistance. Mustang fighter plane has really made a difference. There ain't hardly any Luftwaffe left in the sky and the anti-aircraft flax seems to be less. Maybe they are running low on ammunition. Course we are way too high for it except on our final bombing run. Still need to be careful. I still get scared shitless each time we go up. Still remember what the Major, who gave us our first orientation said. Look to the right and look to your left the probabilities are only one of you will survive this damn war. I do think that it helps mentally to admit I'm scared. We had a flyboy from New York City, Tony, who claimed he grew up in such a tough neighborhood nothing scared him. Each time he finished a run he would come back to the barracks and say, "Man, nothing but a milk run, saw a little flax but it didn't worry me." A few days ago, Tony was gone. Rumor is that the boys in white coats took him out of the barracks in a straitjacket and put him in a Medivac truck.

Another rumor that keeps making the rounds is that we are going to join with the Brits in having a concentrated bombing of one major German city. Like a couple hundred of our B-17s like I fly and a couple hundred of the Brits' big bombers. If we use incendiary bombs, like we are now dropping, it will be a real fire storm. I guess we want to teach that little moustache bastard a lesson. I guess this is war, but after we drop our payload we are usually miles away before we see the blast, but even then, the fireball is so big we can see it very clearly. Each time I see that fireball I can't help thinking there're innocent families down there who had nothing to do with what the Fuhrer wants. What if they are like you, Holly and Junior?

It's funny though what some people think of the Fuhrer's ideas. We have a young flyboy from Alabama by the name of Sherwood Ledbetter, the Third. How's that for a name? He claims Hitler is right about the Negros and Jews. Him and I got into a big argument about that one night. At the end he said, "Ya, I heard a lot of you boys from Minnesota are Nigger lovers." I haven't talked to him since.

Boy, I got mad when I read your last letter. I would like to get my hands on that asshole Rudy. He would think twice about touching a woman like he did to you after I got done with him. You said that Tommy was from 100 miles north of the Twin Cities. If you talk to him again, ask him if he does any ice fishing. Maybe if he lives close to Mille Lacs Lake him and I can do some fishing together. And if he drinks, we can share a bottle. Anyway, tell him thanks from me for taking care of you.

Well it is almost time for lights out. Write soon and give Holly and Junior a hug and a kiss from me. As always, I am kissing this letter as I seal it. That kiss is for you.

Love, Ray

Tommy walked out of the bedroom, naked, to see why Molly was crying so loud. "Is it about Ray?"

"Well, yes—, I mean he is alright if that's what you are asking, but I don't know. This morning was so good for me, and I started thinking, what if Ray was killed and you and I somehow could be together? I was so overcome with guilt and then I got this letter."

Tommy picked up the letter and couldn't help smiling when he got to the paragraph about him. "Come on, honey, let's go back to bed. No sex, let's just cuddle. You need to get a couple hours of sleep so you can work tonight. We can have a little talk about this on the way back to my apartment."

Molly followed Tommy's lead.

After sleeping for a couple of hours Molly still woke up exhausted, so she called her dad and told him she was afraid she was coming down with a bad cold or flu and asked him if the kids could stay the rest of the day with them. Since this was her last work night for the week, she could pick the kids up in the morning and have them for the week-end. Her dad agreed.

She then put a venison roast that her brother-in-law, Roy, had brought down to her the Sunday prior, into the oven. She went back to the bed where Tommy was still sleeping, and whispered into his ear, "Sleep well lover. We have all day until we have to go to work." She then turned off the alarm clock.

Tommy woke to discover the darkness and quickly aroused Molly, "Honey, we way overslept and we need to get going."

"No, we haven't, I made arrangements," she said as she rolled over and kissed him on his mouth. For the second time that day she reached a new sexual high.

After they had showered together, Molly quickly fried some potatoes and heated some canned corn and green beans and served them with the venison roast, which was from a young doe that Roy had shot the opening week-end of hunting season. The roast was very tender and Molly's fried potatoes were delicious. Tommy was impressed and kept fawning over the meal after every fourth bite he took.

As they drank coffee afterwards, he looked at Molly and said, "Shall we talk?"

While Molly sat looking apprehensive, Tommy started. "Since the moment, you turned and looked at me with your smile after I pulled Rudy away from you, I have been living in a world of awe and wonder. I had never believed a relationship with another person could be so enjoyable and all-consuming. I have expected to awake and find it was a dream. Yet when I go home and spend the week-end with Eleanor and the kids, I know it is for real. This morning you cried so hard because of your guilty feelings. Well, I felt strong guilt also, both about cheating on Eleanor and also stealing from a man fighting for his country. Yet, I don't think this relationship is based on our need for passion and sex. I think we both found a partner whom we love. Thinking hard about it, I don't think I ever really was in love with Eleanor. We knew each other, started dating, were sexually attracted to each other and got married. At first the sex was good for me but just basic. We went to bed and did it and went to sleep. Never knew if Eleanor enjoyed it or not. She never expressed much excitement and we never talked about it. Then we started having kids and it became less often. I've tried to bring some new life into our sex life. I found a couple of books, but she had no interest in trying anything different. We got to a point that when she needed sex she would demand I perform and I did but felt like a worker bee servicing the queen bee. After our youngest was born, Eleanor stopped making any demands."

Tommy stopped talking to take a drink of coffee as he let out a deep breath. "Sorry for talking so long about myself," he said as he squeezed Molly's hand. "I don't want to put ideas in your head, but I wonder if you and Ray really were in love. Based on what you told me, I think he took advantage of your innocence, got you a little drunk and induced you to have sex. Sounds like he was good at it, and given your beauty and strong response to him, he made you his one and only. Have you ever thought about what would have happened if you become pregnant? Anyway, we should decide where we go from here and I don't think it should be based on feelings of guilt or remorse."

"You don't know how many times I have thought about not getting pregnant. I would have had two more years of college, had a degree. I always felt that I should be satisfied I had a beautiful daughter, son and a husband who loved me. I guess thinking about it, I've never also said to myself that I had a husband who I loved. Ha, when he told me he was enlisting, I didn't say 'how am I going to get along without you?' My only two concerns were how we were going to survive financially and what would I do without sex. He told me to get a book on masturbation." Molly was crying softly.

"Whose mistake was it that you got pregnant?" Tommy inquired.

"Never thought about that. Was so shocked when it happened. Actually, it was Ray who kept track of when it was safe not to use a condom."

Tommy moved around the table to hold Molly as she began to cry harder. "I think, maybe, what we should do is have a trial separation, you know with Thanksgiving, and Christmas coming up. I expect winter will hit us hard, maybe go to New Years. This has been a pretty intensive three weeks. We should be able to see better with a little break."

Molly, who was a little apprehensive that a little break may prove to be forever, said "You're probably right that we should figure out where we are at. Let's give it a try."

Chapter 5

January 13, 1951

Larry sat listening to the Saturday morning music show on WCCO radio while taking in the aroma of the baking being done by his mom and sisters in the kitchen. He had just finished his Saturday morning barn chores and was waiting for the first batch of hot biscuits to come out of the oven so he could have some with peanut butter and milk. It had been a week since the murder was discovered, but nothing had happened with the investigation as far as Larry knew. As he looked out the window, he saw Sheriff Hewitt driving up the driveway.

"The sheriff is here," he yelled into the kitchen to his mom and sisters.

"Go out and tell him Dad has gone to Isle to buy some cow feed but have him come in for some hot bread and coffee," Larry's mom answered back.

Larry quickly put on his coat and went out into a beautiful January morning. The sun was shining and it felt warm despite the temperature reading on the big porch thermometer of 17 degrees. Larry was excited to hear if there was any news about the murder.

"I sure won't pass up a chance to have some of your mom's great bread, but I need to talk to you first. I have come to see you, not your dad," was the sheriff's response to Larry.

"Did you guys do what I told you to do last week at the crime scene?"

The demanding look on the sheriff's face made Larry decide he better tell the truth. "No, Gordon did go and look at the body in the house. Said he never saw a dead man before. I gave him hell for doing that though." Larry wanted the sheriff to know that he carried out his instructions.

"That's what I thought. The state boys finished their fingerprint check and the only ones they found in the fish house besides the victim's were Gordon's. They had his on file from Jake's battery theft case. I expect the actual killer was wearing gloves. I will have to have a lite talk with Gordon when I see him again. I need to think up an explanation for why I left you boys to guard the house. I suppose the truth is the best."

With the mention of gloves, Larry remembered that Gordon had been wearing big logger's chopper gloves the night they were on the lake. Must have taken them off when he took a leak, Larry thought to himself.

"I have a little job for you if you want to help me further on this investigation. If you do it, you will need to be careful," the Sheriff said. Larry was all ears.

"What do you want me to do?"

"What I am going to tell you, I want you to keep in complete confidence. Don't even tell your buddies if they help you with my plan. Ok?"

Larry nodded his head at the sheriff and said, "Yes."

"When the state boys got done checking out the fish house they took a look at the victim's pick-up. The passenger door had been jimmied open and they found Virgil Larsen's fingerprints on the front seat cushion. I was going to bring them in for questioning, but on the way here to talk to you, I got an idea. I want you and your buddies to get into a conversation with them. While you are talking bring up the murder and see how they react. Maybe they will be dumb enough to say something to prove they were near the fish house around the time of the murder. We think it happened sometime either late Thursday night or in the a.m. on Friday. Also, have any of you three told anyone about the icepick? I should have told you and your two friends not to mention that little bit of information. If Virgil or his two buddies should mention the icepick that would be very interesting. Hey, your dad is coming home," the sheriff said, looking down the farm's driveway. "Does he know about you helping me out last Saturday night?"

"Yaw, I told him about it. Of course I didn't mention anything about our cough medicine."

"Neither will I," the sheriff assured Larry.

As the sheriff greeted Larry's dad and told him he was just visiting Larry to thank him for helping him guard the fish house, Virgil Larsen was walking into the "Bait and More Sport Store" in Brainerd, the largest town near Mille Lacs Lake, carrying an ice auger.

"I understand you buy used sporting goods," Virgil said to Amos, the store owner.

"Yes, we do. What you got?"

Virgil held up the ice auger. "Done ice fishing for the year. Need a little cash."

Chapter 6
November 1943 to July 1944

The weather reports were the focus of all the workers at the Arsenal on Monday morning following the Thanksgiving weekend. A major snowstorm predicted to start at around 10 p.m. had moved in faster than expected, and the snow had accumulated to six inches by 5 a.m. It was still snowing several inches per hour and was going to continue at that rate for a few more hours.

Tommy surprised Molly as she was working on the line by coming up to her and talking. Since the day they had agreed to try a separation to deal with the guilt both of them were feeling, Tommy had avoided any contact, and neither one had gone back to the after-work breakfast group.

"Have you looked outside lately? I don't think you can make it to Eagan in this snow storm. I put my snow chains on my car during my break, so I'm pretty sure I can make it to my apartment. Call your dad and tell him you are snow bound, and are staying here at work, then come with me." Tommy talked in a hushed voice. "We need to talk anyway."

Molly, who had been tempted dozens of times to approach Tommy and ask him to come home with her and had spent the last hour worrying about being stranded on the way home in the snow storm, was shocked how Tommy was fulfilling her desire and relieving her worry in one simple request. "What if someone sees us leaving together?" Molly said trying to not sound overly eager.

"In this snow storm, no one will notice."

Tommy was right. The day shift was cancelled and everyone was preoccupied with how they were going to get home. With all his experience driving in snow storms on country roads, Tommy maneuvered through traffic and around cars which were stuck, mired or sliding on hills due to the snow. Molly was impressed with Tommy's driving and felt a strange sense of excitement. She was on an adventure with the man she knew she loved.

After getting as far into his parking spot as he could, Tommy opened his trunk and picked up a box. "Luckily I packed some food and supplies when I left home." He then led Molly up the back stairs of the apartment building to his third-floor apartment. It was a single room with a small kitchenette to the side, with only two chairs and a small table as furniture.

"Where is the bed?" Molly asked with a stunned look.

Tommy set down the box in the kitchenette, stepped over and moved Molly back, turned a latch on the wall and lowered the Murphy bed. "A bed fit for my queen."

After two hours on the bed where neither could get enough of each other they fell asleep, waking to discover it was almost 1 p.m. "I need to call my dad," Molly said as she jumped up. "Told him I would call by noon."

"We will need to get dressed and go down to the building sup's office. He's an ornery old cuss, but I will bring this down with a glass to give him," Tom said as he pulled a bottle of Seagram's Seven out of his box. "With this he will probably let you talk all afternoon."

After the call to Molly's dad, the couple returned to Tommy's apartment. Tommy made two baloney sandwiches and opened a bag of potato chips. With a couple cans of Seven-Up he had in his small refrigerator he mixed two Seven-Sevens.

"This is the first drink of whiskey I have had in my life." Molly raised her glass as a toast and clinked her glass against his. With a voluptuous overtone she whispered to Tommy, "You certainly have led me down the road to decadence. Here's to decadence."

After their feast of baloney sandwiches and two drinks, Tommy and Molly set the alarm to allow enough time to get Molly's car out of the snow and ready to run before the start of their shift, and then returned to the Murphy bed to talk. Before any real conversation could start they fell into a sound sleep in each other's arms.

For the next seven months, the love relationship flourished. Most of the days they were together were spent at Molly's house, but every so often Molly, feeling naughty, would whisper, "Murphy bed," to Tommy when he walked by her at work, and the day would be spent at Tommy's apartment. On some of those days, the couple would go down half a block to Tiewiski's Bar for lunch and Molly would have a couple of whiskey drinks, as she called them.

As spring and summer weather came, they would enjoy the outdoors, taking a picnic lunch to Minnehaha Falls in Minneapolis or driving along the Mississippi River. When Molly and Janet got together after a ten-year hiatus, Molly told Janet that this seven-month period was, and always would be, the highlight of her life.

Despite the pleasure the couple was enjoying, some incidents were foretelling future problems. On Christmas Day Molly entertained her whole family in celebration of both Christmas and Holly's fifth birthday. One of her sisters and Holly both noticed and commented on Molly's glowing demeanor. "Mommy has never been happier," Holly declared after Molly's sister had said, "Molly, being a working woman must be good for your soul." Later that day, Molly's dad, helping clean up, took a bag of garbage to the trash bin. Just when he was going to walk back into the house, he saw a discarded condom package next to the bin.

Reverend Iverson did not say anything to his daughter directly, but on the third Sunday after Christmas, as Molly sat with the family in their customary seats in the front pew, he did not deliver the normal sermon instead preached about adultery.

In this time of war, when so many of our young husbands have been taken away from their wives, the devil knows how difficult and lonely it is for the wives who have been left at home, especially when they have to sleep alone in the marriage bed. Yes, the devil in his cunning can create situations and opportunities wherein the wives will be tempted to engage in illicit acts of adultery. Just like in the Garden of Eden when, in the form of a serpent, he tempted Eve and not Adam to eat the fruit of the forbidden tree, the devil knows the weakness of a woman with God given desires. Of course, it is not only the unfaithful wife who is committing a sin. The man too is also breaking both the Seventh and the Tenth Commandments. Yet, God in his mercies will forgive this sin. Even one of his chosen, King David, saw a woman of beauty and coveted her. Not only did David and Bathsheba commit adultery, but David ordered that her husband be killed, thereby committing murder. However, upon realizing the extent of his sin, David threw himself on the mercy of the Lord and was forgiven. Let us Pray.

After the sermon, Molly's dad said to her, "Sweetheart, anytime you want to talk, call."

Molly did not take him up on his offer. She was in denial that he was talking about her, even though her mom gave her a pat on the knee, a brief smile and had quietly whispered, "Don't worry, things will be all right."

At work Molly was becoming more aware of rumors about her and Tommy. Often when she approached a group of women who were talking, she sensed that they were suddenly changing the subject. A co-worker, Helen, whom Molly believed had disliked her from the first day Molly worked, sinisterly asked her one day at break, "When is Tommy going to get you a promotion, or haven't you slept with him enough yet?"

These detractors notwithstanding, Molly was certain the relationship with Tommy was meant to be, and without knowing what Tommy would do about his marriage, she decided she would have to end hers. On a warm July Sunday afternoon, she took Holly and Junior to a park near her parents' home, where she had played as a child, and while they played, she wrote, after several drafts, a letter to Ray.

Dear Ray,

After several attempts to make this letter less harsh, I am going to be direct. In your last letter to me you complained that my letters were getting less frequent and less personal. I'm sorry, but it is true. The reason is that since you have been gone I now realize that I never loved you. You may not have noticed, but I have never said I love you, even during our most passionate lovemaking. Yes, there is another man. His name isn't important, but I have discovered a person I love and am experiencing a joy and excitement I never knew was possible. This is not about satisfying my sexual needs. This is about an internal high I have when I am with this man and the lonely low I feel when we are apart. Feelings I have never had in our marriage.

I will be talking to an attorney. Don't know if we can get a divorce before you come home or not. I know there will be questions to settle and all that, but I hope it can be done without too much bitterness for the children's benefit. But whatever ever happens I need to be out of our marriage.

For the Good Times we have had,   Molly

At first planning to send the letter without talking to Tommy, Molly decided to wait until he read it in case she should be saying something she wasn't or not saying what she had. She was sure Tommy would be excited about the letter.

The next morning, after having their usual passionate post-weekend love making session, and sleeping for several hours, Molly got up and finished preparing a meatloaf dinner she had started Sunday night. The dinner included mashed potatoes with gravy and the first sweet corn of the season. Tommy woke to the beckoning aroma of one of his favorite meals. "Wow, sure is better than baloney sandwiches," Tommy said as he finished a piece of the crowning touch to the meal, fresh apple pie.

It was then that Molly excitedly showed Tommy the letter to Ray. After reading it and then looking at Molly and then reading it again, Tommy said with a tone of sadness, "I don't think you should mail this."

Molly, for the first time feeling anger toward Tommy, was so stunned she didn't know what to say. She started to cry. "I thought you would be excited. I spent over an hour trying to get the right words. Why don't you want me to be free? Does that scare you? Why?" She ran to her bed.

Tommy slowly walked into the bedroom, sat next to Molly and placed her head on his lap. "Oh, Molly, what have we done? I guess we both knew this day would come. I have been thinking almost constantly for the last several weeks how to get out of my marriage and then ask you to do the same. But each weekend I spend with my kids I realize that if they were left to be raised by Eleanor the boys would become delinquents. She has no control over them. It is bad enough when I am gone during the week. If I left them so I could marry you, I am sure they would feel abandoned. They are at the age they need a father the most. Besides that I'm afraid we have a problem at work."

Molly, who was crying even harder, raised up to look at Tommy directly. "What are you talking about?"

"Mr. Phillips called me into his office about a month ago to talk about how the Defense Department is very sensitive to wives of servicemen who are working at defense plants being subject to harassment and seduction by male supervisors. He supposedly told me this so I would watch out for employees under my supervision. It was clear to me what his message was. He then said 'Tom you are a good employee I would hate to lose you.' Last week he said to me, 'Tom you have to watch your Ps and Qs'. I realized that without the job we would not be able to continue our relationship. That's when I started to look at the gut-wrenching future without you. It will be the most difficult decision of my life, but it may have to be made. That's one reason I don't think you should mail the letter. I am not sure if the Arsenal would find out quickly about it, but if they did I am sure we would be fired."

"What are you saying? What should we do?" Molly could barely talk.

"Well, as hard as it was I'm afraid we need to have another separation for a while and see if the dust settles."

For the rest of the week they did not see each other or have contact at work until Molly arrived for her Friday shift. Tommy was waiting for her in a light rain at the plant entrance she used.

"It was too late. I've been fired. You will be fired as soon as you punch in. Mr. Phillips said that an agent from the Defense Department's inspection service has been following us for the last couple of weeks. Also, Trudy Benedict heard us the morning of the breakfast when we planned our first meeting. She wasn't going to report anything, but several of the other women complained, so she finally told Mr. Phillips. With the war going well now, there is a surplus of the ammunition we are making so there is going to be a major lay-off in a few weeks. Mr. Phillips was going to wait until then, but the inspection service said, no. However, he is going to put in our record that we are a part of the lay-off so our chance of future employment is not affected."

Through her tears, Molly asked, "Do I even need to go in?"

"Yes, they have your final paycheck. You also have to sign some non-disclosure forms and I think Mr. Phillips wants to talk to you. Apparently, he has gone through something like this himself."

"Are you going right home or can we see each other tonight?" Molly toughened herself as she prepared to go in to be fired.

"I will need to go back to my apartment to pick up the few things I have there and tell the caretaker I won't be back. Then I will come to your house. Guess I better take the few things I have there," Tommy said with a sense of finality.

As the rain fell harder outside, they spent the night both trying to make it an unforgettable last time together. However, overpowering sadness was the only emotion either would feel until they fell asleep.

In the morning, Molly made a big breakfast of eggs, American-fried potatoes, pork sausage, pancakes and coffee. In silence, both of them tried to eat, but neither had an appetite. After just looking at each other for a few minutes, they each reached for the other, held on and cried, knowing once they let go it would be over.

Tommy finally broke the silence as he handed Molly a piece of paper. "This is the address of my brother, Si. If you need to write to me, send it to him for my attention. I explained the situation to him last week in case this would happen. It may be best if we don't write too often. I'll look forward to each letter, but it will hurt reading them without being able to be with you."

"Si, is that his full name?" Molly asked.

"No, it's short for Silas. I also have a brother Peter, who, of course, is called Pete."

"Is there a brother, Judas?" Molly attempted to interject some levity into the conversation.

Tommy laughed and took Molly into his arms. "I can now say I have loved and have been loved. Before you, I was not able to say that. Life takes strange turns. Who knows? Fate may allow us to be together again, so I'm not going to say this is a final good-bye." Tommy left.

Chapter 7
January 1951

Irving Moss, Virgil Larsen and Eddie Johansson's close friendship was like Gordon, Ronnie and Larry's friendship except they were about five years older and at this point in their lives they were better known to the local police. All three had graduated from Isle High School in 1946.

Eddie, who was a year older than the other two, had graduated with them. In 1945 he turned eighteen while he was still in high school and was drafted immediately. He was sent to a training base in Arkansas, along with a large number of other eighteen-year-olds, to prepare for the invasion of Japan. Upon the surrender of Japan in August, all of these draftees were discharged and Eddie then returned to high school and got his diploma. However, after a year he reenlisted in the army and served three years.

Irving got a job at a local saw mill and worked there for four years before getting a construction job in the Twin Cities during the summer and collecting unemployment benefits in the winter.

Virgil, someone you didn't want to be on the wrong side of since he was strong, tough and very mean, decided to be a Marine after watching war movies throughout high school. When he was still in basic training at Camp Lejeune, North Carolina, he got drunk at an off-base bar and beat a black teen so badly the boy spent six weeks in intensive care before recovering. He was charged with assault and attempted manslaughter. An all-white military court martial panel acquitted him on the grounds of self-defense, but he was given a dishonorable discharge from the Corps. Since the discharge, he had worked several jobs including one at the local fish lure factory, another doing highway construction, and some work for local loggers. In between these jobs, he spent 90 days and then six months in jail for several drunken driving offenses, including one that involved an accident where a young boy was seriously injured.

Thursday night, after Sheriff Hewitt had asked Larry to help his investigation, Larry suggested to Ronnie and Gordon, that they go to Wahkon, another small town on the south shore of Mille Lacs Lake, without telling them why. Larry knew that the Wahkon Inn, with its backroom pool hall, was a hangout for Virgil, Irving and Eddie.

"Well, lookie, lookie, here, if it isn't the boys from McGrath. Are you still sheriff deputies?" Virgil greeted them as they walked into the pool hall.

"No, we were only deputies for about half an hour while old Sheriff Hewitt went and had some hot soup and got his ass warm," Gordon retorted. "We didn't even get to wear a badge."

"That's right, the sheriff tried to put your ass in jail when we had that little mix up with Jake about the batteries each of us thought the other one had paid for," Virgil smiled.

"Right," Larry said. "It's easy to get confused like that, especially at 2 o'clock in the morning."

"Shut your smart mouth or there might a second murder for all the old farts in this town to gossip about," Virgil said facetiously. "Come to play a little pool and lose some money? Eddie is just waiting to take it from you." Virgil slapped a five-dollar bill onto the pool table.

Gordon quickly matched it. "Ronnie's our man. The beer this extra five is going to buy sure will taste *good*."

Ronnie, who was the best pool player of the three, sank two solids on the break. "Looks like you got stripes," he said as he pointed his stick at Eddie.

The game continued until each player had one ball left. Ronnie then, after calling his shot, banked the cue ball off the left cushion, ricocheted it off the eight-ball, and kissed his remaining ball, which sunk into the right corner pocket. The eight-ball rolled dangerously toward the right middle pocket but stopped. Ronnie tried to catch the outside of the eight-ball with the cue ball but missed. Calling his shot, Eddie tried to bank his remaining ball off the eight-ball into the right middle pocket but hit the shot so hard his ball caught the corner of the pocket and rolled to the center of the table while the eight-ball went directly into the other right corner pocket.

"Five dollars of beer," Gordon shouted as he grabbed the 10 bucks.

Double or nothing, you and me," Virgil said to Gordon

"I don't play games," Gordon said with such intensity it jolted the comical atmosphere of the night.

Shaking off Gordon's comment, Virgil turned to Larry, "How about you?"

"I don't play for money. Play you for a beer." Larry went to pick out a stick.

While they were playing, Ronnie who was sitting out of view of the bartender in the bar room, drank a beer Eddie had brought him and said to him, "Did you see the Ford pick-up the murder victim was driving? It must have been a 51."

"No," Eddie innocently said. "It was a 1950. Not much change, but the highlights are different. I checked it out. Probably bought it on a year-end close out."

Virgil instantly stopped playing and pointing his pool stick at Eddie, said, "Shut up, Eddie. Remember what they said during the war. 'Loose lips sink ships.'"

The following Saturday morning, Sheriff Hewitt arrived at Larry's house just as the final batch of bread was coming out of the oven. Larry met him outside and before leading him in to get his full fill of the aroma and the bread, gave him a full report on the conversation about the pick-up and Virgil's reaction.

Chapter 8

October 1944 to August 1945

Ray was discharged and arrived home by train on October 20, 1944 before he had finished his full four-year enlistment at the request of his employer, Honeywell. This request was granted by the Defense Department since Ray was needed to work on a contract Honeywell had to build special arming devices for a highly secretive project.

Molly, with both kids, picked Ray up at the Union Depot in St. Paul. Molly was completely perplexed not knowing how she would react. She was trying to act normal, hoping Ray would not detect her apprehension of being intimate with him. She was sure he would take some time off before going back to work and they would be spending a lot of time together which would require her to maintain her dark secret day and night. The words she wrote in the letter she hadn't mailed kept running through her head as she watched Ray disembark from the train. As he walked towards them he was stopped several times by strangers wishing to thank him for his service. Holly, who had started the first grade in September, was the most excited to see him. Ray, Jr., had barely known his dad before he left and was a little scared with Ray in full uniform.

"How is my little sweetheart?" He picked Holly up and swung her around in the air. "You're going to look just like your mom." He then picked up Ray, Jr., and swung him around. "My you are growing. You will be hunting and fishing with your dad soon."

He then turned to Molly. "Talk about a sight for sore eyes." He grabbed her, hugged her hard and kissed her on the mouth. Molly, reacting spontaneously, returned the kiss.

"Honey, I hope it doesn't upset you too much, but I've been ordered, almost like I am still in the military, to report to work tomorrow afternoon. I'm going to be assigned to a top-secret job that I can't talk to anyone outside of work about, not even you. Guess I will be working some long hours, but you won't believe the pay when you see my first check. I know it's been hard financially while I've been gone, but we'll be on easy street soon. By the way, I shipped a box full of gifts for all three of you. Should come next week."

Molly felt a wave of relief; maybe things would somehow work out with Ray preoccupied with his job.

Ray was fully involved with his job for the next nine months. He was working six or seven days a week, 10 to 12 hours a day. He was often too tired to engage in sexual activity when he was home but when he wasn't, Molly's response was less than intimate. Ray was too inattentive to notice.

Another facet of Ray's return home was diverting attention away from Molly's lack of receptiveness to Ray's attention. Ray was beginning to show symptoms of post-traumatic stress. He would jump up in bed at night crying, "They're burning," or "We're hit, we're going down." Sometimes he would just go to the bathroom, urinate and come back to bed refusing to talk to Molly, sometimes he would go into the kitchen and take a shot of Jack Daniel's, sometimes he would yell at Molly when she asked what was wrong and sometimes he would talk. "I see kids' faces looking up at my plane and they're on fire, or I see burning people shooting at my plane with rockets and hitting us." By the end of the nine months these episodes were happening once or twice a week. Ray also began having mood changes and would on occasion yell at Molly or one of the kids over small occurrences that, for no explainable reason, annoyed him. He also reported to Molly about arguments he would have at work, with reports becoming more frequent.

On July 13th, Ray surprised Molly by coming home at four in the afternoon, driving a new Mercury sedan. "I think we should get a babysitter tonight and go out and celebrate." Ray showed Molly a $5,200 check. "It's a bonus check. We finished the secret project. Now I will be working regular hours, but my boss suggested I take a few weeks of vacation. He wants me to check with the VA about some counseling. He says the problem I'm having is common among veterans who had stressful duty."

Molly, trying to digest the bundle of news, said, "What about the car?"

"Oh, I traded our old wreck for this beauty." They both walked around the new car. "I got it at a new Ford dealership up in Bloomington. This is only one of five new cars available now that Ford is able to produce new cars again. Was thinking now that we got some extra money, I would buy a used pick-up to drive to work and for hunting and fishing. This will be your car." Ray grabbed Molly and hugged her hard. "I know it's been hard for you since I got home. Maybe now we can get back to a normal life and start enjoying each other like before I enlisted."

Internally, Molly's body shuddered. The day she had dreaded, the day the truth about her infidelity becoming exposed, was coming near.

"There is that good steak house up on West Seventh in St. Paul," Ray said as he and Molly got into the new car. "How do you like the new car smell?"

"Fine," Molly responded.

Except for a brief conversation about a conference Molly had with Holly's first grade teacher, the couple didn't have any more conversation until arriving at the restaurant 10 minutes before their reservation time.

As they waited for more than forty minutes to be seated, Ray became very agitated. "This way, please." The host led the couple to a table next to the kitchen entrance.

Shortly after being seated, a loud noise erupted when a dishwasher dropped a whole pile of trays. Ray jumped and his face projected a strange look.

"You O.K.?" Molly questioned.

Ray, clearly trying to regain his composure, said, "I'm O.K., just had a memory of the first bombing run during my beginning flight training. We would hear the sound of the explosions. My first thought was, are we going to be dropping these on innocent people. I have never forgotten that worry, each time I made a run. I never mentioned it in my letters, but our crew made 127 bombing runs, dropping over 4,000 pounds of explosives each time. Our targets were supposed to be military targets but I always wondered how many of the casualties were just people like you and me. Were they our enemies?"

As Molly reached over to hold Ray's hand, the waiter came to take a drink order. "Jack Daniel's, with a Hamm's chaser," Ray said without hesitation.

"A Seven-Seven," Molly said just as fast.

"A Seven-Seven, when did you start to drink whiskey?"

Molly, for a second, thought of telling the truth but with Ray already upset about the kitchen noise, lied. "Janet and I had lunch a couple times. It's her favorite drink now."

The night went from bad to worse. Ray's steak was not done like he ordered and was tough. He complained about the steak and drank more. He complained about the service and drank more. He talked more about flying and his fears and drank more, until he became loud.

The restaurant owner came over and said, "Sir, please be more considerate of the other customers when you talk."

This led to an emotional outburst. "Spent my last three years fighting my ass off to protect these fucking customers and now all I get is bad service, noisy seats, and horseshit food."

The owner stepped in front of him before he could say more. "Sir, you have two choices. Shut your mouth and leave quietly or tell your complaints to a police officer, who will be here in a few minutes."

Molly stepped in front of Ray and took his hand. "We're leaving. Where is our check?"

"Your night is on the house, given your husband is a veteran, but don't ever come back."

Molly drove home, as Ray sat in the passenger seat and raged. Once home, Ray went into the kitchen, got his bottle of JD, sat in his favorite chair in the living room and drank until he passed out. Molly slept alone.

On the following Monday, despite being on vacation, Ray got up early and turned on the radio to WCCO and started listening to each newscast. When Molly asked what he was listening for, he said, "You'll see." Then just after 10 a.m., a news bulletin was broadcast.

> This is CBS in New York. Various sources have reported, and by all accounts it seems accurate, that a very large explosion happened early this morning in the New Mexico desert which was followed by a white mushroom shaped cloud. Neither the White House nor the Defense Department would comment, but several experts believe it was a test of our first atomic bomb.

Molly waited for Ray to comment after he turned off the radio in the middle of the latest farm report, but all he said was, "What do you think we should do for our vacation? I was thinking we could drive up to see my family in Buhl. My folks haven't seen the kids since last Christmas."

In reaction to the suggestion, Molly asked, "When are you talking about? We would have to get a few things ready." The idea of being together for 24 hours a day for an extended period of time worried her. Would she be able to maintain her oppressive secret?

"I'm going to call the VA now and see how soon I can get an appointment. If it's not this week, we go tomorrow."

Molly didn't argue. She decided it may be better traveling than being home with Ray for the whole vacation. "I'll get busy and wash some clothes, and then I'll run to the store and buy a few things for the road."

While Molly was talking, Ray got a phone call from one of his co-workers. "Ya, I heard," was his only response.

The next morning the family started on the trip. Ray had made appointments for counseling sessions with the VA starting Thursday of the coming week so they had 10 free days to travel. Molly remained nervous. Last night Ray had been the most amorous since he came home and Molly put him off by saying she was worn out from getting ready for the trip. She was hoping that the sleeping arrangements at Ray's parents' house would be less than completely private, so it wouldn't be conducive to intimacy.

"I think we'll take Highway 65 on the way up, and we can stop in Duluth on the way home." Ray outlined his plan as he drove out of the driveway. "That way we can see some different scenery."

The drive to Highway 65 required going through downtown Minneapolis amid rush hour traffic. This stress on Ray resulted in several verbal outbursts. "Can't the idiot see the light is green?" he yelled when a driver in front of him failed to go the instant a light turned. "You bastard, I should've drove right into you," when another driver cut him off to make a right-hand turn. "If this asshole doesn't speed up, we won't get out of town until dark," when a driver, who was going the speed limit, slowed Ray on a single-lane street. Each time Molly told Ray to control his anger for the benefit of the kids. Ray agreed until the next time. Molly looked at Ray and remembered how mellow he was before the war and how he had changed; a pang of angst ran through her body. How would he react when the time came for her confession of infidelity?

When they finally made it out of the city, Ray drove along at 80 MPH when there were no cars in front of him, and passed them as soon as possible when there were, sometimes taking foolish risks. Twice, if the oncoming car had not slowed, he would have had difficulty getting back into his own lane safely. Molly, who never felt insecure as a passenger before, began to feel nervous. "Ray, be careful. You're going to kill us all. Think of the kids," she said after the second close call.

"What happened? You've became a back-seat driver while I was gone," Ray retorted, but he was more careful in passing the rest of the trip.

As they proceeded north, they passed through the town of Mora. As they were leaving, Molly noticed the sign, "McGrath 26 miles." This immediately triggered a barrage of feelings about Tommy. She had never been to McGrath and did not know where he lived, but she knew it was close by. She had written over a dozen letters to him but had only mailed three. Each letter followed the same format. A description of what events had transpired in her life since the last letter, proclamations, with different adjectives, as to how much she missed him and how much she loved him, and a declaration of her deep desires for him and her hope that someday faith would allow them to be together. Tommy had answered the three letters she had sent with shorter letters containing brief summaries of his activities since the last letter, and an acknowledgement that he also was lonesome for her and treasured the idea of the two of them being together.

In his last letter, which she had received in April, he had informed her that he was going to be starting new employment. He was going to be a crewman on a freighter that hauled iron ore from Duluth to Lake Erie. It was a seasonal job from April to November. He had sent an address that she could use to write to him while he was on the ship. "He's probably not home now anyway—he's probably in Detroit or Cleveland or out on the Great Lakes somewhere," she said to herself. Yet she felt a strong sense of closeness to Tommy as the car drew nearer to McGrath. Then as she looked at Ray, she thought about where she had hidden the box containing all those letters as well as the Dear John letter she had written, but not mailed, to Ray. They were in a shoe box on a shelf in her clothes closet. Ray should never have reason to look in her closet, but now that he was going to be home more often, she needed to find a better place to store the box. She certainly didn't want Ray to find out about Tommy from the letters.

Almost like he was sharing her thoughts, Ray said as the city limit sign of McGrath came in to view, "Did you ever ask that guy who rescued you from that molester—What was his name, Tommy—right, if he lived near Mille Lacs Lake? You said he lived 100 miles north of the Twin Cities and that's about here. The lake is just west some 10 to 15 miles."

Before Molly could answer, Ray had, without slowing down to the 30 MPH speed limit, passed the café, bar, store, and Jake's garage that was the whole town, and was exiting McGrath. "I did talk to him a couple times, and I did ask about ice fishing. But if I remember right, he said he didn't do much fishing." Molly looked at Ray, who was looking at the road not her, to see if the question was just a random thought about being 100 miles north, near Mille Lacs Lake, or a probe of her relationship with Tommy. She was satisfied that it was the former and not the latter, but she also realized she had just told the most direct lie yet about Tommy. It was the kind of direct lie that would complicate telling the truth at a later time.

•••••••••••

Two hours after leaving McGrath, the family arrived at Ray's parents' house outside of Buhl. The homestead was an eighty-acre farm. However as when Ray was growing up, the only agricultural products raised on the farm were a few beef cows, pigs, chickens and eggs, garden produce, and a couple of milk cows. All of this production was consumed by the family or traded or sold to neighboring families. The farm had both hardwood and evergreen trees, which were the source of more income than the agricultural products. The sale of Christmas trees, firewood and logs for both pulp and lumber supplemented the income that Ray's dad, and now Ray's mom, earned working for the mining companies. The tract adjoined 6,000 acres of state forest which was good for deer hunting. During the depression, the local game warden told Ray's dad that he would never bother him for hunting out of season as long as the deer were killed for food for the family and not for sale. The family hunted deer from the end of June, when the deer were first fit to eat, to Thanksgiving Day.

Ray's parents, Randolph and Lillian, had raised a family of six in one house, which they had built in 1913. The downstairs of the house had a large master bedroom, a living room with a player piano, a dining room dominated by a table large enough to seat 10 and a good size kitchen where Lillian and her daughter cooked both Croatian and American meals. The upstairs of the house had two large and two small bedrooms. Ray and his brother Roy, who was two years older than Ray, had shared one of the large bedrooms, and his sister Lois, who was three years younger than Ray, and still lived at home, used one of the small bedrooms, and Ray's brother Roland, the youngest and about to start his senior year at the local high school, had the other. The last big empty bedroom was shared by Richard, now 22 and serving with Patton in Europe, and Roger, now 20, and serving as a crewman on the USS New York, which had just finished shelling the Island of Okinawa.

Lillian, Lois, and Roland came out to meet the family as soon as the car stopped in the driveway. Lillian had taken two weeks off from her job at the mining company's office while Lois was a supervisor at the same office but had taken only a day off. Roland was most excited by the brand-new car: "Best looking car I have ever seen." Lois, who was still single, was excited about seeing her niece and nephew and talking to Molly, who she deemed to be special as the only woman she knew who had grown up in the big city of Minneapolis.

Lillian just hugged her son and cried. "Every morning I would say a prayer that, if you were flying that day, that God would protect your plane. When I got the letter you were on the way home, I went right down to our church and spent over an hour on my knees in praise, and appreciation to our Lord. I suppose you were doing the same thing?" she said as she hugged Molly.

Lois and Roland helped carry the family's luggage into the house as Lillian gave instructions. "Take Ray's and Molly's luggage up to Ray's old room. We have pushed the two beds together. Put the kids' stuff in the other big room. Hopefully they can sleep together."

Molly was hoping that there would be a break between the two twin beds, but they fit tightly together. It would be like sleeping on a queen-size bed.

As soon as their luggage was settled and everyone had a bathroom stop and got cleaned up, Lillian called for them to come downstairs. "We will just have a light lunch. Lois and I worked last night and all morning on a special dinner for tonight. Dad and Roy both are planning on getting off work early. Shouldn't be a problem. All the mines are slowing down, with the war coming to an end."

The light lunch consisted of fresh roast beef or venison sandwiches, scalloped potatoes, fresh garden peas, three kinds of bread, peach sauce, cookies and a choice of blueberry or apple pie.

Randolph and Roy both came home around 4:30. Roy brought in the booze. "Don't know what you learned to drink over in England. Hope it wasn't Scotch; didn't buy any of that," Roy said as he brought in a case of Fitgers, a case of Hamm's, a bottle of Jim Beam, and a bottle of Phillips Vodka.

Ray looked at the supply and said, "What I've been drinking is Jack Daniel's but I have my own bottle."

As Ray got up and went upstairs to get the bottle, Molly watched, remembering the night at the restaurant.

Ray returned with his JD and said with an accusatory tone, "Oh, you should have picked up a bottle of Seagram's. That's become Molly's favorite drink while I was gone."

Lillian who had just come out of the kitchen gave Ray and Molly a concerned look.

"Oh, if that's the case I can run into town and get a bottle," Roy said. He didn't catch Ray's sarcasm.

"No, I will just have a Hamm's," Molly said. She had believed that Ray had accepted her explanation about Seagram's being Janet's favorite drink. Now she worried that he wasn't fooled.

"Hopefully you each will only have one before-dinner drink. Lois and I have worked so hard to prepare this wonderful dinner. Hate to have you too drunk to enjoy it. Besides we have a couple bottles of a special wine to drink with the dinner," Lillian announced. "We will eat at six."

The meal was wonderful. The main course was pasticada, a Croatian tradition. It was made with tender beef cuts, which had been marinated overnight, in the Croatian wine that was being served with the meal, to which was added onions, parsley roots, carrots, figs, apples, cooking chocolate and various seasonings. This was served with a Croatian cucumber salad, Swiss chard, and cooked potatoes. For dessert Lillian served povitica walnut bread, vanilla ice cream and the pies and cookies left over from lunch. She also had a semi-sweet coffee made from a family recipe. "If we eat like this for the rest of our vacation, I'll gain 40 pounds," Molly said as she sipped her coffee and finished her third glass of wine.

The conversation at dinner was mainly anecdotes about funny events that had happened while Lillian and Randolph's kids were growing up. Of course, most of them were about Roy and Ray since they were at the table. When either Randolph or Roy would ask Ray about his experiences flying over Germany, he would not answer directly, or would answer with a darkened mood. Lillian, sensing Ray's uneasiness, would quickly change the subject, often to the slowdown in the mining activities.

"I expect, since I don't have that much seniority, I may be laid off this fall." Roy added to what Lillian was saying. "I may try to get on with the boats in the spring. Even if we aren't digging much ore, there is a big backlog to ship." This comment made Molly cough and spit out a little of her wine, but everyone politely acted like they didn't notice.

As Lois and Lillian started to put away the food and some of the dishes, Molly got up to help. "Sit down," Lois and Lillian said in unison. "You're the guest." Implied was the message was that city girls don't know how to properly clean up.

As soon as the two women had done what they thought necessary Lillian came out of the kitchen and said, "Ok, time for cards."

Randolph, who had lit up a cigar as soon as Lillian had left the room, put the cigar down in an ash tray, and said, "Looks like we have enough for two games of three handed whiz," as everyone looked at Molly.

"I have never played any kind of cards. My dad was against all forms of gambling."

"We don't play for money, just for fun," Randolph responded, as if to defend their actions against a charge of sinfulness.

"Oh, I'm not objecting to card playing, I just don't know how. Also, I should get the kids to bed."

"Let's take the kids into the living room and they can play the player piano. Lois said, acting to prevent any pressure on Molly to learn how to play. That will be fun. You four can play partners then."

After playing piano for about twenty minutes, the kids lost interest, partly from being so tired. Molly, with Lois's help, took them upstairs and put them to bed. The two then came back down to watch the card game.

"Care for another beer?" Lois asked.

"Sure, I'll have another Hamm's," Molly responded.

Ray, who was on his third JD, glanced over as Lois gave Molly the beer. "I would join you, but I have to work tomorrow. If you want more, just help yourself," Lois said while sipping her glass of wine from dinner.

"That was the dumbest damn bid I have ever seen!" Ray slammed his cards down and glared at his mother, who was his partner, as Randolph and Roy won the hand.

Lillian was dumbfounded by the attack. It was the first time Ray had ever raised his voice at her. She got up from the table, trying hard not to cry, and said to Lois, "You better finish the game. I guess I'm no longer good enough to be your brother's partner."

After Ray apologized and Lillian continued playing, the game lasted two more hands with Randolph and Roy winning the first, because of Ray's poor playing, and Lillian and Ray winning the last hand because Randolph and Roy gave the hand away. As Randolph relit his cigar and took two puffs, Lois excused herself and went to bed. The rest of the group sat and talked for another hour, during which Ray downed two more glasses of straight JD, and Molly, who was feeling a high, drank three more bottles of beer, without realizing how quickly she was finishing each bottle. This fact that didn't escape the rest of the group.

"Boy, this sure has been a great night. Glad you are home, Ray. Now if we can get Rick and Rog home safely it will be good, but I'm afraid we might see a lot of lives lost if we actually try to invade Japan," Roy said as he got up to leave.

"I've been working—, I mean," Ray caught himself before finishing his sentence. "I think we may have a weapon that will end the war quickly."

"You talking about that bomb we set off in New Mexico yesterday? I read a little about it in the paper at work today. Do you think it's for real? Well, I'm like Lois need to get up for work tomorrow. Thanks, Ma, that was the best meal I have had since yours and Dad's 20th wedding anniversary dinner." Roy, without looking for an answer to his question, hugged his mom and Molly, shook hands with Ray and left.

"Hope you've shown Molly the portable toilet in the side closet," Lillian said to Ray as the couple headed up the stairs. "I think she'll need it."

The house did not have indoor plumbing. Ray had told Molly on the way up, that his folks had signed up for city water and sewer, but the connection was still a couple of years away.

Ray took Molly by the arm to make sure she didn't fall. As he held her arm, Molly recalled the morning Tommy had helped her down the steps of the Big Ten Restaurant the first day of their relationship.

"Well? Have you become a lush while I've been gone? Ma sure thinks so," Ray said as soon as he had closed the bedroom door.

Molly, who was in the same mood as the morning when she and Tommy had gone to the Valley Lounge for breakfast and drunk several Bloody Marys and beer chasers, the same day she had gotten the letter from Ray and that she had shared with Tommy, quickly unbuttoned and dropped her dress as she turned to Ray.

"Lush, I may be, but tonight I want to be your lust." Speaking in the seductive voice that she had developed in her foreplay with Tommy, Molly continued, "I'll be your whore, your bitch, or whatever you want me to be tonight." She unbuckled his belt, unbuttoned his pants, pulled down his zipper, slipped her hand inside his underpants and grabbed his now erect penis.

During the most exotic lovemaking of their marriage, Molly kept seeing images of Tommy and came close to saying his name, but with her moans and groans, all of her utterances were incomprehensible.

Downstairs, Lillian heard both the squeaking bed and some of the loud wailings. She was even more certain that her daughter-in-law had trapped her son into marriage by intentionally getting pregnant.

The remainder of the vacation was spent doing tourists activities, including touring the large open pit ore mine in Hibbing, traveling to the wilderness area near Ely, and taking a trip to the North Shore of Lake Superior. One day Ray took Junior fishing on a small lake near Buhl.

Ray did drink more frequently and had one incident where he became very upset with Junior's behavior. Lillian interceded on behalf of Junior, out of fear Ray was going to strike the child. He also reacted furiously when Lois started kidding him about an old girlfriend who had dumped him in his senior year of high school for the star quarterback of the football team.

Molly did not drink anymore and worked at making the trip fun for the kids. Ray was not romantic at night and seemed distant during the day. Molly worried that she had mentioned Tommy's name in her drunken state, or that she had talked in her sleep. She also tried to help Lillian with her cooking and housekeeping but was rebuffed. "You're on vacation, I'm sure you need a break from taking care of everything at home." Molly was aware of Lillian's contemptuous body language and Lillian's tone of voice when she talked to her. Lillian did not express any concern to Molly about Ray's changed personality.

Upon returning from their trip on the Tuesday before his appointment with the VA, Ray mowed the front lawn, did other yard work, took the new car into the dealer to be serviced and did other small tasks to keep busy. He was apprehensive about the planned counseling sessions. He had received a letter while he was on the trip, confirming the appointment and stating it would be held in a temporary building just north of the main VA hospital. The letter also requested that his spouse, if he was married, come with him at least for the first session. It was this request that Ray was most apprehensive about. Since agreeing to the counseling, Ray had both consciously and subconsciously worked out a plan in his head wherein he would minimize his problems and would report only a few minor outbursts that had occurred since he had arrived home. With Molly present at the session, this plan would be difficult to carry out.

"Mr. Kelseltz, I am Doctor Levi Kaplan. I would like to have you just call me Levi during our sessions. Hopefully, I can call you Ray or Raymond, your preference. I want you to talk casually about your experiences, how they affect you and which ones make you upset."

"Ray is fine." Expecting an accusatory setting where the doctor would confront him with a list of occurrences that had been reported by concerned people, Ray felt relieved by the doctor's low-key introduction.

"OK, Ray it is. Let me tell you generally how we run this program. I'm glad you brought your wife. I will invite her to join us in a few minutes but I want to make certain this is not a problem with you, and if there are any areas of discussion you need to be kept private from her. We do like to have her input on how she sees any problems you may be having, and also, I believe that it's good to talk about any marital issues that may have developed resulting from your absence."

The good doctor continued to outline the program, which would consist of 10 individual sessions and thirteen weeks of group meetings. The doctor also recommended a voluntary aftercare support group.

Molly was called in to join Ray and the doctor. After introducing himself, the doctor briefly outlined the proposed program for Molly and noting she was welcome to be a part of the sessions except when Ray wanted to discuss some issue in private. He then said, "I want both of you to define the most important problem that needs to be discussed at these sessions."

Ray went first. "I need to learn to deal with the feeling that I was guilty of killing hundreds and hundreds of innocent women and children and I need to stop seeing images that are figments of my imagination. This may be a second problem, but I also feel we have to talk about finding that loving feeling we had in our marriage before I left." He was talking directly to Molly when he made his last statement.

Molly, who was taken aback by Ray's comment said, "Ray's behavior is affecting the children. They are walking on egg shells trying not to upset their dad so he doesn't get mad at them. If he can do what he said he needs to do it would be a real benefit to the kids. I agreed we should have a frank discussion about our relationship and how Ray's decision to interrupt our marriage so he could become a flyboy had a damaging effect on the marriage." This comment brought a glaring look from Ray.

"Good," the doctor said. "I hear some honesty from both of you. We will discuss how each of you see your relationship at the next session. This is always hard for two people who are living together, but if you can avoid having this kind of discussion at home and can wait to do it here it will help minimize any misunderstanding between you. The last thing I want to ask you to consider for the next session is the role of alcohol in your current lives. See you next week."

The couple avoided any direct discussions about what was said at the session during the following week, but there was a distance between them. Ray did not have any violent outbursts, only an aura of depression, which caused Molly to be certain he somehow had found out about Tommy. Ray did not try to instigate any sexual activity but slept over 10 hours a day. On the Monday before the second session he returned to work.

Molly's apprehensions proved to be unjustified. Ray had a major surprise for her. He began the second session by looking at Molly and confessing.

"Molly, I was untrue to you while I was in England. The schedule was set up to give each flight crew a week off after 10 days on duty. This week off was supposed to be the only time we could drink, although that rule was violated more than obeyed. However, during the week off we did spend a lot of our free time in the local pubs. Of course, knowing that there were free-spending flyboys at these pubs attracted many of the unattached women in the area, as well as some who were attached. For the most part the relationships were just platonic, but booze and loneliness were too plentiful and led many, including myself, astray. Sylva was a widow whose husband had been in the rearguard at Dunkirk and was killed in action. She was almost 10 years older than me and had a teenage son and daughter. We met at the pub I usually patronized, and after seeing each other a few times there, she invited me to her house for a home-cooked meal. She had arranged for her kids to stay with friends for the night. So after a good meal and a few bottles of wine she led me to her bed. For my last 14 months of duty I spent most of my free time with her."

As Ray was relaying this tale of betrayal, Molly's mind was barraged with conflicting thoughts and feelings. Her first thought was, "Good, now I can confess about Tommy and we will be even." But, as Ray continued, a new feeling intervened. It was anger, it was hate, both at herself for the guilt she had felt, which she now saw as a reason Tommy was not willing to leave his family, and at Ray for his unfaithfulness. This was replaced by a new feeling before Ray finished his tale. A feeling of relief. She was now free to leave Ray at the appropriate time.

"Do you love Sylva?" was Molly's only response, which she asked unemotionally.

"No, No, No!" Ray was crying hard as he moved and got on his knees in front of Molly. "I never loved her. I love you. It was just about sex and the need not to be alone. Please, say you can forgive me."

"I'm sorry Ray. I'm sort of in a state of shock. I will need some time to get my mind around this."

Doctor Kaplan then intervened. "Ray, why don't you go out into the reception area and have a cup of coffee. I want to talk to Molly alone for a few minutes."

"Do you love Ray?" the Doctor asked as soon as Ray had left.

"No."

"Have you ever told Ray you loved him?"

"No."

"Those are pretty quick and unequitable answers. When Ray was confessing, I was waiting for you to react. But you just sat there like he was talking about the weather, like what he was saying did not affect you in any way. Tell me what's going on."

Molly finally let go of her emotions and said as she cried hard, "I too had an affair while Ray was gone. It was with a co-worker who from the first time he touched me I felt a response I had never felt with Ray. I always believed, based on what I felt and what I have heard other women talk about, that I had a good sex life with Ray. It may have been a little better with Tommy, but that was not the important thing. It was something else. Maybe affection is the feeling,—just small things that happened between us that made me feel wanted for being me, just the looking forward to being together. I don't know. It's hard to put into words. I guess I never had that with Ray. He introduced me to sex when I was a little drunk and never let me have any other relationship. He just possessed me as if I was his property. I got pregnant and was basically told I had to get married by my parents, although Ray was also gung ho to do it. I was never asked if I wanted to get married. I just went along with the flow. Tommy has told me he can't leave his kids for fear of how they will grow-up without him at home. When Ray confessed, it opened up a new pathway for me to get out of this marriage. But I don't want to act too impulsively. Also, there are the kids. What do you think I should do?"

"You are right. I don't think you should rush into any quick action. Ray is very troubled now with his reaction to the memories of the bombing and the damage it did. He took a big risk with his confession. We will need to work through this, but at some point, you will need to tell him your feelings and decide how to deal with the fall-out from the truth, both for Ray's benefit and your own mental health. But I want to finish today with the question about alcohol use I brought up at the end of the last session. I will have Ray come back in." Doctor Kaplan got up to go to the door.

Ray came back into the office, walked over to Molly and kissed her on her cheek. "I'm so sorry but I had to get this off my chest. I didn't love her. As I said, it was about sex and not being alone."

Molly did not react.

"Ray, Molly has to process the information you disclosed today. We will talk more about this at later sessions but now I do want to talk briefly about alcohol use. Do you think you have been using it more in dealing with your bad memories of the war?" Doctor Kaplan took control of the session.

"Ya, I'm probably drinking more now than I drank before I enlisted. Also, I am drinking more straight whiskey. I don't think I am an alcoholic though. I know this is not about me but Molly has surprised me with how much she is drinking. She never drank before I left and I wonder why she started during my absence." Ray was defensive.

"This is not about being judgmental or trying to label you. I'm just going to point out that your reactions to recalling the war can be made more problematic with alcohol use. To the extent you are aware of this effect and can minimize your alcohol use we can make more progress on improving your overall mental health. Molly do you want to comment on Ray's observation?" Doctor Kaplan asked.

"I never drank in my life until the night I met Ray and I guess I do drink a little more now. But what Ray is referring to is the first night of our recent vacation when I was in a holiday mood and drank more than I realized. Also, while he was gone, I went out with some friends from work and learned about a new drink with whiskey and 7-up. It sort of surprised him." Molly was pleased that she was able to be fairly accurate in the lie she just told.

"Well, I just brought this issue up now because if alcohol is a major problem, any work we do with other issues will be in vain. I think next week I should just work with Ray on his anxiety issues. If you can try to record anything you think triggers your angst or causes some type of outburst on your part it would be helpful. See you next week, Ray, and you, Molly, in a couple of weeks. Again, I want to caution you both on trying to solve any of these problems outside of these sessions." Doctor Kaplan led both of them to the office door.

Chapter 9

August 1945

Ray did not have any outbursts during the week before his next session but appeared to Molly to be stressed out as he read the newspaper about the destruction of Hiroshima on August 7th, two days before his appointment. After the session, he was not talkative and Molly did not question him about the session. The next day life changed again for the relationship.

"Hello, this is Molly." It was mid-afternoon as she answered the call.

"Mrs. Kelseltz, this is Cecil Murphy, your husband's team leader. I believe we met at the office Christmas party last year. I have some troubling news. I need you to keep what I am about to tell you completely confidential. Ray may have told you that he was working on a top-secret project. I can't tell you too much about it, but it was connected to the bomb we dropped on Nagasaki yesterday. Our working group was provided some classified pictures of the results of the blast. As soon as we began reviewing these pictures Ray became very agitated, and as he saw more he began to rant "more deaths, more innocents killed, more suffering, all my fault, all my fault," and then he became hysterical. He tried to destroy the pictures, threw a desk lamp at the wall and was totally out of control. We called security to subdue him. We then contacted some medical doctors at the Minneapolis Clinic of Neurology and they have admitted him to the psychological clinic at the Golden Valley Hospital. He is being evaluated there. I talked to his doctor and he believes it's best if you wait until tomorrow morning before you go to see him. He has been given some medication and he will be sedated for most of the night."

Molly immediately called Doctor Kaplan and was surprised he was available. After hearing what had happened he assured Molly that the Golden Valley Hospital was the best psychological clinic in Minnesota and that he would contact the staff and get the name of the doctor treating Ray.

"I want to make sure he is not given too strong a psychotic drug. That may exacerbate his condition. I will try, if you agree with me, to have him put under my care. I can get him admitted to the hospital here." Doctor Kaplan spoke in a comforting voice.

Molly agreed. She went to see Ray the next morning, but he lay in his bed with a blank stare and was non-responsive to Molly's comments or questions. Doctor Kaplan was successful in having Ray transferred to the VA hospital the next day. It was three days before he would communicate with the staff or Molly.

Ray spent five weeks in the VA's mental health unit, where he had several hours of therapy each day, working through what he was logically responsible for, and what he did not have control over. The therapy addressed questions such as would the bombs still have been dropped if he had not been part of the flight crew over Germany, or if Nagasaki still would have been destroyed had he not worked on the secret project? Then in a session during the last week, Ray had a revelation. He was simply a cog in a war machine. The way to compensate for his servicing as this cog was to work the rest of his life for world peace. He committed himself to this new purpose in life.

One of the last sessions included Molly. The purpose was for Ray to discuss what he intended to do to ensure his ongoing recovery.

"My goal is to live for the future. I'm going to avoid recalling the past and the memories, nightmares, and dreams of what transpired in my life since my enlistment. I have talked to Cecil Murphy, at Honeywell, and we both agreed that continuing to work there would not be in my best interest. He will give me a strong reference and, apparently, my hospital stay will be classified as treatment for a war injury. So, with his reference and my extensive amount of flight time, I should have a good chance of being hired as a pilot. After I'm settled in at home, I'm going to apply at both Northwest and North Central Airlines. Cecil has heard that neither one can get enough qualified pilots with the way travel by air is taking off—sorry for the pun—but some people are predicting that passenger train travel will be done in ten years." Ray, tired of doing all the talking, turned to Molly. "What do you think of these plans so far?"

Molly, surprised by Ray's new plans for employment and knowing that if he were able to be hired as a pilot he would have a great deal of free time, was scared and thought quickly. "I considered the possibility that you may be unemployed for a while and since I always wanted to work as a nurse, I want to qualify for a nursing position. If I hadn't become pregnant, I would have become an RN. Using those two years at the U I can be certified as an associate nurse with a three-month program at the Vo-Tech."

Ray was taken aback. "Well, I'm sure if I get a pilot's job, the pay will be plenty so you won't have to work. I sure don't want everybody to think I'm not able to support my family."

Dr. Kaplan interjected to head off any argument. "I think it's always good to get as much education as possible. I would encourage you to take the refresher course, Molly. We can talk at a later session about working outside the home. This would be a good time to bring up any other matters that either of you feel is important to air out before Ray is done with these sessions."

Molly, knowing what the doctor was referring to, started to formulate a way to tell Ray about her infidelity, but could not bring herself to disclose it to Ray.

After Ray had left the session for his room, Dr. Kaplan caught Molly before she left and asked her to stop in his office for a few minutes. "I was hoping that you would talk about your affair with Tommy. I felt this would be the best time to bring it out into the open before Ray is discharged from this treatment program. However, it has to originate from you. I won't violate your confidentiality. The longer this is not talked about increases the possible damage from the actual disclosure."

"I know." Molly's tears started, although she was trying to be tough. "I just don't want to face the possibility of Ray reverting back to the state he was the first day he came into the hospital. Also, I just didn't know where to start."

"I understand, but let me give you my perspective. I think holding onto this secret gives you a reason not to try to be close to Ray and lets you hold onto your hope of leaving this marriage and being with Tommy. If I am correct, it is not fair to Ray, but more importantly, it is very unhealthy for you. You either have to clear the air with Ray or decide to leave the marriage. You believe you are doing this for the kids. I know from my experience that a marriage that is kept together 'for the kids' ends up being destructive to both spouses and the kids. If you don't tell Ray, you will never have any possibility of closeness with Ray. There is an old adage that goes like this, 'I have harmed you, therefore I need to blame you.' So, think about what I have said and if you want I will schedule a session before Ray is discharged." Dr. Kaplan escorted Molly to the door as he finished talking.

Molly spent the next two days thinking about Dr. Kaplan's advice and was on the verge of having him schedule a session to tell Ray about Tommy; but before making the call to Dr. Kaplan, she got a call from Ray.

"Molly, you can come and pick me up at the hospital as soon as you can. I am being discharged today. Apparently, the VA is having so many new patients with my condition they are shortening the program for patients who are doing better."

After Ray returned home, he did apply at both of the two local airlines and, as Cecil Murphy had predicted, both companies offered him employment. He accepted the offer from Northwest and started his training three weeks after being discharged from the hospital. Molly followed through on her plans and started her nurses training. With this sudden active schedule for both of them, neither brought up any of the past problems, but there wasn't any close connection between them either. When Ray wanted sex, Molly submissively went through the motions without any real feelings. Ray finished his training and was flying by Christmas. Molly completed her training in February and without asking Ray for his opinion or approval took a nursing job at a St. Paul hospital. They did coordinate their schedules to the extent that was possible for one of them to be home with the children. Except at night, they were seldom home together. Several times, Molly made a commitment to herself to confess to Ray, accepting Dr. Kaplan's advice that any real closeness would be impossible until she did. Despite these commitments, she never could find the courage to tell Ray.

Molly was at work when Ray received the call from Molly's sister. A March snowstorm had dropped about six inches of snow overnight. Molly's dad went out after breakfast and shoveled off the sidewalk in front of their house. He came into their house and told Molly's mom that the shoveling had worn him out and he was going to lie on the couch to rest a little while. Mrs. Iverson had gone into the kitchen to put away the breakfast dishes when she heard the thump as her husband fell to the floor. The police who responded to her emergency call said he was probably dead when he hit the floor.

"Honey, I have very bad news. Maybe you should come home before I tell you."

"No, what is it? Is it one of the kids?" Molly's mind was racing with the belief that because she insisted on getting a job outside the house, God or some other Higher Power had punished her by inflicting harm on the kids.

"No, it's your Dad. He died suddenly this morning."

Molly dropped the phone and began to wail uncontrollably.

A couple of co-workers came to her aid.

"Molly, Molly, are you still there?" Ray shouted into the phone.

One of the co-workers picked up the phone and held it for Molly as she said between wails, "I'll be home in an hour or so. I'm going to go down to the chapel here at the hospital to pray. If the kids get home from school wait until I get home so we can tell them together."

As Molly knelt and started praying, the hospital chaplain came and, after finding out why she was grieving, joined her in a prayer and read her a passage from a book of reflections he often used for people who had lost loved ones at the hospital. She found him to be very comforting. However, she was not able to stop reliving the Sunday her dad had given his sermon on infidelity. She had always planned on sitting with him in his study at the church and confessing as, she knew, other members of the church had done. She also had planned to then bring Ray into the office and confess to him with her dad's support.

It was a very large funeral. The bishop of the synod presided at the service, assisted by four ministers whom Pastor Iverson had mentored. Both the main floor and the lower level of the church were full and an additional group waited outside on a cold March day. Ray was very attentive to Molly and tried to be comforting to her and her family during the period of grieving, but Molly was aloof to his support.

Ray, feeling the distance between him and Molly, he assumed was a response to his affair with Sylva, began to look for outlets to his loneliness. The first thing he did was join a group of "Ban the Bomb" protesters. In the spring of 1946, *The New Yorker* magazine published an issue that was devoted entirely to the effect of the bomb America had dropped on Hiroshima. This energized the whole movement and Ray spent most of his weekends went he wasn't flying taking part in downtown marches. He even led several protests at the military production plants of his former employer. He also joined a "Veterans Against Wars" group who wrote letters to the editorial pages of the Twin Cities newspapers, took part in radio talk shows and made appearances at several of the American Legion and VFW clubs around the area criticizing the expanding military buildup and the arms race with the Soviet Union. Often the group's appearances at veteran's clubs were met with hostilities. They were booed, called names, accused of being communists and sometimes physically assaulted. Ray was sure that the endless amount of propaganda being fed to these groups by the weapons manufacturers was the source of the hostilities. This anti-war effort soon brought Ray a taste of reality. After being interviewed on WCCO radio, which had the largest audience in the state, about his idealism, he was summoned to the office of the CEO and major shareholder of Northwest Airlines.

"Ray, I have been reviewing your work record and your performance evaluations since you began flying for us. You have an excellent record and I can only foresee that you will have a long and rewarding career with this organization. However, I did hear your radio interview and saw some of the press coverage of the peace efforts by you and your group. I certainly commend you on your efforts to express opposition to what you, individually, see as a bad course of action by our government. But I am required, for the good of the company, to point out that what you do individually reflects on this company. So, I must give you a choice. Either cease your anti-war activities or submit your resignation."

Ray, seething with anger, got up, walked in a circle, held back the barrage of hateful words rampaging through his head, and said, "Can I talk to my wife and let you know tomorrow?"

"No, I need the answer now. If you have loyalty to this company it should be an easy choice."

Ray realizing how much he enjoyed flying and the great benefits of his job, responded, "Sir, I will cease all my peace efforts."

As he drove home, Ray made a mental note to research the number of contracts Northwest Airlines had with the military.

Molly, after talking to the hospital chaplain the day her dad died, had resolved, for what seemed to her the hundredth time, to tell Ray about her affair. Ray's strong support after her dad's death made her more determined to confess until the unexpected happened.

"Ma, Ma," Junior yelled, "there is a truck coming up the driveway."

It was a week after the funeral and Ray had left that morning on a flight to Japan. Molly looked out the window and saw a truck with a load of firewood parked in front of the house.

"Is your Dad home?" Tommy asked Junior, who had run out to see the truck.

"No, it's just me, Mommy and Holly."

Molly ran to grab and kiss Tommy but stopped, realizing Junior was watching and said, "What a surprise. Why did you come without calling? What if Ray had been home?"

"I didn't want to chance a call. Well, to be honest, when I decided to come I wanted to surprise you. I would've just acted like a firewood seller if Ray was home." Tommy moved around the side of the truck, out of Junior's view and squeezed Molly's hand. "I needed to see you," he said softly.

"Here, meet my second son, Gordon." Tommy opened the truck door and Gordon jumped out. "He's going to be thirteen in two weeks and he's already helping me like a man. Can you use this wood? It's really good stuff."

"Hello, Gordon." Molly, without any hesitation, hugged him. She saw Tommy's resemblance in all his features, and the idea that he could be her stepson someday kindled an excitement in her brain. "I would love the wood," she said as an afterthought.

"Where should we unload it?" Tommy asked.

"I'll show you, but first come into the house and I'll make coffee for you, Tommy. I have some cake and ice cream for Gordon." Molly led the way to the door.

After serving her guests, Holly and Junior, Molly went to her bedroom and changed into her nursing scrubs sans of any under clothing.

"Holly and Junior, can you get some of your card games out and ask Gordon if he will play with you? Gordon, can you keep the kids occupied while I show your Dad where to unload the wood? I will help him with the unloading." Molly put on a long coat, nodded to Tommy and headed out the door.

"Back your truck up to the woodshed. It's almost empty. I'll go and get ready." Molly smiled the same smile she had smiled the first day of their romance.

Tommy entered the woodshed to find Molly standing nude, except for the opened long coat, against the wall. He went to her and without any words the two of them made love standing up, with a release of passion that had smoldered within them for the two years they had been apart.

After the loving, the two of them dressed and started the task of unloading the wood. "Where's Ray? You didn't seem too worried about him coming home."

"No, he's probably just landing in Tokyo about now. You picked a good day to come. Was it just to bring wood and to see me?"

"No, I came to tell you I've made a big decision. I'm prepared to leave Eleanor if you're still willing to divorce Ray."

Molly dropped the firewood she was stacking and grabbed Tommy. "When?"

"I'm scheduled to start back on the boats in two weeks. We usually finish in late October. We can work out some of the details by letter over the summer. We'll need to figure out where we will live. I assume you will get custody of Holly and Junior so it will be best if I get a new job in the Cities. I want to keep close contact with my kids. Maybe Denny and Gordon will live with us. That's the kind of details we will need to think about."

"How much does Gordon know about us?" Molly was crying tears of joy.

"I told him we were friends who worked together at the Arsenal. He's old enough to figure out that it may be more than that, but he won't say anything to his mom. But we should get this wood unloaded before he gets too suspicious."

Molly kissed Tommy hard. "It would be wonderful if you could stay the night!"

"It would be heaven, but I can't. I'll have to go home."

"OK, I'll make some hamburgers before you go." Molly was

disappointed but her excitement over what Tommy had said overrode any negative feelings. By Christmas she would be living with the man she loved.

For the rest of the spring and early summer Ray became more and more aware of the distance separating him and Molly. She with greater frequency, was rebuffing any sexual overtures he initiated and was not interested in anything he suggested as activities they could do together. One of the perks of his career as a pilot was free air travel to anywhere in the world yet Molly was not willing to go to places he suggested, like a week in Florida at the end of April, or a weekend trip to New York City without the kids. Ray became more perplexed.

One day when Molly was working and the kids were in school, Ray was home preparing to leave that afternoon on a trip to the Orient. While thinking about what might make Molly happy, he decided he would buy her some clothes and shoes from Japan or Korea. Given he had never purchased any apparel for her, he went into her closet to look at the sizes of her dresses and shoes. After writing down her dress and blouse sizes he reached up on the upper shelf and took down a shoe box, the one that Molly was always going to conceal in a better place.

Ray discovered the letter that Molly had written to Tommy but hadn't sent. After reading these letters he got to the letter she hadn't sent to him about asking for a divorce. Then he found a letter she was waiting to mail to Tommy.

> *Tommy, my love,*
> *I have waited to write this letter until you were back at work on your ore carrier. Hopefully when you receive this you can read it and reread it at night in your cabin. If so, I hope you can share the excitement I'm feeling as the summer passes and we get closer to being together for the rest of our lives. As I think of that, I feel over and over the height of the ecstasy I had against the wall of the woodshed the day you delivered the wood. The smell of your body in your work clothes, the joy of your touching and kisses as you once again worked my body into a frenzy and then you entering me and bringing me to a rapture so strong I would have collapsed if I had not been in your arms. Often since that day I go*

*into the woodshed and stand against the wall at the same spot
and fully relive that moment although it is never as good as it
was with you. Write to me with any more ideas you have about
our future together. More Later.*

To the only man I have ever loved.
Molly

Ray, stunned, didn't know what to do. His first instinct was to destroy all the letters. Instead he got up and walked around the bedroom.

"Stupid, naïve, idiot, you believed it was just your little fling that was the problem. She was cheating on you the whole time you were gone and she is still cheating on you," Ray yelled out loud with no one to hear. His anger gave way to self-pity as he broke down and cried. Then a wave of sadness overtook his other emotions. "I love her, I love her," he cried. He looked around the room as if he could find something to relieve the gnawing sense that he had just lost the one thing in the world he needed most. He went back and started to reread some of the letters, especially the one to him where Molly said she had never loved him. Then he saw the address on the envelope Molly had prepared to be mailed to Tommy. As he stared at the address he knew what he would do.

Chapter 10
February 1951

Sheriff Hewitt spent the last Saturday morning in February on the lake. At the insistence of both the county attorney and the state investigators he had agreed to have the fish house moved from the lake to the parking lot of the County Courthouse. He was not sure what value it would be, but he had agreed. A house mover was hired and the sheriff supervised the loading to minimize any disruption to the inside of the house. The victim's pick-up truck had been taken to the county's garage shortly after the murder. After the truck carrying the house had left, the sheriff stopped at several of the fishing houses near the murder scene. He had talked to most of the fishermen near the victim's house several times since the murder but he knew that additional inquiries sometimes lead to someone remembering something they had not remembered before. Also, a fisherman who may have been on the lake the night of the murder and was not around the other times he was investigating might be on the lake now. The sheriff found such a fisherman who had a house 400 yards toward the shore.

"Hello, I'm the County Sheriff, Oscar Hewitt." He put out his hand as the fisherman opened his door. "Don't know if you heard about the murder we had here about six weeks ago; it was on either the night of January fourth or the following morning. I'm just checking if you may have been fishing that night, and if so, if you heard or saw anything."

"Glad to meet you Sheriff. I'm Carl Newsom. I'm from Wisconsin and only get up here about five or six times a year. I was up here for New Years and left that Friday, I guess before the body was discovered. Ole told me about the murder last night. I didn't think too much about it, but now that you have asked, something a little strange did happen my last night here. It was just before midnight. I remember checking my watch to see how late it was, knowing I had to get some sleep so I could get going in the morning. I had to take a leak, and as I did, I saw what appeared to be small circles of light, in the distance, reflecting off and on off the snow. The circles were moving around the fish houses a couple hundred yards toward the shore. Then I thought I saw a black object move. I didn't think it was a person, more like a bear. Given that the reason I had to relieve myself was the six to eight Pabsts that I had drunk, I dismissed what I saw as an illusion. Now thinking about it, I did hear what sounded like a car starting just as I went back into my fish house."

"Is this your car here, Carl?" The sheriff nodded toward the new black Cadillac sitting next to the house. "It's a beauty."

"Yes, mine and the bank's," Carl chuckled.

"Thanks, this has been most interesting." The sheriff went back to his car and made a recording of what Carl had reported. On the way out, the sheriff jotted down Carl's license plate number.

After leaving the lake, the sheriff drove to the Oien's farm. He managed to time his arrival so he got there just as the noon time dinner was being served. Larry's parents, brothers Howard and Chet, and sisters Louise and Beverly, who were home from the cities where they both had jobs, and Larry were just sitting down at a table filled with food. As the sheriff walked in Irene, Larry's mom, quickly made a place at the table next to Albert, Larry's dad, for the sheriff to sit down.

"Sure didn't want to interrupt your dinner," the sheriff said, although he did not hesitate in taking off his winter coat, cap and gloves so he could sit down. "How are you all?" He said as the various plates of food were passed to him.

"Fine," Albert said. "You've met all my family, haven't you?"

"Yes, has Jerry gone to Korea, yet?"

"No, he's stationed in Alaska. He's serving as a radio operator in the radar defense system and since it's a fairly high-tech job he is pretty sure he will not be sent into combat." Albert handed the sheriff the platter with the roast beef and the bowl of potatoes along with the bowl of gravy. "Eat up. We have plenty."

"Just save room for some rhubarb and strawberry pie. I used some of my canned sauces and it came out really nice," Irene injected.

"You must be relieved. Your four sons who served in the big war all made it safely home. It would be a shame to lose a son in this little flare-up." The sheriff was making quick work of his full plate of food.

"How's your murder investigation going?" Howard asked. "A lot of gossip going on about it."

"Well, I did spend the morning out on the lake. Nothing too much new, except there was a black man who said he was from Wisconsin who had a strange tale about what he may have seen the night of the murder. He believed he saw some small lights going off and on that appeared to be headed toward the shore. He also saw something move, which he thought was a bear. I got his license number and will check him out. Stopped at Ole's though and he said that the guy is a fairly regular customer."

"Maybe someone was walking and turning a flashlight off and on," Larry speculated. "Pass me some more squash, Bev."

"Never thought of that. I'm going to have to make you a regular deputy yet."

Albert laughed. "Ma wants him to become a preacher, but all he's interested in is football and politics. I told him he'll be hurt either way."

"Other than that, the investigation is proceeding. I can't mention any names but there are some local boys being questioned." The sheriff gave Larry a look when he said no names should be mentioned. "The case has drawn the interest of the FBI. Boy, talk about people taking their job seriously. I guess all the agents have law degrees and they sure think they know everything and us locals are just bumpkins. They see complicated plots to most crimes and everyone is guilty until proven innocent. They have some real crazy ideas about the reason for the murder."

"Apparently, the victim, who was a pilot, hadn't gone home after he flew in from Korea before driving up to the lake. So the FBI is looking into the possibility that he was involved with illegally importing something from Korea. With all the witch hunts going on about communists and the war starting, one theory they have is he was involved with espionage. He got access to some South Korean secrets and delivered them to an agent for the North Koreans who then killed him so he would never report the spying. The victim did engage in a lot of anti-bomb and peace demonstrations after he returned from bombing Germany during the war."

"I guess I more or less laughed at the agent who told me this theory. I said, 'Wouldn't it be the other way around? He would be taking secrets to Korea and not home from Korea.' That didn't make me too popular with them and they sure cut me a new asshole. Oops, I'm sorry I got carried away and forgot there are ladies present." The sheriff's face reddened.

"Don't worry, Sheriff, with eight brothers we have heard worse than that," Louise stood up. "I'll get some more coffee and the pies."

"Anyway, what I was going to say was that they read the riot act to me about leaving Larry and his two buddies alone to watch the crime scene that first night when I went into Ole's to warm up and make my calls."

"Didn't the victim's wife know why he came straight up to the lake?" Howard asked.

"That's another strange twist to the case. His wife would not talk to the Eagan Police Chief when he started questioning her. She went and got a criminal lawyer from South St. Paul and everything has to go through him. He did confirm that the victim did come right up to the lake and he also claims that the wife did not know he was home from his flight. The Eagan chief, who is a close friend of mine since he has gone deer hunting with me a couple times, is pretty sure the couple were having marital problems. However, we have no evidence she had anything to do with the murder. She was working the night shift at her nursing job both Thursday and Friday of the week of the murder."

"Well, that's enough talk about the investigation. The reason I came by today is to let you know, Albert, that I have decided not to run for reelection next year. The more time I spend on this case I realize how much police work has changed since I was elected twenty years ago. I used to interview people and know who was lying and who was truthful and be able figure out the facts. That's harder to do now and criminal investigations are becoming more technical. And with a bigger population there is more crime. I was a little critical of the FBI agents, but some of their new techniques are really amazing. Besides I'm getting old and twenty years is long enough. Since you have been one of my biggest supporters, I wanted to tell you first. Also, I'm trying to talk my deputy, Earl, into running. If he does, I hope I can count on you supporting him."

"It will be sad not to have you as the sheriff, but I understand. Anyone you recommend will have the full support of our family. Right boys?"

"Sure will," Larry's brothers mumbled with their mouths full of pie.

Later that afternoon, while he was out helping his dad cut firewood, Larry began thinking of all the things the sheriff had said at dinner. He recalled what the black fisherman had said about thinking it was a bear moving away from him. He then remembered kidding someone about how they looked like a big bear as they walked away from him. He immediately killed that thought in his head.

Chapter 11
Summer 1946

Tommy stood at the rail of the Johnathan Stevenson, an ore carrier, as it moved through the channel connecting the Duluth Harbor with Lake Superior. Standing with him were Arvin Berg and Hans Thompson two other crew members, who were from McGrath. Hans had told Tommy about the opening for employment on the ship and had helped him get the job. This trip to Cleveland and back was the first voyage of the season.

A small group of spectators, including three busloads of school kids, were waving and watching the ship leave the harbor on a cool April Fool's Day, as the fog horn cautioned that the aerial bridge over the channel was being raised. Tommy waved back at the crowd and looked up at the Duluth hillside while his mind concentrated on what he had promised Molly. How was he going to tell Eleanor and the kids when it was time to leave home? Would he have the willpower to keep his promise? Would he do what he wanted for himself or make sacrifice for the welfare of another? "It has to be done. It has to be done," he said to himself.

"Hello fellow sailors," Roy Kelseltz pushed his way to the rail between Tommy and Hans Thompson. "Since I worked with all of you last season and really didn't get to know any of you I thought I would introduce myself right from the start. My name is Roy. As he turned his head away from Tommy, he added, "Kelseltz," under his breath. "I'm from up on the range. Live near Buhl. Understand you three are all from down near Mille Lacs Lake. I been down there and done a little fishing on that lake."

"The name is Hans Thompson. This is Arvin Berg, and Tommy Haas. I knew your name was Roy, but you're right. We didn't really get to know you last year. Of course, it was near the end of the year when you started."

"That's right but I enjoyed it. Doesn't pay as well as the mines, but it's a less stressful job, as long as we don't have to sail through any big storms, of course. You been on this boat for a while?"

"Yuh, my eighth season, third on this boat," Hans Thompson answered.

"I understand you are like third or fourth in command. You must know this boat pretty well. How about you, Tommy. Have you been sailing quite a few years too?" Roy asked.

Tommy, still thinking about his commitment to Molly and not paying attention to the exchange between Roy and Hans, responded to Roy without really looking at him. "No, this is just my second season and it may be my last since I'm thinking about getting a full-time, year-around job when I'm done this fall."

Hans looked at Tommy in surprise. He didn't know he was thinking about quitting. He wondered what would lead him to change his lifestyle.

"Well, now that we are on the lake, I better get to my post in the engine room. Do you play pinochle? Hard to find any good players on this ship. Arvin and I have to play each other all the time and it gets tiresome beating him. We can't get Tommy to take time to learn." Hans gave Arvin a little poke in the ribs as he mentioned beating him all the time.

"Just a minute," Arvin said. "My recollection is that I won the last five games we played last year."

"I'm good at most card games. The boys I worked with at the mines played a lot of pinochle. Maybe I can teach Tommy a little. I guess it's time for my shift to start too. Talk to you all later." Tommy didn't notice the strange smile Roy had as he mentioned his name.

●●●●●●●●●●

Molly could not quell her uneasy gut feeling. Although she was excited about the promise Tommy had made, she sensed something was wrong. A major concern causing this feeling was Ray's behavior and responses to her. He had not done anything specific, but he seemed to be unresponsive to her questions, appeared to be avoiding her, and to drink more after almost quitting following his counseling at the VA. Other little things were happening. When she opened the shoe box to get the letter to mail to Tommy, she believed someone else had been looking at it, but if Ray had looked at the letters he surely would have confronted her about them.

There was also the fire that burned down the woodshed. About two weeks after Tommy had delivered the new wood, and a couple hours after

Ray had left for a flight, Junior came running into the house yelling, "Mommy, Mommy the woodshed is on fire!"

Molly looked out the door and flames were coming through the roof of the shed. She quickly called the volunteer fire department, and although they responded amazingly fast, the shed and all the wood was lost. However, coming so quickly allowed them to confine the fire to the shed. The fire chief told her that most likely some wood at the bottom of the pile may have been very green and started drying quicker than the very dry wood and caused spontaneous combustion. He said it's more common in hay loft fires in barns, but it also may happen in wood piles.

Molly questioned Junior, "Have you ever played with fire?" The blank look on Junior's face (which Molly read to mean, "What are you talking about?") convinced Molly that he had nothing to do with starting the fire. She had always kept all matches away from the kids' access.

"Can you check for arson?" Molly asked not accepting the chief's theory.

"We can, but it is expensive. Unless you had the shed insured, we have no reason to incur the cost. Of course, if you did have insurance the company would require us to do it, but they would pay the cost. You can have it done at your expense of course."

"No, that's O.K. How long could that fire have been smoldering before it became visible?"

"Several hours." The chief began helping his crew in putting away their hoses and cleaning up.

Molly remembered the unfinished letter to Tommy. Had Ray read it and the part about the woodshed?

Molly finished the letter, telling Tommy about the fire and adding more about her impatience for the summer to pass. She also purchased a lock box, placed all the letters in it and kept the box locked in the trunk of her car. When Ray returned home she told him about the fire and the fire chief's theory about the cause. When Ray was disinterested, Molly became certain that he had read the letter and had started the fire, but she didn't confront him. Maybe this knowledge would make Ray more agreeable to her leaving him in the fall.

As Molly thought about the arrangements that would have to be made, she was sure her mom would not approve of her leaving Ray, so she believed telling her now may help her adjust. On the first Saturday in May, while Ray was on a weekend flight, Molly called her mom to ask if the kids could stay with her for the night and go to church with her, since she had to work the night shift at the hospital. She also told her mom she would be coming over early so the two of them could spend a little time together.

Upon arriving at Grandma's house, Molly was surprised when her mom, Martha, introduced her to Kelly, a sixteen-year-old neighbor girl.

"I asked Kelly to come over and take the kids to play in the park since it is almost like summer out. I made a small lunch for all of us and then they can go. You said you wanted to spend some together, so I assume you have something to talk about. If not, I have something to tell you and it would be hard to talk with the kids around."

Molly was intrigued. She was glad when lunch was finished and Kelly and the kids went to play.

Martha, who at the age of 48 was almost a mirror image of Molly, said, "I'm glad you came over. Don't tell your sisters, but I always felt you were the daughter who was most like me. It is amazing how our physical appearances are so similar, and I believe that you and I have the same mental and emotional traits."

"I know about the same physical appearances. So many times when I have been to Dad's church, women would come up behind me and call me Martha and then be surprised when I turned around. At first it was embarrassing since I'm twenty years younger, but now it gives me hope I will look as good as you when I get to be your age," Molly said.

"Come on dear, don't make me sound that old," Martha laughed. "So, I am sure you didn't come over to tell me you resent looking like your mother."

"I don't resent that at all, but I want to talk about something very personal. I am going to divorce Ray. I hope you're not too surprised and you won't disapprove."

"Sweetheart, the only surprising thing is that it has taken you this long to make the decision. Will you be marrying the man you had the affair with while Ray was in England?"

Molly stared at her mom. She was both stunned and dumbfounded. "You knew?"

"Of course, we knew. Remember your father gave a sermon about it? I didn't say anything at the time, but you did look the happiest you ever looked. Your sister commented on it at the Christmas dinner. When do you plan on making this change?"

"His name is Tommy. He is working this summer on an ore boat on the Great Lakes. The season ends around November 1. Then he is leaving his wife. We hope to be together by Thanksgiving."

"I can tell you are excited. Do you love him?"

"Yes! Yes! Yes! I'm more certain about this than anything in my life." Molly was euphoric. "I'm glad you approve and hope you will support me. I am sure it will be a trying time."

"O.K., now it's my turn." Martha took Molly's hand. "I don't want to demean your father or damage your memory of him. He was a wonderful man, a great father and grandfather, and a very powerful minister to many parishioners at seven different churches, and I lived with him for over 30 years. I never loved him."

Molly's eyes opened wide as she looked at her mother and realized she had now seen her for the first time. She was not there as the person who gave her life and had been her safe harbor from whatever storms, big or small, life had bestowed on her. She was there as another woman who had experienced the same and probably more of the feelings and emotions she had in her almost 28 years of living.

"You know my history of coming to America from Sweden with your Aunt Hannah in 1914. I was 18 years old and we went to live with our Uncle Simon in Dalton, Minnesota. Well, at the time besides Swedish, I could speak better Finnish than English. I had only been in Minnesota for about two months when there was a Fourth of July celebration in Dalton. As my uncle was introducing us to as many of his friends as possible, most of whom were members of the small Lutheran church in Dalton where my uncle was the main elder, I saw this handsome man. I'd guess he was about two or three years older than me, and I was sure he was Finnish. After Uncle Simon left Hannah and me on our own, I told Hannah about him and that we had to find him, which we did at the bandstand. His dad, uncle and brother had a three-piece band consisting of an accordion, guitar and fiddle. They provided the music for the celebration and were going to play at the street dance that night. Nervously I walked up to him and tried to say 'hello' and 'how are you' in Finnish."

"He looked at me with a look of wonderment and said in fluent English, 'Hi, my name is Bruno and yours must be Helen of Troy since you have to be the most beautiful woman in the world.'"

Without another word being spoken I knew I had just found the love of my life. His full name was Bruno Happala and he lived on a large farm about 15 miles north of town. That night Hannah and I went to the street dance. Bruno, when he wasn't helping with his family's band, stayed with us. He got me to dance, after I got over my fear of trying, and then we danced often. I still remember one wild polka where everyone stopped to watch us." Martha looked out the window, but she was looking at a memory.

"Wow, Mom! I never knew you danced, besides having a secret love all these years."

"Back in Malmo, Sweden, where I grew up, we did have a local dance hall. Hannah and I did go there often since there were frequent dances for teenagers. But let me finish my story. On the Sunday after the Fourth, just after we had finished the after-church dinner, I looked out the window and saw Bruno sitting in a two-seat surrey which was being pulled by a beautiful bay colored horse. Uncle Simon saw him at the same time and both of us walked out to talk to him. He said he was coming into the house but hadn't yet found a place to hitch the horse. Then he asked Simon for permission to take me for a ride. Simon gave Bruno a good looking over and walked up to the surrey to smell his breath and then said, 'Yes, you can, but be back in an hour. Also, make sure you stay on the road. I want you to always be visible from the road.'"

"That became our little joke. *Always be visible from the road.* Later as we rode together we often found rural roads where no one would come by for hours, but if they would have we would have been visible." Martha was now smiling.

"So, what happened to Bruno?" Molly asked.

"I'm getting to it, I'm getting to it, dear. Our romance became more serious. After asking Simon for permission, Bruno proposed and we made

MURDER ON THE LAKE

plans to be married the following June after I finished my one year of school that I was taking to learn better English. But what happened almost led me to suicide."

"Every fall the Happala family would have a barn dance after the grain crops had been harvested and another when the corn had been harvested. Bruno took me to both of them. The family band played, there was dancing and unlike the July Fourth dance there was alcohol at the barn dances. Most of the other farmers in the area who had come to the dance brought their own bottle and the Happalas had both home-brewed beer and home-distilled alcohol. Everyone called it White Lighting. Bruno offered me a beer and I refused. He drank a couple beers and took a straight shot of the White Lighting. I then told him, if he wanted to drive me home, I didn't want him drinking anymore. He agreed but was clearly upset and our ride home was not a fun and romantic ride like we normally enjoyed. The second dance was even worse. Bruno started drinking earlier and more often. I confronted him and, since he was already drunk, he yelled at me that he wasn't going to be hen-pecked before we were even married. I never felt more hurt in my life before or since and couldn't control my crying. I found Hannah, who was there with her boyfriend who she later married, and they took me home."

"So that caused the end of the relationship?" Molly was sad and disappointed for her Mom's lost love.

"No, that's not the worst part of the story. In early August of that year, the church where my uncle was the head deacon hired your dad as its minister. He had just graduated from the seminary so it was his first church. My uncle owned the local general store and had the largest house in Dalton; therefore he agreed that Pastor Iverson could live with us in his house. As you well know your father was always forceful both in his sermons, in taking charge, and having things done his way. Of course, it was why he progressed up the hierarchy of the Synod. He was always hired by bigger and bigger churches. Anyway, I digress. So, having him living in the house seemed like a wonderful addition. It was like having a personal counselor who was not afraid to tell you what was right or wrong. Oh, there were warning signs. He would often brush up against me in the hallways acting like he didn't have enough room to miss me, though he did. One time when we were alone in the living room he said to me, 'The Bible says man was created in the image of God, but you must have been created in the image of the most angelic angel.' I thanked him for the compliment, but the way he said it and the look he gave me made me feel uneasy."

"It sounds like you weren't attracted to him at all. How did you end up married to him?" Molly was now anxious to find out the end of the story.

"Well, you may be able to guess what happened. Have you ever noticed the amount of time between our wedding anniversary and your sister Marie's birthday?"

"He got you pregnant!" Molly's memories of the day she learned for sure she was pregnant with Holly flooded her whole being: The fear she had of telling her dad, the feeling she had about knowing it meant she would have to marry Ray, a feeling she now knew was trepidation.

"Yes, he raped me," Molly's mom continued. "The first time I got upset with Bruno over his drinking, I briefly talked to your father about being upset. He suggested that we pray about it in my bedroom, but I told him we could do it where we were sitting on Uncle Simon's front porch. After we prayed he gave me a hug which was clearly sexual. But just as he released me Uncle Simon came home from a meeting and gave us an accusatory stare. Your father quickly said, 'Martha and her boyfriend had a little argument tonight and I was trying to comfort her.' Then when I came home after the big fight with Bruno, I was so upset I wasn't even thinking about your dad or the fact that Uncle Simon and my Aunt Bertha had taken the train to Minneapolis to buy winter inventory for their store. If I had I would have asked Hannah to stay home with me, instead of going back to the dance with her boyfriend."

"You were actually scared of him." Molly moved to embrace her mom.

"I guess so. Well, maybe it would be more accurate to say I just didn't trust him. Anyway, my concern proved to be justified. As I entered the house I was still broken up and crying hard. Your father came to me as soon as he heard and we both sat down on the living room couch and I told him the whole story. He stroked my hair and face and said things like, 'Oh, you poor dear, I feel your hurt,' and other words of comfort."

"Then he said, 'It is probably the Lord's will that a woman as beautiful as you not spend her life on a dairy farm in northern Minnesota.' Those were his exact words. I can still remember almost every detail of that terrible night."

As her mom started to break down, Molly, who was also crying, gave her a hug. "Oh, Mom I wished you would have shared this a long time ago. Have you ever told anyone about this?"

"Just your Aunt Hannah. To quickly finish the story, when your dad said that I jumped up and responded, 'Don't say that. I love Bruno. I'm sure God wants me to be happy.' I ran to my bedroom and got my nightgown on and got into bed after I checked to see if there was a lock on the door, but there was none. Then your dad came into the room and said, 'I just want to say a prayer for you and Bruno.' Then he began stroking my face and neck again."

"I said don't, please go. He placed his hand on my breasts. As I was crying and trying to say, no, no, stop, please stop, I realized he was on top of me and was naked. I felt the sharp pain as he entered me."

"Oh Mom, that must have been awful. At least when Ray seduced me, he was gentle and it was a joy."

"After it was over, I was filled with anger. If I would have had a weapon of any kind, I'm sure I would have killed him. I was crying hard as I beat on him with my fists and yelled, 'Bruno and I had agreed we wouldn't do this until our wedding night. Now you have ruined me, Bruno won't want me.' Then your dad said, 'Don't you tell anyone about this night. If you tell Bruno or anyone I will tell them you seduced me and I tried hard to resist the temptations of the devil as you undressed and pressed your body against me. Bruno won't know at least until the wedding night and I doubt he will know then. But if you tell anyone, I'm sure they will believe me, and Bruno will never have you.'"

"I guess it was good you never told me. I assume you never told my sisters either. It would have been hard to not hate Dad after hearing this story. I still don't understand how or why you ended up married to him. Didn't you hate him?" Molly was still holding on to her mom.

"How did you end up married to Ray? When your dad ordered you to marry him, I relived this whole nightmare. I wanted so much to tell you what happened to me and not to marry Ray unless you knew you loved him. In my case I didn't sleep much that night and considered suicide. I took three baths trying to get rid of my feeling of being dirty. I couldn't go to church or anywhere near your dad. Then before your dad came back after the last service, Bruno came with the surrey and got down on his knees and begged me to forgive him. He promised never to drink when we were together. I hugged and kissed him and we went for a Sunday afternoon ride. By the time we rode home I was sure everything would be fine and I would still be marrying Bruno in the spring. I made a decision that I would not tell anyone and I would make sure I was never alone with your dad again. That all changed six weeks later. I knew I had missed my period and started to be sick in the morning. I confided in Hannah and she and her boyfriend took me to a doctor in Fergus Falls who confirmed that I was pregnant."

"Couldn't you have told Bruno the whole story? If he really did love you as much as he claimed, he could have married you even with you having another man's baby." Molly wished she could change the outcome of her mom's sad story.

"I never considered that since I never had a chance to talk to him. Hannah and I decided on the way home from the doctor that we should tell Uncle Simon as soon as we got home since he was going to find out anyway. I never expected his reaction. He immediately started yelling mainly about his reputation and how my pregnancy would affect his store business and his position as the head church deacon. Without telling me what he intended to do, Uncle Simon went and got his horse from the stable and rode off. He rode out to the Happala's farm and confronted Bruno. Of course, Bruno was more surprised than my uncle, who accused Bruno of lying. Bruno broke down and started crying and yelled that I must have been two-timing him and he would never want to see me again."

"How cruel of Uncle Simon. I guess I never knew him. I was so young when he died."

"Well, he was crueler. Upon returning home, he demanded to know how I became pregnant. I told him about the rape. His first response was disbelief. Then he told me how your dad had made some comments to him the last couple weeks about my seductive actions around him. That I would lift my breast with my hand when I walked towards him, smiling as I did, that I would wait until his bedroom door was opened and then walk by in just my bra and underpants and the night Simon had caught us in the hug, that I was the aggressor. Of course, I denied everything and said he was lying, so my uncle took me right down to the church. We found your dad in his office counseling a woman whose husband had a reputation of being a rounder. My uncle did not waste time. He told the woman she would have to leave and then he asked your dad if he had raped me."

"He continued to lie. 'I had intercourse with Martha but it was consensual. In fact, she seduced me. After I had comforted her because she was upset about her boyfriend getting drunk, I was getting ready for my final prayers before I went to bed, and she came into my room completely naked and started kissing and caressing me. She then led me to her bed. I was asking the Lord for strength, but I was not a match for the devil.'"

"My uncle was watching both of us while your dad was talking. He didn't say anything but I knew he didn't believe the story your dad was telling. Despite that, what he did next was the cruelest thing he could do. He said to your dad, 'Will you marry her?'"

"Your dad's face lit up and he said, 'Of course I will marry her.'"

"I yelled and screamed so loud I am sure half the people of Dalton heard me. 'I'm not marrying him. I'm going to marry Bruno. I refuse to marry anyone if Bruno won't have me.'"

"My uncle looked at me hard with a stern, unsympathetic look and said, 'Martha, I sponsored your immigration, and since you are not a citizen yet, if I withdraw my sponsorship, you would be sent back to Sweden. Either you agree to marry Pastor Iverson or I will withdraw my sponsorship.' I ran home, crying all the way, with a strong death wish. Hannah was home and kept me safe. The wedding took place three weeks later and your dad got a call, which he later told me was arranged by Simon, from a new church in Breckenridge, Minnesota. We moved there a month after the wedding. It was the town all three of you girls were born in."

"So, you never saw Bruno again?" Molly asked sadly.

With a big smile, Martha said, "That's the main reason I told you this long sad story. About a month after your dad's death, the doorbell rang and I opened the door. Although it had been over thirty years, I knew. It was Bruno! He started to say something, but I just grabbed him, hugged him and kissed him. He had seen an article in the Fergus Falls paper about your dad dying and not wanting to be improper waited a month before coming to find me. He had never married and had moved up to Warren, Minnesota, to escape the memories of Dalton. He then became one of the biggest potato growers in the Red River Valley, and without bragging, he said he had become fairly wealthy. After talking for hours about what had happened, he said despite it being thirty years his proposal was still good. Without hesitation, I said 'Yes, Oh, Yes!'"

"Did you get married?" Molly was so excited.

"No, I told him I had to tell all three of you and I do have some things to take care of regarding your dad's estate."

"I just had a brilliant idea." Molly was now bubbling over with excitement. "You may not want to wait, but if so, after Tommy and I are divorced, we could have a double wedding. Of course, you wouldn't have to wait until then to go up to Warren," Molly added with a wicked little grin.

"Don't worry about that dear. I have already been up to Warren several times," Martha smiled.

"Given what happened, why didn't you divorce Dad?" Molly felt the need to justify her actions in planning the divorce from Ray.

"During most of the years of my marriage divorce was almost not heard of except for among the idle rich. Also, I didn't know how I would survive. I had no idea if Bruno would even talk to me let alone marry me. I guess in a lot of ways I was scared—scared of your dad, scared of being sent back to Sweden, scared of being alone. Also, raising you three kids kept me busy so I didn't have time to feel sorry for myself. After your sister Marlene was born, we moved to the first church your dad had in Minneapolis. I had a lifestyle change. By then your dad was obsessed with advancing as high as he could in the church hierarchy so we agreed to avoid any hint of marital problems to the outside world. I demanded and got a separate bedroom and had minimal contact with your dad in our private lives. I took on the role as the active minister's wife and came to enjoy the contact with the women of the church and the challenges of making the church a better place for all the parishioners. So the bottom line was I was content and did not think of Bruno or what might have been. Maybe that's why God has given me this blessing."

"After you made the change in your lifestyle what did dad do for his sexual needs? I didn't know what it was as I grew up but looking back, I guess he always had a high testosterone level."

"I didn't really care. There were some women at the various churches who acted in a way towards me that led me to believe they knew details of our private lives that could only have come from your dad sharing personal information. I suspected that it may have been pillow talk. I also had reason to believe there may have been some women outside of the church but again I didn't care."

As Martha was finishing her last comments, Kelly and Molly's kids returned.

"I'm sure glad we talked. The idea of a double wedding really excites me." Molly's whole body showed that excitement as she hugged her mom.

For Molly, the rest of the summer seemed to drag on as if it would last forever. By the end of September, she started marking off the days until Thanksgiving on a private calendar she kept in her lock box.

Chapter 12
October 1946

The surface of Lake Superior was as smooth and reflective as a mirror. Despite this Captain Hall of the Johnathan Stevenson was apprehensive as he stood at the wheel with his first mate, looking at the red morning sky. He called down to the ship's radio operator for the second time since he had come up to the foredeck an hour ago. "Any change in the timing?"

"No, sir, the weather report has just been updated. Rain and winds of 15 to 20 knots beginning at about 22:30 hours then increasing to 50 to 70 knots by 1:00 hours tomorrow, October 30th."

"How far do we need to go?" the captain asked the first mate as he continued to scan the skies.

"One hundred sixty-six nautical miles will put us two miles into Whitefish Bay."

"We need to be there by midnight. Sixteen and a half hours, 10 knots per hour, can this old girl do it?" The captain was talking to some power in the sky more than to the first mate.

"Yes sir, she's a good ship and we will have calm seas at least until 12:00 hours."

The thing that the captain most liked about the first mate was his positive attitude. It was the main reason he made him the first mate.

Captain Hall took the mike. "This is the captain. I'm making this broadcast to update everyone on the coming storm. If I hear anyone say, *Red skies in the morning, sailors take warning* I'll dock them a week's pay. I want every crew member to be fully confident that this ship will pass through the coming storm with flying colors and at this time tomorrow morning we will be sailing on calm seas, like now, except we will be in Whitefish Bay, safe from all storms. Now as you finish your morning mess, I want all of you to prepare for one long, hard work day since we are going to maintain maximum speed until we are in Whitefish Bay. Also, as you work your respective shifts, I want everyone to be alert to any problems or malfunctions that could slow this great ship down or increase the chance of damage from the storm as we pass through it. I'm putting First Mate Winters on the mike now to report about the predicted timing and strength of the storm and our distance from our goal. He will be making updated reports throughout the day. Pay attention so we all can be fully prepared for any changes that may happen."

The ship continued over the smooth lake. At the noon mess Tommy, Arvin and Hans ate together.

"How bad will it be?" Tommy inquired.

"Seen worse," Hans nodded as he ate. "Four years ago on the final run, we got hit early in the morning, and it didn't let up all day. Thought that was it. We wouldn't have made it except around 20:00 hour the storm moved quickly north and the captain sailed almost straight south. We lost a boiler. Limped into Whitefish Bay and had to have a tow boat bring us into Sault Ste. Marie. Going to get some more meat."

"I was on that trip. No one ate, but everyone was throwing up." Arvin kept the story going until Hans returned. "Heard you're getting off at Detroit?"

"Ya, Captain gave me permission. Didn't need me on the final run from Detroit to Cleveland. Have some business I need to take care of as soon as I get home." Tommy made room for Hans to sit back down.

"What are you going to do for a new job?" Hans took up the questioning.

"Not sure. Applying at several places in the cities. Hope to get something like the supervisory position I had at the Arsenal." Tommy wished he had a better answer.

Hans and Arvin exchanged glances knowing there was more to the story.

The afternoon was busy. All hands who didn't have a regular shift at their job spent the time checking and rechecking all the hatches and other exposed areas of the ship to make sure everything was as secure as possible. The evening mess was cancelled. Cookie said, "Ain't no use in feeding you guys. Just make you sicker, quicker."

"I raised you two bucks," Hans said. "Listen to the wind pick up." It was 20:00 hours and the rain had begun at 19:00 hours.

I'll call and raise you two more," Tommy said, looking stone-faced at his cards.

The winds were creating heavy waves. All the seamen not on duty were advised to stay in their cabins. Tommy had joined Hans, Arvin and Carl, another crewman, in Hans' cabin for a few hands of poker since no one was planning on sleeping.

"Tommy-boy, I can tell a bluff when I see one. I call. Give me one card," Hans said to Arvin who was dealing. Both Arvin and Carl had folded.

"I'm good." Tommy nodded at Arvin.

"Oh momma! Just what the baby needed," Hans looked at his cards. "Bet five."

Without changing his expression, Tommy said, "Call and raise you five."

"I'll save myself five," Hans said as he threw down his cards, the seven through ten of spades and the jack of hearts. "Can I see what you have?"

"Sure." Tommy, now smiling, showed his hand. "Just like Wild Bill Hickok when Jack McCall shot him, aces and eights, the Deadman's Hand."

"Don't say that in this storm." Carl wasn't smiling.

"Have to get down to the boiler room." Hans picked up his remaining money and started putting on his storm coat and rubber waterproof boots. "We will pick this game up when we are on smooth seas. Need to get my money back home in my pocket. You guys all hang tight. In three hours it will be so quiet we can all sleep like babies."

"Think I will do some letter writing," Tommy said as he left to go back to his cabin.

Forty-five minutes later Roy knocked on Tommy's cabin door. "Need your help, Tommy. Got a call from the first mate, worried that the number three hatch is working loose. Said I should get some help and check it out. Better put on your full storm outfit. Really nasty now."

They descended down the steep steps to the ship's deck and slowly worked their way across the wet and slippery deck to the number three hatch. The wind howled. The waves smashed the side of the ship and rocked it like a toy in a bathtub. Roy moved close to Tommy's side and talked directly into his ear. "You ever pay attention to my last name, Kelseltz?"

Tommy looked directly into Roy's eyes. "You're Molly's brother-in-law!"

"You got it buddy. Here I have a message from Ray." Before Tommy could react Roy's, right arm came full force across his body and hit Tommy squarely between his eyes just above his nose.

Tommy staggered backward gaining speed on the wet, slippery deck as he desperately tried to grab ahold of something. His back hit the ship's railing, as he failed. Upon impact with the rail Tommy's body did a complete somersault, hitting the deep, black, cold, violent, waters of Lake Superior head first. Thunder roared. A titanic wave rose up as if it was feasting on Tommy's body, hitting the ship. Roy grasped onto the lock of the hatch to prevent himself from being swept overboard, and he waited for the wave to subside.

After carefully working his way back to the steps, Roy climbed back to the cabin level and ducked into Tommy's cabin. He quickly found a nearly empty half pint of Seagram's Tommy had on his closet shelf. Roy took the bottle and spilled just enough on the cabin floor to create a scent. He left the cabin, without noticing that he had dropped the paper bag that had held the bottle nor the letter that Tommy had started. Once he was out of Tommy's cabin, he called the captain on the ship's phone.

Excitedly, he said, "Sir, this is Roy Kelseltz! There's a man overboard, a man overboard, Tommy Haas was washed overboard!"

"Roy, pull yourself together. I'm going to give some orders and then you can calmly tell me what happened."

"Engage all searchlights, We have a man overboard," the captain's voice boomed over the ship's sound system.

"Shall we launch lifeboats and cut our engines?" First Mate Winters had already placed the procedure manual on the captain's console above the ship's control panel.

The captain shook his head and said privately, "No, the world's strongest swimmer couldn't survive more than five minutes in these waters. We need to make the bay within the next hour. I can't risk the ship and whole crew by slowing down to do a search. What is the latest reckoning?"

"Seven point two nautical miles, sir. Fifty-two minutes at our current speed to enter the bay."

"Any reports of serious damage?" The captain repeated the same question he had asked every five minutes.

"No sir, but several reports of extreme stress at various locations. We are being battered, but all the hatches are holding."

"Very good." The captain got back on the phone with Roy. "Roy, in a concise manner tell me what happened and then go back to your cabin and write out a full report. When we are safely in the bay, I will have you come up to the command deck and we will review this whole matter."

"Sir, at 23:05 hours—I know the exact time because I was checking how long it was until my shift—Tommy knocked on my cabin door. He said he had gone down to the deck to look for any damage and he believed the number three hatch was coming loose. He requested that I assist him in going out on the deck to verify that the hatch was secure or to report any problem with the hatch. I agreed, and we determined that the hatch was secure and were going to return to our cabins when a gigantic wave hit us. Tommy lost his footing and I tried to grab him but almost lost my own. If I hadn't held on to the hatch lock, I also would have been washed overboard. Sir, I don't know if I should put this in the report, but I believe I smelled alcohol on Tommy's breath."

"I want a complete report. We will have to go over every fact fully and be accurate in what happened. See you later. Now I have to get this ship into Whitefish Bay."

"Any sightings with the searchlights?" The captain turned to the first mate.

"Only heavy seas."

"This is the captain," he broadcast to the entire ship. "Tonight, we lost a fellow seaman. Tommy Haas was washed overboard as he was making sure the ship was secured. Given the very minimal chance he would survive in this storm, I made a decision not to risk the lives of the whole crew and instructed that the ship will continue with the maximum speed possible into Whitefish Bay. All search lights can be turned off. I request that all hands stop for a moment of silence. God, bless the soul of our fellow seaman, Tommy Haas."

Chapter 13

March 1951

Larry hurried into the house after being dropped off by the school bus. It was the first Thursday in March, two weeks from the day when he, Gordon, and Ronnie would be going to the Minnesota State basketball tournament. The three of them were going to sleep on the floor of Larry's sister Ruth's house on Minnehaha Avenue in south Minneapolis.

Ruth and her husband, Chuck, married last June, had purchased the house under the GI Bill. Chuck had served as a Seabee in the Pacific. This would be the first time Larry would be staying overnight in the Cities. The few other times he had been down to, Minneapolis and St. Paul, were either day trips to the Minnesota State Fair or school trips. Larry was excited to be going.

"Ma, where is the Duluth paper? I want to read the sports page about the district playoffs for the basketball tournament."

"On the living room table, along with the Aitkin paper. How was school?"

"Fine, got an A on the history test."

"That's good. Your lunch is ready. You can read the papers while you eat. Pa isn't back from his shopping trip to Aitkin. You'll have to get out and feed the cows their silage and then clean the barn. It might be milking time before he gets home." Larry's mom set down a plate of ham sandwiches in front of him, along with a bowl of blueberry sauce, cookies and cake.

Larry grabbed the papers, got a cup of coffee and sat down to eat. Then he saw the headline on the front page of the Aitkin paper.

Arrests made in murder case

Larry quickly read the article.

County Attorney Jim Ryan and Sheriff Oscar Hewitt announced at a press conference on Tuesday that Irving Moss and Virgil Larsen, both of Isle,

Minnesota, and Edward Johansson of Wahkon, Minnesota, were arrested and charged with second degree murder in the death of Raymond Kelseltz on January 5, 1951. Mr. Kelseltz, of Eagan, Minnesota, was found dead in his fish house on Mille Lacs Lake, a mile north of the south Aitkin County line. He had been assaulted with his own ice pick. Mr. Ryan stated he would be convening a Grand Jury within the next month to seek a first-degree murder indictment. The two officials would not comment any further, but this reporter did obtain a copy of the arrest warrant.

The warrant stated there was sufficient evidence to place the three defendants at the scene of the crime. The owner of the resort from which the victim had entered onto the lake testified that the three defendants were in his resort drinking beer shortly after the time the investigators believe the crime was committed.

Additional evidence presented in the warrant include fingerprints of one of the defendants found on and inside the victim's pick-up and an ice auger that was identified as belonging to the victim which was sold by one of the defendants to a bait shop in Brainerd shortly after the murder.

"Ma, did you read this! I can't believe it."

"What can't you believe? That they killed someone just to steal an ice auger or that they are guilty?"

"I don't know. It just doesn't make sense. I didn't know about the ice auger. Maybe they believed he owned something more valuable. Irving and Eddie wouldn't hurt a flea. If Virgil did it, he would have used his fists."

"Well the truth will come out. It always does. You better get to the barn. The cows need to be fed." Larry's mom was starting to make supper.

Larry started to head out to the barn when he saw a new car coming up the driveway. He stopped to see what stranger was coming to visit then realized it was his dad.

"How you like it?" Larry's dad proudly walked around the 1951 black four-door Ford. "Didn't plan on this when I stopped at the Ford dealership. But John Recka, the owner, made me a deal. I called the bank and got financing. Now you will have a decent car to drive to the Cities."

"Wow! Only 45 miles on the odometer, really new. I will have to be really careful driving in city traffic now. You didn't see the sheriff while you were in town?" Larry started the car to listen to the engine, and then he checked to see if the radio worked.

"I made sure it had a good radio." Larry's dad was smiling. "Yes, the sheriff was in the Tip-Top Café when I stopped for a hot beef sandwich."

"Did he talk about the arrests?" Larry turned off the car so he could hear his dad better.

"Not much, but based on his demeanor as we talked, I don't think he's too certain he has the right suspects. He complained about the County Attorney wanting to do something before the fall election. Let's get Ma to see the car."

●●●●●●●●●●

As Larry drove into the driveway of Gordon's house, he looked for Gordon's car but it was not there. The boys had plans to go down to Tony's Dance Hall on Pine Lake, east of McGrath. It was half way between Finlayson and McGrath so it was a different crowd than the dance hall near Isle. There was a beautiful Finnish girl Larry was hoping to get to know better who lived east of Finlayson. Maybe tonight she would be at Tony's.

As Larry got to the front door, Dennis, Gordon's brother hurried out. "Out of the way, Larry, got a hot date." Dennis, who was two years older than Gordon was a known woman's man.

"Gordon's not home," Eleanor said while she held the door open for Larry. "Come in. We had dinner without him. I have some coffee and cake left over. He should be home soon. I suppose you three have big plans for the night."

"Just going down to Pine Lake to a dance." Larry walked into the house.

Eleanor, who looked more haggard and older every time Larry came over, said, "He was just going over to Melvin Smith's to see if he could hire him to haul a load of firewood down to the Cities. I'm worried. You know how Melvin drinks."

Melvin Smith, a sixty-year-old bachelor, made a living by hiring himself and his truck out to haul whatever needed hauling. When he wasn't driving, he was usually drinking.

"I'm really getting worried about Gordon. I know he's been drinking a lot harder ever since the first of the year. I used to blame you and Ronnie, but I assumed you guys just drank a few beers. Now, he's spending more time with Melvin and his crony, old Joe Sandusksi. They drink nothing but whiskey. That was his dad's problem especially in the early years of our marriage." Eleanor's spoke as if she was trying to wipe out a memory.

Larry sat down at the dining room table while Eleanor went into the kitchen to get the coffee and cake. As he sat there he noticed a book with a picture of the Johnathan Stevenson on its cover. Larry picked it up and was looking at it as Eleanor returned with the cake. "Is this the boat Gordon's dad was on?"

"It was the boat that Tommy was washed overboard from," Eleanor said sharply with the same bitterness Gordon expressed anytime he talked about the question of how his dad vanished.

Larry continued to page through the book while he ate his cake. On page 7, the 1946 crew was pictured, with their names listed below. First, he found Tommy's picture and then noticed a name.

"Roy Kelseltz, that's the name of the guy who got murdered on Mille Lacs. No, wait, it was Raymond Kelseltz. Funny the names are so close. Can't be too common of a name," Larry said to Eleanor.

"Not too uncommon. When Tommy worked at the Arsenal, he worked with a Molly Kels..." Eleanor said with venom hanging on every word. She was unable to finish the sentence. She turned and quickly went back into the kitchen to avoid Larry seeing her come apart.

Larry looked at the kitchen door for a minute, then back to the picture. Taking the book out to his car, he found his school notebook and made a diagram.

Ray Kelseltz   Roy Kelseltz,

Arsenal

Molly Kelseltz

Johnathan Stevenson

As Larry was going back into the house, he saw the headlights coming up the driveway. It was Gordon driving way too fast for the icy road. He hit his brakes and did a complete wheelie, just missing Larry's dad's new car by a few feet and then plowing into a snowbank.

Gordon got out of his car, slipping and falling right on his ass. Larry ran over to help him up but could not help laughing. "Tough day buddy?"

"How the hell are you, asshole? Damn near get killed and you laugh your ass off. Man, I'm drunk. Can't do no dance tonight. Hold on to me. Ma's going to be pissed. Watch out! I'm going to throw up." Gordon kept talking and swearing as Larry led him into the house.

●●●●●●●●●●

"So we're going home alone again," Ronnie chided Larry as they left Tony's. "What happened with your little Finnish beauty?"

"We did our little dance again. I told her that she was the most beautiful woman in seven counties and she said it would be nice to hear that from me sometime when I was sober. Maybe I should surprise her and show up at her house with flowers, cold sober." Larry contemplated what would happen if he took that risk.

"Boy, if you did that I would have to look for some new drinking buddies. Gordon will be in the army and you will be a married man," Ronnie said, partially in jest.

"What about you? You danced all night with that chick from Askov." Larry was enjoying driving the new car.

"I was sure I was going to score. She kept telling me how she loved the way I danced, especially when we danced slow and close. Also, I tried to impress her by telling her how my buddy had a brand-new car with a big back seat. Then as we danced the last dance and I sweetly whispered in her ear that we should beat the crowd and head for your car, she stopped and tearfully told me about how her fiancé had just written her that he was sure he would be shipped out to Korea as soon as he finished his basic training. 'It wouldn't be right to be unfaithful to him just seven weeks after he left.'"

"I expect that in a few more weeks being unfaithful won't be such a problem. Hopefully. I'll see." Ronnie opened their last beer.

"Since we're alone, I have a question for you that you never heard me ask. I will totally forget your response." Larry looked at Ronnie with a pained expression. "Do you think Gordon is capable of killing someone?"

Ronnie choked as he finished drinking the beer. Startled by the question he said, "You mean the guy on Mille Lacs?"

"Well, first, in general, is he capable of murder?" Larry was nervous.

"Remember when Gordon got into that fight up in Barnum, after the basketball game last winter? If you and I hadn't pulled him off that Barnum kid, I think he was mad enough to kill him." Ronnie looked straight ahead out the window as he recalled the fight. "He didn't know the guy on Mille Lacs, did he?"

"Again, this conversation never happened, but I believe the dead fisherman has something to do with Gordon's dad's death. I doubt Gordon will go with us to the state tournament. If he doesn't, I have a couple ideas for some investigative work you and I can do while we are in the Cities." Larry's body suddenly shook with the idea that his best friend was a murderer and he may be the one to prove it.

Chapter 14
November 1946

The loud sound of the mailman's car muffler woke Molly. She had worked the night shift at the hospital. After picking up the kids from her mom's, she got them off to school and had gone to bed. Ray had gone up to Buhl for two weeks of deer hunting. She quickly pulled on her slacks and a warm pull-over sweatshirt, without bothering to put on her underclothes, and hurried out to get the mail. She failed to notice the cold of the mid-November day. Something was very wrong. Tommy should have been home from his final voyage two weeks ago, yet she hadn't received any letters, phone calls or other communication from him. Everyday her rush to the mailbox had become more urgent. This day there was a letter postmarked from McGrath without a return address. Molly resisted the urge to open the letter until she was back in the house.

Dear Molly, My Love,

As I am preparing to face the storm of telling Eleanor that I'm leaving her and moving to be with you, a major storm is making our last night on Lake Superior a real challenge. The winds are battering our ship with such force the whole crew is on alert. About two hours from now we sail out of Lake Superior into Whitefish Bay of Lake Michigan and the storm will be behind us. Then I will take on my personal storm.

I have received permission to leave the ship in Detroit and have bus tickets back to Duluth. I will call you when I'm back. I have an appointment with a lawyer in Aitkin and will meet with him on the way home. I am hoping to get some type of joint custody arrangement so the boys can spend time with us when they are not in school.

I am so looking forward to having the separation from Eleanor behind me and being with you for our new life together. Since that night at the Arsenal when you turned and smiled at me, I have held on to a dream of you and I being together. Now I see a clear path to it happening.

Got to go. My shipmate Roy just told me that the captain wants us to check out a hatch door latch that may be coming undone. The storm is causing problems. I have a lot more to tell you when I'm done checking out the problem.

Molly reread the short unfinished letter a second time before looking at the second letter in the envelope.

You Home Wrecking Little Bitch,

I guess Tommy was writing this to you. I got your address from some of the letters you had sent to him. This unfinished letter and the other letters were with Tommy's personal effects that the Coast Guard officer brought to me when he came to tell me in person that Tommy was washed overboard during the storm. I hope I never get to see you in person cause I don't know what I would do.

You not only would have robbed me of my husband, if he had lived, but you have caused me to live the rest of my life with only bitter memories of the man I was married to for 16 years.

Eleanor Haas
A widow unable to grieve.

Molly reread the letter from Eleanor. Her eyes kept focusing on one phrase, *if he had lived*. "What does she mean?" Molly yelled out loud. "If he had lived. Of course, he lived. Of course, he lived. Tommy isn't dead. He isn't dead. He will come to my door any minute." Without her even realizing it a primeval scream came out of Molly's mouth, a scream so loud and anguished that any neighbor living closer than a half mile would have called the police.

She ran into the kitchen. The kids' two cereal bowls still sat on the table from the morning. She picked them up one at a time and hurled them against the far wall. Her coffee cup, the one Tommy had always used when he was staying with her, was next. It shattered like the two bowls as it hit the wall. Then she saw the long sharp knife on the counter. She ran to the outside door, stopping to pull off her sweatshirt and then continued in the cold toward the new woodshed with the knife in her hand. As she got to the woodshed she saw the school bus coming. Hoping the driver had not seen her half nude body, she ran back into the house, and dropped the knife. Quickly putting on her sweatshirt, she hugged her two children as they came into the house.

"Do you two remember the man who brought Mommy a load of firewood?" Molly was crying hard.

"You mean before the woodshed burned?" Junior asked.

"Yes, he was Mommy's very close friend. He died." A more intense wave of crying erupted as she said "died."

"Did you love him?" Holly asked.

"Yes, I loved him."

"More than you love Daddy?" Junior asked.

Molly looked at Junior not knowing how to answer him.

"Come. Mommy has to call Grandma to see if she can come over to help us."

Molly's mom brought two sleeping pills when she came over and got Molly to take them. She called the hospital and said Molly was too sick to work. After Molly and the kids were asleep she cleaned up the mess in the kitchen.

The next morning Molly was immobile with depression. After her mom got the children off to school, she got Molly to call the hospital to arrange a week's vacation.

"I don't want to live. I don't want to live," she turned to tell her mom as soon as she hung up the phone.

"Molly dear, listen to me. I'm so glad I told you my story of Bruno and your dad so you will understand how I experienced the same pain you're going through now. The night I was forced into marrying your dad he demanded sex. I refused and he raped me. He then fell asleep and I went into the kitchen to cry. There was a butcher knife laying on the counter. I picked it up and put my wrist on the counter and was ready to chop down with the knife when I felt Marie move in my womb. I dropped the knife, bent over the counter and cried the hardest I ever cried and promised Marie I would be strong and survive for her. Please do the same for Holly and Junior."

Molly looked at her mom and for several minutes said nothing, thinking about what she had been told. Then her face transformed, as if a plastic surgeon had operated, from a weak, beaten manifestation to a determined, hard, powerful appearance. "Oh! Thank you, Oh! Thank you, Mom. I want to live so I can be a Mom to my children like you are to me. Also, I'm sure Ray and Roy are responsible for Tommy's death. I'm going to live to make sure his death is requited."

●●●●●●●●●●

"Hello, honey, are you home?" Ray returned from his hunting trip the Sunday afternoon before Thanksgiving. Silence was his only answer. Then he found the note Molly had left for him.

> *Ray,*
>
> *I was called into work. The kids are at Mom's for the night. I know you are flying out early tomorrow morning. Leave a note when you will be home. Molly*

Ray felt the coldness of the note and a wave of loneliness overtook him. He quickly scribbled a response.

> *Molly,*
>
> *Sad I missed you. Will be home Wednesday night. Roy is coming down for Thanksgiving. Bringing down the venison from our hunt.*
>
> *Love, Ray.*

Ray arrived to a dark, empty home from his flight just after midnight. It was Thanksgiving Day. The house was cold since the fire in the wood furnace was almost burned out. After filling the furnace with wood, he looked around the kitchen and realized that there wasn't any sign of preparation for a Thanksgiving Day dinner. Puzzled and exhausted he went to bed without noticing the changes to the bedroom furnishings. He awoke in the morning to the sound of Roy knocking on the front door.

"Hello brother, you look confused and tired," Roy said as Ray let him into the house. "Where's your family?"

"Don't know. Got home after midnight and no one was home." Ray, still only half-awake, looked around for a note hoping for an explanation. "I haven't talked to Molly since I got home. Just exchanged notes. Sure expected to have a big Thanksgiving dinner."

"Think she knows about Tommy?" Roy's voice spoke with trepidation as he mentioned his name.

"Don't know who would have contacted her." Ray tried to conceal his anxiety. "I'll make some coffee."

"Hope you have some JD for cream. Long drive down." Roy followed Ray into the kitchen.

Just as they sat down with their cups of coffee Molly came home and stormed in.

"What do we have here? Two brothers plotting another murder?"

"WHAT THE HELL ARE YOU TALKING ABOUT?" Roy shouted, his face turning a whiter shade of pale.

"WHO are you talking about?" Ray tried to keep his composure while attempting to have an innocent not knowing look on his face.

"Both of you shut up. The game-playing is over." Molly's voice rose several octaves but remained calm and strong.

"I have Tommy's last letter, the one he was writing when you came to get him onto the deck so you could knock him overboard." Molly looked right into Roy's face without any hint of bluff in her words.

"I have the name of the investigating officer with the Coast Guard and will provide him with my information and your motives unless you do what I want," Molly continued.

"Still don't know what you are talking about, but what do you want?" Ray smiled weakly. "Molly, I love you."

"Cut the bullshit. If you want, I will agree to a divorce on the following terms. I keep this house, have full custody of Holly and Junior with you having normal visitation rights, you pay half your take-home pay for child support, maintain a life insurance policy with me as beneficiary, and I get half of your retirement benefits. If you don't want that I'm willing to stay in this marriage since now I don't have any reason to get out." Saying the last few words broke Molly's curtain of steel and she choked hard, tried to wipe away her tears but failed. She turned away from Ray and Roy and partly regained her composure.

"If I stay, we will be living apart in this house. If you didn't notice, I have moved all my stuff out of our bedroom into the spare bedroom. I installed a lock on the door. You're never to come into that room. You will have to deposit half your take home pay into an account in my sole name and pay half the household expenses besides. Except when we do joint things with the kids I don't plan on having any contact with you. These are your two choices. If you don't want to do either I'll schedule a meeting with a Coast Guard guy. You have all weekend to decide. The kids and I are having dinner with my family and then we are going to Warren in the morning. Mom is getting married Saturday." Molly turned and was gone.

"Pour me some of that Jack Daniel's straight." Roy was sweating. "What could he have written? I'm sure he had no idea what I was going to do. He didn't write anything after he went over the rail."

"Maybe she's just bluffing. How did she even know? I think everything I enjoy in life is over." Ray ran into the bedroom, fell face down on the bed and cried for two hours until falling into a troubled sleep.

Roy sat and drank the rest of the bottle until he too fell asleep, interrupted by nightmares of red lights and police sirens coming after him in an endless chase.

Chapter 15
1946 to 1947

After giving Ray his two choices, Molly went to her mom's house for Thanksgiving dinner. All her family was there, but no one asked about Ray being absent. The next morning everyone made the seven-hour trip to Warren.

Bruno Happala, Molly's mom's fiancé, was the most respected man in Warren, and in Marshall County, of which Warren was the county seat. In the 25 years he'd been farming in the county he had been a prime mover in the development of the Red River Valley potato trade and was now working on the development of the sugar beet industry as an alternative crop. As his farm prospered and grew, many of the local mothers tried to devise ways to interest Bruno in their daughters. Many unmarried women tried to attract his attention. Bruno's complete lack of attention to any of these women caused a few rumors about him not being interested in the opposite sex. However, all the men who worked with or met him admired his masculinity and knew he had no sexual interest in them. When there was talk in the bedrooms and the bars throughout the county about Bruno's sexual preference, the conclusion was, in most cases, that he was just not interested in sex, and hard work was his only enjoyment. So when the story broke that Bruno had gone to Minneapolis and proposed to his teenage sweetheart who had just become a widow, the news spread like wildfire. The wedding of these two lovers became the most anticipated wedding in the county's history.

The bride's wedding party arrived just after dark on Friday night. Bruno, who had built a very large farmhouse for a bachelor farmer, had arranged for extra beds so Molly's whole family would be able to stay in his house. Although Molly's mom had spent most of the prior two months with Bruno and moved most of her clothing and personal effects into the master bedroom, Bruno and she decided they wanted to make the wedding night seem more special. So Molly and her mom slept together, and Bruno slept alone in his bedroom.

After unpacking what they had brought from Minneapolis for the wedding and eating a small supper, Molly's mom turned to her. "Oh, my poor dear child. I have such conflicting feelings running through my brain. Tomorrow will be the happiest day of my life. Yet, I have such a pain in my heart thinking about how you were cheated out of the same happiness."

Years later, when Molly remembered that point in time and what her mother had said, she was able to identify it as the moment some portion of her thinking process changed: It hardened. She thought that she would have to avenge Tommy's death, but then she realized she was not avenging Tommy's death, she was avenging what had been taken from her.

In the morning, the three daughters kicked Bruno out of his own house while they helped their mom prepare for being a bride a second time.

Upon his return, Bruno asked, "Where's my bride? I want to see how beautiful you three have made her."

"You can't see her until the wedding. We don't want this marriage to start with any bad luck," Marie said. As she was speaking the first snowflakes began to fall.

Bruno spared no expense in having a large wedding. He was a member of a small Finnish Lutheran Church, so Bruno rented the Grange Hall, the largest public meeting place in Warren. The ceremony was scheduled for 2 p.m. followed by a large buffet dinner prepared by the ladies aid group from all three of the Lutheran churches in Warren. Then at 6 p.m. the party was to start and last until "It's time for the morning milking," as the invitation stated. Bruno hired the best old-time dance band in the area and was also having his family band play. The Happala Family Band now included the next generation of the family and played both current and old-time music.

Bruno told several people, "I might be allowed to take a few turns on the fiddle. Had plenty of time to practice, living alone. Been working on playing a lot of Bob Wills' stuff. So, you might hear a little Texas swing. Thinking about doing 'Keeper of My Heart' for my new bride."

The guests started to arrive early. The talk was not about the wedding, but about the snow. The Friday night forecast was for four to five inches after midnight Saturday. By 1p.m. the four to five inches were already on the ground and the snow was getting heavier. Bruno, the county sheriff, Warren's police and fire chiefs huddled and made arrangements. Several farmers who lived close to town and who still had horses and sleighs brought them to town and stabled them in a barn near the hall. All the town's people who had room in their house for guests signed up on a poster board, and the county's three snow plows were brought to the hall to be ready to clear the roads to the town's people's homes.

After the arrangements were made and the delayed ceremony was to begin, several things went wrong. Bruno, in his haste to make arrangements, had left the rings at home and the road to his house was now impassable. The bridal flower bouquets were still at the florists and the minister, who had arrived late because of the snow, came without his prepared wedding sermon. Despite these problems, the bride looked stunning, the music was superb, and the minister ad-libbed a sermon that was much better than the one he'd prepared.

The dinner was consumed by a roomful of spirited guests who, demonstrating their pioneering attribute, did not worry about the snow making them captive, instead enjoyed an event that they knew would be a part of the town lore for a long time.

After dinner, Bruno jumped onto the bandstand and announced, "Thank you all for coming to share the greatest day of my life. The love and support you have shown me the last 25 years has been indescribable, but it pales in comparison to the love and support I have experienced this afternoon. Now I want you to let loose and I want you all to have the best time of your life. Don't even try to guess the amount I spent on beer and booze. We're not going to run out, and no one need worry about driving drunk tonight because no one will be able to drive. Start the music."

The town mayor approached Bruno after his announcement, and said, "My wife and I would be honored if you and your bride would use our master bedroom as a honeymoon suite. She braved the snow and went home after the dinner and has everything ready. The sheriff will haul you in his pick-up anytime you're ready."

Bruno, after taking a few turns with the band, took the mayor and sheriff up on their offer. On the way to the mayor's house he asked the sheriff, "My real problem is how can I get to Fargo? We have tickets to fly out to Minneapolis and then on to Havana. When I was working developing sugar beets, I spent some time in Cuba and decided it's where I would want a honeymoon."

"What time is your flight?" the sheriff asked.

"Three tomorrow afternoon," Bruno replied.

"Well, the state roads should be open well enough by 10 in the morning. I'll clear it with the highway patrol and being in Fargo by two shouldn't be a problem."

As predicted the party did last until milking time. The several farmers who had dairy cows were taken by snowplow, horses or sleighs to their farms and all of them had several volunteer farmers to help. As daylight broke, the guests were anxious to get outside to see the amount of snow. The Grand Forks radio station was reporting snow amounts of 18 to 22 inches with wind gusts of 35 to 45 miles per hour.

One person who didn't party until morning was Molly. The more she saw the excitement, joy and happiness surrounding her mom and Bruno's wedding, the more she became bitter and depressed that it was not the double wedding she had planned and dreamed about. She started to drink. Beer at first, 7-7's next, and then straight whiskey. The drunker she got, the wilder she danced, which didn't go unnoticed by the single men with whom she was dancing.

"Where's your husband?"

"Home, he's a pilot and had a flight this week-end," was her response early in the night.

"Where's your husband?"

"Home, he wasn't invited," later in the night.

"Where's your husband?"

"Home, I guess. Who the fuck cares?" much later in the night.

"Where's your husband?"

"Dead, if I had my wish," near the end of the night.

A few minutes after three, Molly wandered out into the storm. Marie was, by this time, keeping a watchful eye on her sister. She followed Molly out and after Molly barfed up all the dinner and alcohol that was in her stomach and then spent about 10 minutes with dry heaves, she led Molly into the office of the Grange where there was a small couch. Molly immediately stripped off her maid of honor dress, and all her undergarments and fell into a deep sleep on the couch. Marie covered her nude body the best she could with the discarded clothes, and found a notepad on which she wrote, "DO NOT DISTURB" and taped it to the office door. For Molly, the party was over.

Chapter 16

January 1947

Upon their return from Warren, Molly and the kids found, much to Molly's relief, that Ray was gone and had left a note that he was flying. She also found a notice, in the mail, from the Dakota County Court that she had been selected for jury duty. She was to report on January Fifteenth.

After waiting as part of a jury pool for three civil cases, she was selected for a high-profile criminal case. The case involved the death of a successful stockbroker's wife who had been shot after returning home from an afternoon grocery shopping trip. The back door of the couple's large house, in an exclusive neighborhood of Sunfish Lake, Minnesota, had been broken into and it appeared that the wife had interrupted a home robbery. A retired neighbor, walking his dog, heard the single shot and saw a man run from the house to a car parked on a nearby side street.

He quickly hid behind some bushes and memorized the make of the car and the first four numbers on the Illinois license plate. Then, not daring to go to the victim's house, he hurried to his own house and called the police. The police did not arrive for 15 minutes and spent over two hours investigating the crime scene before interviewing the neighbor. It was three hours before a bulletin was issued for the get-away car. No one was caught, but after two weeks a known Chicago mob member was identified as the owner of the car. Before he could be interviewed he was shot in a gang-like shooting in Chicago.

Daily reports in the Twin Cities newspapers detailed evidence of the stockbroker's infidelity with various women, the large life insurance policy on the life of the victim and possible connections between the stockbroker and the Chicago mob; this evidence led to a grand jury indictment for first and second-degree murder.

Molly sat together with her 11 white male co-jurors for four days as the county attorney and his main assistant criminal prosecuting attorney worked on building a case based strictly on circumstantial evidence. The neighbor was called to testify about the man he saw running from the house. The victim's sister testified about how her sister had endured years of her husband's infidelity but was determined not to let him out of their marriage. The victim's best girlfriend reinforced the sister's testimony and added details about who the victim perceived as the latest and most serious threat to her marriage. She relayed the wife's story about how her husband had scheduled an office staff meeting where his firm's staff was going to be reorganized at the Holiday Inn near the airport. Then his firm was to buy dinner for the staff. The wife, believing this would be a good time to meet the whole staff, went to the hotel at 8 p.m. assuming she would be welcome for dinner. When she walked into the restaurant she found the whole staff merrily enjoying another round of drinks with her husband's office manager sitting so close to her husband she may as well have been on his lap.

After this testimony, the office manager was called to testify.

"Your Honor," the assistant county attorney addressed the judge "we request that this witness be declared a hostile witness. We had to subpoena her to get her to testify."

"Request granted," the judge responded. He then turned to the witness and told her, "You being declared a hostile witness doesn't mean we are judging your personality. It just means that the state's attorney can basically cross-examine you. I will remind you that you are under oath and must answer each question fully and truthfully."

"Will you state your name for the court?" the assistant county attorney began.

"Mary Jo Mahoney."

"Are you single or married?"

"Single."

"Have you ever been married?"

"Yes."

"Did your marriage end in a divorce?"

"Yes."

"How long ago?"

"Two years ago."

"Now Ms. Mahoney, by the way, is that your married name or your maiden name? If I were to ask your former husband, who would he say was the cause of your divorce?"

"Objection," Steven Mitchell, the handsome defense attorney quickly said, "if opposing counsel wants to know what the witness' husband would say, he can call him as a witness."

"Objection sustained," the judge declared. "However, the witness may tell the court if Mahoney is her married or maiden name."

"It's my maiden name," the witness stated.

"Now, Ms. Mahoney," the assistant county attorney continued, "where do you work?"

"JBS Investments."

"Does the B in JBS Investments stand for Bellows, the name of the defendant?"

"Yes."

"Isn't Mr. Bellows the head of the firm?"

"Yes."

"How long have you worked for JBS Investments?"

"Just over six years."

"What were your duties during the first three or four years of your employment?"

"Objection," The defense attorney jumped to his feet, "This whole line of questioning is irrelevant."

Molly thought it may just be her imagination, but she felt like the defense attorney was looking at her instead of the judge each time he addressed the court.

"Your Honor," the assistant county attorney responded, "I believe it is very clear where my line of questioning is going."

"Agreed. Objection overruled," the judge said.

"I worked as a financial data typist for three years and then became a supervisor of the overall typing pool," Mary Jo responded.

"Is that when the defendant first noticed some of your other abilities?"

"Objection," Mr. Mitchell quickly said.

"Objection sustained. The jury is to disregard the question. Mr. Collins, you know better than that," the judge admonished the assistant county attorney.

"Sorry Your Honor," the assistant county attorney said. Then he asked the witness, "Did you get promoted more after that?"

"Yes, I became Mr. Bellows' personal secretary and then I was made overall office manager."

"How long ago were you promoted to personal secretary?"

"About two and a half years ago."

"When did your divorce proceedings first commence?"

"Two years ago."

"Were you the Petitioner in that action?"

"Yes."

"Now, Ms. Mahoney, have you ever been to the Highway 10 Motor Inn in Anoka, Minnesota?"

The witness didn't answer. She looked at Mr. Mitchell for help, but he did nothing. "I, I really don't recall."

"Ms. Mahoney, remember what the judge told you. You're under oath," Mr. Collins admonished the witness.

"I have been there."

"How many times?"

"Maybe six or seven times."

"Were you alone?"

"No."

"Who was with you?"

"Mr. Bellows," Mary Jo said softly.

"Mr. Bellows and you? Right? Was anyone else with you? Speak up so the jury can hear."

"No, it was just me and Mr. Bellows." Mary Jo tried to be loud and clear but her feelings of betraying the defendant who gave her with a wounded look, made it very hard.

"What was the purpose of these motel visits?"

"Well, we wanted to get away from the office where there was always interruption when we tried to do planning for reorganizing the office staff." Mary Jo was proud of her quick thinking to come up with a logical explanation.

"Where is Mr. Bellows' office?"

"Downtown Minneapolis." Mary Jo's faith in her answer began to fade.

"So you and Mr. Bellows drove from downtown to Anoka to avoid any interruptions. Also, isn't Anoka almost on the other side of town from Sunfish Lake?" Mr. Collins said, while facing the jury with a mocking look.

"Objection, your Honor, the state's attorney is now testifying." Mr. Mitchell was on his feet. Molly once again felt he was looking solely at her.

"Objection sustained."

"Ms. Mahoney, did you and Mr. Bellows engage in sexual intercourse?"

The witness looked at her attorney, at the defendant, the jury, and the judge.

"Ms. Mahoney, do you want me to repeat the question?"

"No," she said.

The judge leaned over his bench and with a sympathetic tone said, "Ms. Mahoney, you will have to answer the question."

"Yes," she said quickly.

"Every time you were at the motel?" Mr. Collins followed up the answer.

"Yes," Mary Jo said weakly.

"Your Honor," Mr. Collins rose from his table with a collection of papers in his hand, "I wish to enter the state's exhibits 1 to 12. These are the log book entries from 11 dates during the last 30 months and an affidavit from the motel owner who was working the front desk on the dates for all the entries. The affidavit certifies the entries as being accurate. It also states that the two individuals, Paul and Helen Jones, listed in the entries, looked identical to the pictures of the defendant and Ms. Mahoney. The attorney for the defense has agreed by stipulation that he has no objections to the entry of these exhibits."

"Yes, Your Honor, I agree," Mr. Mitchell responded to a look from the judge.

"For purposes of the record, I would like to note that the date on the first exhibit was six months prior to Ms. Mahoney filing her petition for divorce. The date on exhibit 10, the next to the last one, was one week prior to Mrs. Bellows' murder. The date on exhibit 11 was 10 days after the murder."

"Now Ms. Mahoney, are you in love with Mr. Bellows?"

"Yes," she answered without any reservation.

"Has he told you he is in love with you?" Mr. Collins continued.

"Yes."

"Do you hope to marry Mr. Bellows?"

"Yes."

"No further questions of this witness," Mr. Collins addressed the judge.

Molly, sitting in the jury box, felt a strong sense of empathy with Mary Jo. All the feelings of joy she had experienced looking forward to being with Tommy that were destroyed by his death flowed through her brain.

Attorney Mitchell, on cross examination, never mentioned the relationship between his client and Mary Jo. Instead, he introduced a ledger book for Mary Jo to verify, in her capacity as office manager of JBS Investments, as being the complete listing of all the company's current clients. After Mary Jo verified the list and explained the procedures used to make certain the list was complete, he then proceeded.

"Ms. Mahoney, can you check whether the names George Alfonso or Frank Green are included in the client list of JBS Investments?"

"Yes, I can." Then after she looked under "A" and "G" in the client listing, she said, "They are not included."

"Have you ever, in your capacity as office manager of JBS Investments, heard of or known of any connection between George Alfonso or Frank Green to JBS Investments or Mr. Bellows?"

"No, I haven't."

"Have you heard of George Alfonso or Frank Green anywhere else?"

"Yes, I have read newspaper articles reporting that these two men are connected to the Chicago mob and were also business clients of Mr. Bellows; but I believe I know most of Mr. Bellows' clients and have never heard of these two men except for the newspaper articles." With that Ms. Mahoney's testimony ended.

Following this testimony, the prosecutor called a ballistics expert to establish that the gun used in the murder was the same gun found on Little Jake Kelly, the mob member who was shot in Chicago.

The next witness for the state was Mr. Jarvis, a Chicago homicide detective investigating the murder of Little Jake. After establishing the foundation for his testimony, the prosecuting attorney, asked the detective, "Do you have any leads as to who shot Mr. Kelly or why he was shot?"

"Yes, we located Little Jake's girlfriend and she said he left her to go and collect some big money, a payoff for his last job."

"Objection Your Honor! Objection!" Mr. Mitchell was on his feet. "Hearsay, clearly hearsay."

"Your Honor, Mr. Jarvis is just relating his notes from his file." Mr. Collins clearly wanted to get this testimony to the jury.

"That doesn't matter. It is still hearsay. I can't cross-examine his file." Mr. Mitchell sat back down and clearly made eye contact with Molly. "If the state wants to get the girlfriend's testimony into the record, have her testify."

"Your Honor, we can't find the girlfriend." This was Attorney Collins' last hope of having the testimony approved.

"Is she dead?" the judge asked.

"We don't know," Mr. Collins answered.

"Well, if she was dead, the 'dead man exception' to the hearsay rule might apply. Since we don't know, objection sustained. The jury shall disregard this testimony," the judge ruled.

After failing to get this evidence in, the state finished its examination of the Chicago detective, mainly about the fact that Little Jake's murder was, in the detective's opinion, a gang-related killing.

Upon cross-examination, Attorney Mitchell solicited testimony from the detective that five valuable pieces of jewelry were recovered from Little Jake's car. This jewelry was returned to the Dakota County Sheriff's Office and was identified as Mrs. Bellows' property.

The prosecution then called an FBI agent, who in conjunction with an investigator from the Security Exchange, had conducted an investigation of mob connections to stock brokerage and investment firms. On direct examination, he testified that JBS Investments was part of this investigation.

On cross-examination, Mr. Mitchell asked, "You testified that JBS Investments was part of this investigation?"

"Yes," the FBI agent answered.

"How many stock brokerage and investment firms were included in this investigation?"

"Nationwide, five hundred sixty-five," he responded.

"Five hundred sixty-five. Would you characterize this as being a fishing trip?" Mitchell asked sarcastically.

"No, definitely not," the agent answered, acting like the question was an insult.

"As for your investigation of JBS Investments, did you uncover any evidence where there was any contact between Mr. Bellows or any employee of JBS Investments with any persons you have identified as being connected to the Chicago mob?" Attorney Mitchell was on his feet, talking with a slightly raised voice, glaring at the FBI agent for a moment and then looking directly at Molly.

"No," the FBI agent answered while looking down.

"So," Mitchell, still on his feet and talking a little louder, asked, "What was the purpose of your testimony? Are you suggesting there is some casual connection between the FBI investigating JBS Investments along with 565 other firms and this murder trial?"

"Objection, Your Honor, the defense attorney can save his comments about the evidence for his final argument," the state attorney said.

"Objection sustained."

"No further questions for this witness." Mitchell sat down.

The state finished its case by introducing evidence of a $700,000 insurance policy on the life of Mrs. Bellows. Mr. Mitchell, on cross-examination, clarified that the policy was taken out seven years prior to the murder and it was part of a package of insurance that was used to fund a buy/sell agreement between the partners of the firm. He also got the insurance agent to testify that Mr. Bellows had not exercised three separate options to increase the amount of the coverage, including one only four months prior to the murder of Mrs. Bellows.

Mr. Mitchell then presented his defense. He called three friends of Mrs. Bellows who testified to the frequency of Mrs. Bellows wearing and flaunting her expensive jewelry. She often wore it to lunches with friends, shopping, and always when she went out at night, which was quite often. He also called a Dakota County deputy sheriff who had interviewed Mr. Bellows. Using this interview, which the state had chosen not to enter into evidence, he was able to present to the jury complete denials by the defendant that he had anything to do with his wife's murder and statements by the defendant that during their thirty-four years of marriage he and his wife had various problems with his infidelity, but he knew of at least two affairs his wife had during the marriage. He also had, several times during the interview, stated that he had never asked his wife for a divorce nor had he planned to ask her for one at the time of her murder.

Mr. Mitchell then asked the deputy sheriff about the interview process. "Deputy Freeman, do you have a nickname in the sheriff's department?"

"Yes, I guess I do," he answered.

"Can you tell the court what it is?"

"The Closer."

"In the parlance of the law enforcement community, what does 'The Closer' mean?" Mitchell asked.

"It means a person who can get a suspect to talk," Deputy Freeman answered.

"An interviewer who can get a suspect to confess, right?"

"Well, in most cases." Seeing where Mitchell was going with his line of questioning, Deputy Freeman tried to hedge his answer.

"Since you have earned the name 'The Closer,' in what percent of cases have you been successful in obtaining confessions?"

"I'm not sure."

"Come on Deputy Freeman. I'm sure you have bragged about your success rate to a lot of people."

"Objection, Your Honor, the defense attorney is badgering the witness," Attorney Collins interjected.

"Objection overruled. I think the witness is avoiding answering the question. Deputy Freeman, answer the question truthfully, with your best estimate," the judge instructed.

"Ninety-five percent," Deputy Freeman answered quickly.

"Ninety-five percent. Did Mr. Bellows confess?"

"No, he did not." Deputy Freeman seemed ashamed.

"Now, Deputy Freeman, you have your notes from the interview in front of you. Can you tell the jury how long the interview lasted?" Mitchell continued.

"Just over 20 hours."

"Twenty hours. Did you have any breaks?"

"Just two. I had to relieve myself." Deputy Freeman clearly looked like he would welcome a break from Mr. Mitchell's questioning.

"Did, Mr. Bellows get to relieve himself?"

"Once."

"Did Mr. Bellows have anything to eat?"

"No."

"Did Mr. Bellows have anything to drink?"

"One glass of water."

"Did Mr. Bellows ask to have an attorney?"

"Yes."

"More than once?" Mr. Mitchell pushed on.

"Yes."

"Deputy Freeman, did you grant him that request?"

"I told him he could call as soon as we finished the interview."

"Which you believed would be after you had a confession."

"Objection, Your Honor, the defense attorney is answering for the witness," the state's attorney said.

"Sustained," the judge ruled.

"How did the interview end?" Mr. Mitchell continued.

"The suspect passed out," Deputy Freeman said looking down, away from the jury.

"He passed out without confessing?" Mitchell asked with a note of triumph, looking directly at Molly.

"Yes," a defeated Deputy Freeman answered.

"No further questions for this witness. The defense rests," Mr. Mitchell said.

"Mr. Bellows, your attorney has rested your defense without calling you to testify. Are you in agreement with your attorney's decision?" The judge addressed the defendant directly.

"Yes, your Honor," Mr. Bellows replied.

The judge then addressed the jury. "Mr. Bellows has a right to testify or not testify. His decision not to testify shall not be taken into account during your deliberations."

After final arguments by the state and the defense the jury got the case.

"Well, it's time for us to go to work," Carl Hanson, the 63-year-old retired dairy farmer, elected as the jury foreman, spoke to the rest of the jury.

Besides Carl, there were four other farmers ranging in age from 32 to 57 on the jury. The other jurors included a 27-year-old accountant, a 41-year-old high school teacher and coach, a 36-year-old hardware store worker, a 43-year-old factory worker, a 50-year-old truck driver and a 23-year-old construction worker.

"I guess we all know each other well enough now to address each other by our first names. Now, Molly, I am sure that you, as a married woman, were quite upset about the defendant's affairs outside his marriage. I hope that doesn't prevent you from having an open mind while we examine the evidence," Carl, in a clearly condescending tone, said, looking directly at Molly.

Molly, feeling the negative vibes, responded, "No, Mr. Hanson, I believe I have a good understanding as to what happened between the defendant, his wife and Ms. Mahoney. I plan to be very objective about reviewing the evidence."

"Good, but please call me Carl," the foreman replied. He was clearly offended at Molly's sharp response.

"Before we start our discussion, I think we should get a sense of where we are, based on what we heard in the court. I will pass out these index cards and ask if each of you will mark, without looking at your neighbor's card, either 'G' for guilty, 'I' for innocent or 'NS' for not sure at this point." Carl passed out the cards.

"Arnold," Carl said to one of the other farmers, sitting to his right, "Will you collect the cards, then mix them up, so we won't know whose card is whose?"

After he tallied the results Carl announced, "Five 'G', six 'NS' and one 'I'. I guess we will have a little longer deliberation than I thought."

The deliberations did last longer than Carl thought. In his opinion, he strongly favored a guilty verdict based on the evidence that the defendant and Mary Jo had been at the motel a week before and 10 days after the murder and the evidence that Little Jake had told his girlfriend he was going to get a big payoff for his last job, evidence which had been stricken from the record. He was surprised that only five jury members indicated a guilty verdict on the first vote. He was more surprised that one had voted for a innocent verdict. He tried to determine which juror it was. He was still sure that Molly voted for a guilty verdict because of the infidelity.

"It's most likely the accountant. He probably identifies with Bellows as a fellow professional," he thought to himself.

"Since we have some disagreement, I think we should all discuss what evidence is the most important. Why don't each of you express what you see as the piece of evidence that led you to vote the way you did and what information you feel is necessary to change your mind," Carl spoke to the other jurors. He then asked Ted, the accountant, to go first.

"Well, I think, based on the evidence, there was a substantial motive for the defendant to arrange the murder. The reason I voted that I'm not sure is I believe there is reasonable doubt as to any connection between the defendant and the shooter or his mob bosses."

Carl, surprised that Ted wasn't the juror voting for an innocent verdict, proceeded to call on all the other jurors except for Molly, still believing she had voted guilty. The four other guilty votes had come from the two oldest farmers, the factory worker, and the construction worker. All four of them expressed the same reasoning in their own way.

"That Bellows was up to hanky-panky with that young girl and there was enough evidence to show he arranged for the hitman," one farmer stated his opinion.

The other five jurors who had voted they were not sure agreed with Ted that the affair with Mary Jo was an ample motive and a couple of them also believed the $700,000 life insurance was important. They also agreed with Ted that the state had failed to prove the connection between the shooter and the defendant beyond a reasonable doubt.

Carl, realizing Molly must be the one who voted for acquittal, finally called on her.

"I am just stunned that I was the only one who voted 'I' for innocent," Molly started. "It was clear to me that Mr. Bellows was trapped in a loveless marriage, but that is not necessarily a motive for murder. If you accept that, the state has no case whatsoever. It failed to prove any connection between the defendant and the mob. I think all of you are overlooking the fact that there was a jewel robbery that did happen, which Mrs. Bellows invited by flaunting her jewelry. Also, the fact that Mr. Bellows did not break during his 20-hour torture session creates for me way more than reasonable doubt. I don't think he is guilty, but if he is, the state certainly didn't prove it." Molly was forceful.

"Mrs. Kelseltz, I'm shocked that your morality doesn't think sleeping with a younger woman outside your marriage and knowing your wife will not grant you a divorce isn't a motive for murder. I don't want to be personal, but I wonder about your religious background." Carl started to respond to Molly but was interrupted by Ted.

"Sir," Ted said, "I don't think the comments you just made are proper. Molly was just stating her opinion and you don't need to make a personal judgement about her."

"Huh?" Carl said to Ted, "Trying to impress her because of her looks?"

"Whoa," the school teacher said to Carl, "if you keep this up, I may call for a new vote on who should be the foreman."

"O.K, I'm sorry," Carl said, without conviction, while looking at Molly. "I think there was plenty of motive and as for the mob connection, let's remember that Little Jake told his girlfriend 'he was going to go get a big pay-off for his last job.'"

"That's not even in evidence," both Molly and Ted said simultaneously.

"Not in evidence! The hot shot defense lawyer kept it out because of a technicality," Carl retorted.

"Come on Carl," Arnold, the farmer sitting next to him, said. "You know we can only use the evidence that the judge allowed."

"You're right. I think I'll let someone else lead the discussion for a while," Carl said.

The high school teacher agreed to take over and he led the jurors in examining all the evidence in detail. It took two days for Molly, who was now being supported by Ted, to create a perspective that the only thing that the state had proved was the defendant was cheating on his wife, the wife was killed by a jewel thief, and there were insurance proceeds from a seven-year-old policy. Further, the state had failed to establish a connection between the shooter and the defendant. After two days, nine of the jurors had agreed to this analysis. Only Carl and the two older farmers were holding out for a conviction.

On the morning of the third day, the farmer who had labeled the affair between Mary Jo and the defendant as 'hanky-panky' announced as the deliberations started that he, after sleeping on all that had been discussed the two prior days, now agreed with the nine and would vote for acquittal.

Arnold quickly said, "I think the guy is guilty as hell, but I agree that the state's attorney sure in hell didn't prove it."

Carl, giving Molly a "well you won" look, said, "Well, given my age, I know when I have been beat. I guess we should take a formal vote."

After the announcement was made in court about the unanimous vote for acquittal and the jury was leaving the courtroom amidst the loud hubbub, a paralegal for Attorney Mitchell handed Molly the attorney's business card. On the back of the card, he had written a message in beautiful handwriting.

> Mrs. Kelseltz,
> I would be honored if you would have dinner with me at your convenience.
> Please call me at my office. Thank you for your service.
> Steven Mitchell

As soon as she walked into the restaurant, she saw Steven Mitchell standing at the bar. He saw her at the same time. It was a Tuesday in February so there weren't many customers in the Golden Steer Motel and Restaurant.

"Molly, is it O.K. to call you Molly?" Steven asked with an infectious smile. "Call me Steve. Can I buy you a drink before dinner?"

"Sure, I'll have a 7-7. Molly is fine," she said as Steven led her into the bar.

He ordered her drink and another vodka gimlet for himself. "Thank you for coming. I have talked to a couple other jury members on the phone and understand you were the main reason we got an acquittal."

"Well, I just stood up for what I felt was right." Molly sipped her drink. It was her first taste of alcohol since she had passed out at her mom's wedding.

"We can talk more about the deliberations later at dinner but tell me a little about yourself." Steven clinked his new drink against Molly's glass. "Hope, you don't think this is too personal, but when I questioned you on voir dire, I felt you weren't just another happily married suburban housewife. Besides being the most beautiful juror I have ever picked, something told me that my client's infidelity wouldn't be an issue with you."

Molly, again slightly embarrassed as she always was when someone commented on her beauty and stunned by Steven's on-the-mark insight, said, "I guess you're not really my attorney, but I assume anything I tell you will be kept confidential. Also, what does 'voir dire' mean?"

"Absolutely, anything you tell me will be kept confidential. 'Voir dire' is the term for the selection of a jury." Steven motioned to the bartender for two more drinks. "We will get a table that's fairly private for dinner then you can tell me if I was right. Any kids?"

"Two, a daughter nine and a son seven."

"You are still married?" Steve knew the answer but wanted to hear how Molly described it."

"That will be part of my story." Molly looked around at the bar. "This is a nice place. Haven't been to South St. Paul that often."

"Hook-n-Cow. That's what it's called because of the stockyards, biggest in the country. My senior partner always jokingly refers to this as the 'Golden Pig' just to be different. Lot of business deals have been made in this place." Steven nodded to the hostess to take them to a table.

"So, what's good?" Molly looked over the menu.

"When you are in cow country you have to have steak. The New York cut is my favorite," Steven said with authority.

"Sounds good. Order what you are having for me too. I like my steak medium. I need to use the ladies' room," Molly said as she stood up.

Upon her return, Steven said, "I ordered this bottle of wine. I really like it. Goes well with steak."

Molly took a couple of sips. "I'm not a wine drinker, but with the taste of this I could really become one."

Molly then started her story. She told Steve most of the details of her marriage, the affair with Tommy and Tommy's death. She also told him about her certain belief that Roy knocked Tommy overboard at the request of Ray and her current living arrangement with Ray. The story lasted the whole time it took to eat dinner and drink two bottles of wine. Upon finishing the story Molly asked, "Would you have any suggestions as to how I could find out what happened, and, if possible, prove what I believe?"

"I've just been retained by a new client from Duluth who has been charged with his wife's murder. I'm afraid it will be a much tougher case than Mr. Bellows', unless you want to move to St. Louis County and somehow get on the jury?" Steve joked. "My main investigator will be spending the next month or so up there. I can have him dig into Tommy's death while he's working on our current case. No charge to you, of course."

"Oh, that would be so great. If you were able to find something out, I wouldn't know how to thank you." Molly, besides being high on the wine, was excited.

"We'll figure something out," Steven said with a mischievous smile.

"So, I've been talking about myself all night. I know you wanted to talk about the deliberations a little." Molly smiled back at Steven knowing what he meant but wanting to change the subject. "But first I have a question. All through the trial I felt you were looking directly at me, almost every time you made a statement. But was that just my little fantasy, or were you?"

"No, it wasn't a fantasy. At first, I was stunned by your beauty and of course looking directly at you was more pleasing to my eyes than looking at all those old farmers and other boring looking men. However, the real reason was, as I told you earlier tonight, I really felt, when I seated you on the jury, you would be my key to preventing a conviction. Call me psychic, but I believed you had an experience in life like what you just told me. I was hoping you would not be judgmental about my client and would be able to zero in on the key points of our defense. Having the ability to read jurors may be my strongest skill as a defense attorney."

"I did zero in on you completely destroying the state's effort to tie Bellows to the mob or to Little Jake. Without that the state didn't have a case." Molly leaned over the table to be nearer to Steven.

"So if you murder someone using a hitman, the trick is to make sure the connection between you and the hitman can't be proven." Molly ended her observation with a soft gentle laugh.

Steven stared at Molly for several moments. "Hopefully you are joking."

Molly looked at her watch, "I should get home. I work the afternoon shift tomorrow."

Then, in an effort to stand up, she lost her balance. Steven quickly jumped up and caught her. Holding her close he said, "Little too much wine? Maybe we should get a room here so you don't have an accident or get stopped by the police."

Molly returning Steven's embrace whispered, "Help me to the ladies' room so I can pull myself together. Then we can talk about that idea."

In the ladies' room Molly, for the first time since she and Tommy made love in the woodshed that Ray later burned down, was overcome with sexual excitement. Looking in the mirror she said, "Oh, Tommy, I miss you. I'm going to be faithful." Then, as she was going back out to Steven, she also had the realization that an affair with Steven would complicate a possible future need to have Steven as her attorney.

As Steven watched Molly come out of the ladies' room, he knew from her body language what her answer would be. So, he just reached out and held her hands.

"Steve, my body wants nothing more than to share a bed with you, but it's too soon. I wouldn't be able to respond without thinking of Tommy. Hopefully you and I will stay in touch and we will see where the future leads."

"That's a better refusal than I expected. I'll have the hostess call you a cab and my law clerk and I will bring your car to your house first thing in the morning. Let's have some dessert and coffee and talk about something light. What kind of music do you like?" Steven led Molly back to the table.

"Sinatra, big Sinatra fan," Molly gave Steven a tender kiss on his cheek.

Chapter 17
1949

Ray drove slowly up Cedar Avenue toward downtown Minneapolis. It was 1:30 a.m. and he had flown in from Los Angeles. He knew Molly was home with the kids sleeping in her own bedroom. To avoid the mixed feelings of anger, bitterness and self-pity that he felt every time he slept at home with Molly a room away but unreachable, he delayed returning home. It had been over two years since Molly left him without leaving the house. As he often did, Ray considered getting a divorce so he could find a new partner. He missed the aspects of companionship that flowed from a normal marriage, but on nights like this he missed conjugal relations the most.

Ray pictured Molly sleeping in the nude, like she always did, alone in her bed and wished he could touch her. Outside of a few unsatisfactory experiences with prostitutes in the Orient during layovers, he had not had any sexual affairs since the separation. He had been tempted to seduce a couple of the flight attendants but did not want the complications that arose from affairs with co-workers. On tonight's flight, he and his co-pilot got into a discussion about sex. The co-pilot told him about the Exotic Dance Studio of Love on Cedar Avenue. The first time he passed it he missed the small neon sign on the side door of the two-story brick building, which housed a neighborhood grocery store and meat market on the first floor. Knowing he had gone too far he turned around and then saw the sign.

"Must not want to attract much attention," he said to himself as he parked, after some hesitation, a block away from the door. He took off his pilot's jacket and put on a winter flight jacket. The radio DJ had just announced that it was two above zero, but the excitement of the unknown shielded Ray from feeling the cold. He had never been to a sauna and he was unsure if he was safe. Ray entered the side door which opened to a flight of stairs. At the top of the stairs he found another door with a bell. He rang.

"Been here before?" A hardened female voice spoke through an intercom.

"No," Ray said, fighting the urge to turn and leave.

"Know someone?" The interrogation continued.

"Jimmy Hagberg, he's my co-pilot." Ray immediately realized that his relationship to Jimmy was completely irrelevant to the current conversation.

"You a cop?"

"No, I'm not a cop. I'm a pilot." The door opened.

Ray was stunned by the beauty of the woman who projected the hard voice. It was hard to know her age. Was she younger than she looked because of her hard-living or was she older but still retaining her youthful beauty? She stood in front of Ray, A 5-foot 4-inch brunette wearing a lace gown covering a revealing bra over her buxom breasts and miniature panties below her slim waistline.

"Welcome to our fun club. Hope you weren't looking for dance lessons. Our sign is a little misleading, I guess by design. You can call me Eve." The complete change in the voice of the woman now speaking, from the voice that came over the intercom, created an excitement within Ray.

"No, I'm not looking for dance lessons."

"What would you like?" Eve softly asked as she twitched her lips slightly, tilted her head and smiled.

"Well, I—" Ray didn't know how to or if he even should just come out and ask for sex.

"Here's our normal deal. Forty bucks you can have a great sauna and then a really great massage by one of our young ladies." Eve walked towards a small desk in the corner of the front hallway.

"Don't you give the massage?" Ray felt rejected.

"No, I'm the night manager here, although I have some special clients. One is coming in shortly. I'm sure you will enjoy your massage with any of our girls. Are you ready?" Eve again tilted her head and smiled her naughty smile.

Ray enjoyed the sauna for half an hour, not knowing what would come next. He was unsure if he should move to the massage room Eve had shown him at any particular time. Then a drunken sixty-some-year-old man joined him in the sauna.

"Looks like you're ready to enjoy the exotic dance of love," the drunk slurred with a hardy laugh as he looked at Ray's hardened penis. Ray, both embarrassed and nervous, quickly wrapped a towel around himself, headed into the massage room and laid down on the bed, the only piece of furniture in the room.

While Ray lay there alone he replayed, for the hundredth time, the whole scenario that had caused his current state of despair. With Tommy now out of her life, it was pure stupidity to think Molly would be the same wife she was before he left for the war. But how did she know Roy was responsible for Tommy's death? Or did she? Was her whole act nothing but a guess and a bluff? Did she devise the current arrangement just to punish him? Was it worse than if she had just left and gotten a divorce? Was there any hope for the future? Sometimes when the two of them did things together with the kids Ray felt some acceptance and joy in Molly's behavior. Was this just a mirage? Ray was so consumed with his thoughts that he failed to notice the tall young blonde woman enter the room until she was sitting on the foot of the bed.

"Hi, I'm Amber," she said with a soft, seductive, angelic voice.

Ray was stunned. He had always considered Molly to be the most beautiful woman he knew. Here on the bed with him sat a woman even more beautiful. She was wearing a gingham dress. The one button holding together the top of the dress invited to being unbuttoned so her breasts could come out.

"So," she said, "I am good at massages, but I am also good at other things." As she spoke, she stood up on the bed, threw back her long blonde hair which had fallen over her breasts, unbuttoned the button, and slowly started to pull up her dress, her only item of clothing. "For eighty dollars, I'll entertain you with a night you will never forget."

An hour later, Ray walked to his car. The temperature had dropped 12 degrees since he entered the Exotic Dance Studio of Love. Ray didn't notice. He knew it wouldn't be a cure for his loneliness, but he had found a remedy for his need for companionship and sex.

Ray slept until noon after he got home from the sauna. Molly had left a note for him.

> *Ray,*
>
> *Mom and her new husband Bruno will be in town for the weekend. I am having everyone over for dinner on Sunday. If you will be home you're welcome.*   *Molly*

Ray held on to the note for several minutes trying to divine a deeper meaning other than it just being a polite invitation to dinner in his own house with his family. Then he quickly scribbled a reply.

Molly,

I'm going up to Mille Lacs Lake this afternoon. I'm buying a fish house from a fellow pilot. I will probably spend tomorrow ice fishing, but I will be home for dinner on Sunday. It will be good to see all your family again.

Love, Ray

As Ray and Stan, the pilot who owned the fish house, drove out onto Mille Lacs, Ray was stunned by the number of houses and the activity on the lake.

"It's a city by itself up here," Stan said. "You can fish quietly alone in your fish house or you can get together with some of your neighbors and make a party out of it. During the week-ends you can always find some action, going on either on the lake or at Ole Johnson's bar. I've never checked it out, but there's rumors that 'ladies of the night' work the lake."

Ray gave Stan a probing look. He couldn't know about his night at the sauna. Why did he feel so guilty about that night? "Well, I just plan on using this house for fishing. Why are you selling?"

"Don't know if you heard. I'm retiring in two months, but I have some leave time I need to use up. Wife and I are taking a couple weeks trip to Florida to look for a winter home. We'll spend the summers here and winters in Florida. I plan to become a Florida resident to avoid the Minnesota income tax. Let's catch a few of those famous Mille Lacs walleyes and then I'll buy lunch at Ole Johnson's bar. Ole's a great guy, full of information about the fishing. Fun bar too." Stan opened two beers and raised his in a toast "Here's to your new home away from home and many years of great fishing."

Ray spent the night fishing and enjoying the solitude. As he drove home from the lake, he envisioned a new life of ice fishing to occupy his spare time and an occasional session with Amber when he was lonely. But as he got closer to home the endless hope arose again. Maybe this invitation to dinner was a real change in Molly's feelings and would lead to a new start in their relationship and the need for ice fishing and Amber would be gone.

"Ray, I want you to meet my new husband, Bruno," Molly's mom greeted him as he joined the family just before dinner was ready. "Bruno grew up in Dalton, a small town up by Fergus Falls. Now he farms near Warren. You're also from a small town, aren't you?"

"From Buhl, up on the Range." Ray shook Bruno's hand. "Good to have you in the family."

As the dinner proceeded the conversation was carried by Molly's mom, Bruno and Ray. It was mainly about growing up in small towns with Ray telling some anecdotes about life on the Iron Range and Molly's mom and Bruno sharing some funny tales about their early relationship.

"Let me tell you about my ice fishing house." Ray turned to Junior. "I caught four nice walleyes through a hole in the ice. You and I can fillet them later today."

"Can I go with? Can I go with the next time you go?" Junior yelled.

"Sure, the next weekend I'm off." Ray waited for Molly to join in his exchange with Junior. She was silent. To break the ice with her, Ray turned, intending to compliment her on the great fried chicken. But when he turned he saw her staring at him with a look in her eyes so strong it felt like it could burn a hole in him, a look of hate.

The last two years of Ray's life spiraled down into bitterness. During the winter months, he spent most of his free time alone in his fish house drinking heavily. The first year he did bring Junior with him a few times, but Junior got bored with the long nights and lost interest in going.

During the summer months Ray would go home to Buhl and stay with his family. For the most part, these visits would consist of him and Roy drinking at a local bar until closing. Neither one ever mentioned Tommy or what happened the night Roy knocked him overboard. Yet, like a ghost, that moment in time hung in the air without acknowledgement, creating a cloud of despair.

The only real enjoyment Ray experienced was his fairly expensive relationship with Amber. Several times a month Ray would have a session. Although the sex was good, the companionship became more important. Ray unburdened his sadness about his failed marriage. Amber also began confiding in Ray. Trusting him with her real name, Eileen, and talking about coming to Minnesota in response to an ad from a modeling agency. During the first month, everything appeared to be authentic with her posing for photos for her portfolio. Then she was sent on her first job as an escort for a local politician on a trip to Washington D.C. It was then that she discovered that the modeling agency was a front for the Kid Kahn crime mob. She tried to quit but was told directly that, although she may not be killed, her face would not be pretty enough to do any more modeling after she left. So, for several years she did what she was told. Then she met Becky White, who owned the Exotic Dance Studio of Love.

Becky White grew up in a single parent home with her two sisters, one two years older than her and one a year younger. Her mother kicked her dad out two months after he came home in his usual drunken stupor, forced her to have sex and got her pregnant with Becky's younger sister. The family was having a hard time surviving the depression, given their dad never held a job for more than two months, when he was lucky enough to find one. The idea that she would now have to feed and care for three children under the age of four caused Becky's mom to be depressed for a period of time. Then, realizing that the no-good man she had married was the biggest drain on the family resources, she snapped out of her depression and considered her options. Her strong Catholic faith eliminated any thought of aborting the unborn child. It was her husband who had to go. He woke up one night after again passing out from drinking, to find his wife holding his testicles in one hand and a very sharp knife in the other.

"So," she said coolly, "you're going to agree to get up and leave this house and to never come back. How quickly you say yes will determine if you leave with or without your balls." As he hurried out the door Becky's mom yelled, "I was able to get ahold of a gun, so if you ever come back through that door it will be the last steps of your life." She knew he was too weak a man to ever call her bluff.

The four women survived with help from the church and food lines. Becky's mom worked parttime jobs, mostly domestic jobs for wealthy families, and took in laundry. Then she started taking in men. Most of her customers were mobsters who didn't want to risk being caught in raids on a whorehouse by some cops who were not on the take.

By the time Becky turned nine she and her older sister found a way to help with the family's finances. They became panhandlers. First, they started on the street and then they discovered a gold lode. They worked the bars and restaurants where members of the mob hung out. They would light their smokes, laugh at their jokes, and sometimes sing and dance, and they collected big tips. Several of the men had been guests of their mom and knew the girls. The girls also became adept at fostering competition between the mobsters to be the biggest tippers. It was with this background that Becky developed her view of equality between the sexes. She firmly believed that there were few men her equal. After spending her young life working the bars, she found one. Just after she turned sixteen, she was working her act at Danny's, a restaurant and bar on Chicago Avenue in Minneapolis. She turned and was face-to-face with a young, handsome, impeccably dressed male in his early twenties. Both of them stared at each other and the chemistry in each of their brains triggered a feeling of love.

"Hi, I'm Aaron. I'm new in town. Just came in from Miami."

"I'm Becky. I have always lived here." Her face reddened in embarrassment at her dumb response.

Aaron quickly picking up on her feelings said, "This looks like a great place, but I don't know if I would like to live in a bar all my life."

For the next 10 years the two of them were together. During this time Becky accumulated a small fortune from Aaron's gifts of expensive jewelry and from the loose cash Aaron left lying around. She also acquired something more valuable. Every time Aaron left to carry out his assignments as the top enforcer and hit man for the mob, Becky wrote down notes on index cards of what Aaron had shared with her in their pillow talk. She had started the note keeping with the idea that she would write a book. As she accumulated more and more notes she realized that she could never print the information without putting her life in jeopardy, but she knew how she would use it if Aaron was no longer around.

What Becky knew would happen, finally happened on a quiet Sunday night. Aaron and a new guy, who had just come in from Kansas City, were assigned the task of taking care of some competition from Chicago who were trying to move into the territory. Aaron had worked his way up the hierarchy of the job by being very meritorious and careful about how he did his job but he got careless. He didn't check with his contacts in KC about the new guy. If he had, he would have found out no one in Kansas City knew him, and maybe someone would have connected him to the Chicago mob. As Aaron stepped out on the street to take care of the Chicago competition, he heard the gun shot from behind him and felt the pain of the bullet piercing his brain.

Shortly after Aaron's funeral, Becky met Kid Kahn in a private meeting. She showed him some of her index cards and informed him that she had sent letters of instructions to two different individuals as to where they would find sets of these cards if something happened to her. Then she made her demands.

"I have plans for a massage parlor. I'm going to name it the Exotic Dance Studio of Love. I need 50G's to get it started. More importantly you will need to tell the local politicians under your control about these cards and that if I have any problems running my club some of the cards about them may be leaked to the newspaper. I'm not going to flaunt the club and will just rely on word-of-mouth advertising. I'm sure some of your boys will become regular customers. Also, I want to hire several of the girls you have working for your modeling agency. I understand some of them are not very well treated and are not happy but have been told they can't quit."

Kid Kahn was bitter but he agreed. Becky started her club. Amber and Eve became two of her girls.

●●●●●●●●●●

Ray drove to the Exotic Dance Studio of Love as soon as he had landed from his latest flight. It had been several weeks since his last visit. His sessions with Eileen had become more about talking and less about sex, which was starting to bother him. Was he going to become personally involved with a whore? It was 10 o'clock, Tuesday morning, but this was a day Eileen usually worked. Upon entering the club, Ray was greeted by Becky.

"I'm sure you are here to see Amber, but she's not here. Her stepfather, who raised her, died back in Long Island. She wasn't going to his funeral because of some abuse when she was a teenager. I convinced her to go to find some closure. I'm a little short of girls today, but if you don't mind a little age, I am willing to do a session. I know you are one of Amber's favorites."

Ray was intrigued. Since he had been coming to the club he had read two newspaper articles about Becky campaigning to have prostitution legalized. He wondered why she wasn't worried about drawing attention to her operation and having it shut down by the vice squad.

"I'm here for some action. I'm sure I will enjoy my time with you." Ray was excited.

Becky used her experience to satisfy Ray's needs and then said, "Would you like to talk a little?"

Ray laughed, "I was just thinking on the way here how my sessions with Amber have become more about talk, less about action."

"Don't worry about that," Becky said. "One of the few regular clients I had over the last few years was a Lutheran minister. His wife had quit sleeping with him years ago, but sex wasn't his greatest need. Some sessions were all talk. Poor guy died a couple years ago. I miss him. Had a lot of problems. One of his biggest concerns was for his daughter. She got pregnant in college and he forced her to get married. But she then fell in love with someone else while her husband was fighting in the war. He knew she was unhappy in her marriage but was hoping she wouldn't get divorced, to protect his own reputation."

Ray was stunned. He broke down and cried in Becky's arms.

Chapter 18
March 1951

The wooden bench seats at Williams Arena were hard and the place was crowded. Ronnie and Larry were sitting with their classmates, Lois, Bev, Irene, Gerald and George. Another six members of their class were sitting a few rows closer to the basketball floor. This was the first night of the state tournament. Everyone had come to the city that morning. After driving down to his sister's house with Ronnie and leaving the small amount of clothes they had brought for the weekend, Larry accepted Ronnie's dare and drove around downtown Minneapolis. Except for having other drivers blow their horns at them a few times and stopping just in time to avoid turning onto a one-way street, Larry successfully drove past the Foshay Tower, Dayton's Department Store, The First National Bank Building and then found his way over to the University campus in time to walk around before going to the first afternoon game. The other classmates had similar adventures around the big city. An aura of excitement about being in the big city without adult supervision encompassed the group adding to the excitement of the tournament. This was not unique to the kids from McGrath. It was a feeling shared by the other 8,000 plus kids from small towns in Minnesota who were now filling up the second level of Williams Arena.

"See why this is called 'The Barn.'" Larry said.

"Who calls it a barn?" Bev asked.

"All the sports writers," Larry responded with an air of superiority. "Can't read an article about Minnesota Gophers basketball or about the state tournament without several references to 'The Barn.'"

"Doesn't look like our barn," Bev retorted. "The sports writers must be city boys."

That brought a collective laugh from the group.

"Who's playing today?" Gerald asked.

"I have the program." George read off the schedule.

"Brainerd plays East Grand Forks in the first game. Then it's Canby against Hopkins. Tonight, it's Gilbert and Austin. Then Mountain Lake plays St. Paul Monroe. Who's everybody picking?"

"Which school is smaller, Brainerd or East Grand Forks?" Lois asked. "Whichever, I want them to win along with Canby, Gilbert, and Mountain Lake, all the small schools."

"That would be great," Larry said. "But I doubt Gilbert can beat Austin. They're undefeated. Gilbert has a big center, but so does Austin and they have twin brothers as guards who are really good."

"I'm still going to yell for Gilbert. What's everyone going to do tomorrow during the day?" Lois wondered.

"We should all get together and go around downtown. Should be a lot of stores and other things to see," Irene suggested.

"Other things? Boys you mean," Ronnie joked.

"So what? It's not my fault all the boys from McGrath are boring," Irene shot back.

Ronnie quickly defended his honor. "Well, if your mom would let you go out with us McGrath boys some Saturday night you wouldn't be so bored."

"It would be fun to go around downtown together. My sister has some plans for Ronnie and me tomorrow. So if we do something together, we have to do it Saturday morning," Larry lied, not wanting anything to interfere with his plan to poke around Eagan on the small chance of finding a connection between Molly and Gordon.

The afternoon games were exciting, especially the Canby and Hopkins game, which Canby won by a score of 45 to 43. After the games, the group walked around the University campus and found a restaurant serving mainly hamburgers, which was a treat for all of them. They returned to Williams Arena for the night games.

"Boy, that center for Gilbert is big. If we had him on our team, we would be playing here instead of them," George said. Both George and Gerald played on McGrath's basketball team, which won six games during the season.

"That's Boots Simonovich. He's 6-foot-8," Larry said, trying to be the source of all knowledge. "Let's see how he plays against these better teams."

Boots showed them how well he could play against better teams as Gilbert upset Austin by a score of 67 to 56. With most of the fans pulling for Gilbert, "The Barn" was rocking and loud. It got even louder in the second game as the small school Mountain Lake led by a 5-foot-5 guard upset the only city school in the tournament, St. Paul Monroe, by a final score of 47 to 46.

"Boy, that was exciting!" Lois yelled above the loud noise of the crowd. "All my teams won."

"Can't wait until tomorrow night. Gilbert may win the whole thing," Larry yelled even louder.

It was 11 o' clock Friday morning, the second day of the state tournament. "Are we lost?" Ronnie asked, surprised that he and Larry were driving on a gravel road.

"No, this is Pilot Knob Road. Her address is 4429 Pilot Knob. Watch the numbers on the mailboxes. This is just like driving in Aitkin County."

"There it is, the next driveway. You better keep moving. There's a car coming out." Ronnie was looking past Larry as he drove.

"I'm speeding up. Look and see if it's a woman driver." Larry felt his adrenaline increase as he drove past the driveway and the oncoming car. It turned onto the street in the direction the boys had come from.

"I'm sure it was a woman and I think she was alone. Hard to see with the dust, though," Ronnie said, looking back.

"I'm going to follow her after I get turned around. Don't want to be too close." Larry turned into the first driveway past Molly's.

He followed just close enough to see the car turn left about a mile from her driveway.

"Yankee Doodle Road, now that's a different name. I wonder where this comes out," Larry said, pulling closer to the car he was following. "Don't want to lose her with these hills."

"She's going to that bar across the highway up ahead," Ronnie said as they came over the last hill.

"I'm pulling over for a few minutes, then we'll go in, too. Hopefully they serve food. Maybe we can get into a conversation with her." Larry pulled over to the side of the road.

The sign read "Valley Lounge—World's Best Hamburger." Molly was at the bar, with a drink, talking to the bartender. The only two other customers were sitting at a table finishing what looked like breakfast.

Larry led the way and went right up to the bar where Molly was sitting. "You serve food, right?"

"Best food in town. And right now, the only food in town." The bartender chuckled as he pulled out two menus. "We also have breakfast until noon, if you're interested."

"Your hamburgers must be good if they're the best in the world," Ronnie joked.

"Try them. I'm sure you'll agree." The bartender winked at Ronnie.

"They are good," Molly chimed in. "You boys aren't from around here, are you?"

"Two hamburger plates then, right? I'll put your order in. What town are you from? You look like farm boys." The bartender took back the menus.

"McGrath." Ronnie answered. "Have you heard of it?"

Molly. who was just taking a slip of her Bloody Mary, choked. "McGrath? Do you know anyone by the name of Haas?"

"Sure. Gordon Haas is our best friend. Do you know Gordon?" Larry asked quickly while it seemed natural.

"Ah, no, well maybe I met Gordon. I worked with his dad during the war at the Arsenal." Molly finished her drink in one gulp and motioned to the bartender for a refill. "A year or so after the war I bought a load of firewood from him. He did have his son with. Yes, I think his name was Gordon." An ashen look came over Molly's face. "You boys live near Mille Lacs Lake?"

"About six miles from it," Larry answered.

"You probably heard about my husband's murder then." Molly was no longer looking at the boys but was looking at something only she could see.

"There was a fisherman killed right after New Year's. Everybody in the area knows about that. Was that your husband?" Larry watched for Molly's reaction.

"Yes, I'm Molly Kelseltz. Ray was my husband. Weren't some local guys arrested? Do you know them?"

"Sure do. Have a hard time believing they did it." Larry was now looking directly at Molly, watching her body language. "You know about Gordon's dad's death? Got swept off an ore carrier."

"Yes, it's a small world. But my brother-in-law works on the boats. He knew that I knew Tommy, so he told me about it."

"Was he on the same boat?" Larry probed.

"No, I don't think so. Well, I don't know." Molly guzzled her second drink and jumped up. "I'm late. I have to go." She rushed out of the bar without looking back at the boys. She didn't want them to see the tears streaming down her face.

The boys ate their hamburgers without talking. It was the best hamburger they had ever eaten at a restaurant, which admittedly was a small sample. Larry replayed the conservation with Molly over in his head several times as he drove back to Minneapolis. Then he said, "Well Ronnie, what do you think? Whole lot of lying?"

"Well, first thing on my mind is 'Wow,' what a beautiful woman. It was hard to concentrate looking at her. But back to your real question, she was sorry she asked if we knew the Haas family the minute she said it. She knows Gordon." Ronnie looked straight ahead not wanting to confirm what that meant.

"Yes, she is beautiful and she was really in love with Gordon's dad. When she mentioned his name, I felt her emotions. Thought she was going to break down. But she definitely lied about her brother-in-law being on the same boat. Where do we go from here?" Larry let out a deep breath of air relieving the tension that had built up during the conversation.

"Let's enjoy the rest of the tournament and talk about this next week." Ronnie was also anxious to relax.

"I'm going to write down some notes when we get back to the house. Then we'll forget about this for the weekend." Larry suddenly realized he was going 90 miles per hour across a bridge. He quickly slowed down. "Don't want a speeding ticket as soon as I'm allowed to drive this car."

The second night of the state tournament was even more exciting than the first. After Canby had won the first game Gilbert faced off against Mountain Lake.

"If Austin couldn't stop Boots, he shouldn't have much of a problem against Mountain Lake," Larry announced to the group. Since he was rooting so hard for Gilbert to win, he almost regretted his words. Mountain Lake had a three-point lead with a minute left in the game, Boots got a basket and Gilbert's star guard, playing on a bad leg, scored another basket for a one-point win.

The next morning the group did meet downtown and spent time looking at all the merchandise for sale in Dayton's, Donaldson's and the other department stores.

"Hard to believe there is this much stuff to buy," Lois commented to Larry. Without Larry being very aware of it, Lois was spending most of the morning walking with him. Larry did notice that Irene and Ronnie were often paired up and one time when Irene was pointing out something to Ronnie, Larry noted they were holding hands.

In addition to window-shopping, the group did a lot of people-watching. They walked down Hennepin Avenue past bars like Augie's and the Gay Nineties. They were reading all the show bills with pictures of scantily dressed women in suggestive poses.

While they were looking at one of the show bills, a man who was about to enter one of the bars approached George. "Man, you are a fair-haired looking boy. Come inside with me and I'll get Bruce to serve you a drink."

It took George a minute while he looked at the man smiling at him, to realize what he meant. "Come on everybody," he yelled. "Let's get out of here."

The group finished the morning by having lunch at the Nankin Restaurant. It was the first time any of them had eaten Chinese food.

On the way back to Larry's sister's house, Ronnie turned to Larry and said, "Here's the deal. Irene and Lois want to ride back to McGrath with us."

Larry smiled remembering Ronnie and Irene holding hands. "That's fine with me."

"Well, the other part of the deal is they want to go home right after the game," Ronnie continued.

"What?" Larry said. "We're not dropping Irene off at her house at two in the morning. Her mom will shoot us."

"Not a problem," Ronnie answered. "Irene is staying with Lois for the night. She also suggested maybe we could get a couple six packs for the ride home."

"Maybe my brother-in-law will let me 'steal' a couple. Irene doesn't think you are so boring after all?" Larry laughed.

As Ronnie and Larry walked up to their seats at "The Barn," Lois and Irene were standing waiting for them. Ronnie smiled at them. "It's all a go."

"Good," Irene said as she took Ronnie's hand and led him into their row. Lois reached out and led Larry in next.

Bev, already sitting near George and Gerald, watched the four of them enter and said, "Ah, the sweet smell of love is in the air." A festive mood fell over the group.

"This should be a good night of basketball. The Minneapolis paper said the tournament expects a new record attendance. Hope Gilbert learned their lesson last night." Larry wanted to turn the group's attention back to basketball.

"Who's bigger, Gilbert or Canby?" Lois asked.

"Canby, I think," Larry answered. "But we need to yell for Gilbert anyway. They're from our region."

"Go Boots," Gerald yelled, mocking Larry.

Larry didn't have to worry. Although Canby had three players guarding Boots, Gilbert's injured guard took over and scored 30 points and Gilbert won by a score of 69 to 52.

Lois turned and hugged Larry. "Rah, rah, rah for Gilbert. I should go down and lead their cheerleaders."

"Let's hit the road," Ronnie said. "We can do our cheering in the car."

"Who's going to have time for cheering?" Irene gave Ronnie a little kiss on the cheek.

By the time Larry worked his way out of the traffic jam of people leaving the tournament and out of the city, Irene and Ronnie were engaged in loud heavy petting in the back seat.

Lois, who was sitting tight against Larry and was helping him shift gears when he had to whispered while nibbling on his ear. "Sounds like they're having fun back there."

"I'll find a good place to park soon, and we can have our own fun." Larry gave her a quick kiss.

"Don't worry about that. Didn't Ronnie tell you? My parents and those two brats I have for siblings are on a trip to California. When we get to my house we have it all to ourselves." Lois returned Larry's kiss hard on his cheek.

"Tell him about the condoms," Irene yelled from the backseat.

Lois started laughing and told the story.

There's a small drug store a block from where we were staying with my aunt. We got the idea it's better to be safe than sorry. The only person in the store when we went in was an old man behind the counter. After looking around for a few minutes to get our courage up, Irene asked him if he had any rubbers.

He looked at us for a few minutes startled, and said, "Do you girls mean condoms?"

"Yes," Irene answered, fighting the temptation to run out of the store.

He looked at us over his glasses, "How old are you girls?"

"Eighteen." Irene started to pull out her driver's license.

"That's OK. What kind to you want?" he asked.

"The kind that keeps us from getting pregnant," Irene blurted out between giggles.

"Here is a pack of six. Hopefully, that's enough," he said with a final look of disapproval."

Lois then pulled out the pack they were able to buy.

Larry looked in the rearview mirror and said to Ronnie, "Guess we should have gotten to know our classmates a little better." He sped on toward McGrath.

Chapter 19
Autumn 1950

Molly remembered the trip she and Ray took to Buhl as she drove up Highway 65. Ray, still suffering from his post war trauma, drove like a madman the whole trip. She also recalled what she felt at Ray's mention of Tommy as they neared McGrath. When he asked if she had asked Tommy about ice fishing on Mille Lacs it had triggered all the guilt and fear she was harboring about her and Tommy's relationship. Again, she ran through the scenario in her head. What if she had been honest with Ray as soon as he had returned home from the war and asked him for a divorce? Would Tommy still be alive?

It was a perfect mid-October day. All the hardwood trees had lost their leaves so a hint of winter was in the air, even though the temperature was in the low sixties. Molly knew in another five to six weeks the lakes would be frozen and ice fishing would begin. For the past four years Molly and Ray had maintained their married but unmarried status. Ray was spending more time in Buhl during the summer and ice fishing in the winter when he wasn't flying. Molly expected he had found some love interest but she didn't care. He was always polite, tender and seemingly hopeful when they were together. He also continued to be a good father and would make arrangements to be available to take care of the kids when he had to. The only thing that kept Molly from being receptive to Ray's clear desire to resume their normal married relationship was the driving pang of hate she would experience when she looked at him that arose from her certainty that he was responsible for Tommy's death.

After the completion of the Bellows murder trial and the dinner with Steve Mitchell, Molly maintained a relationship with Steve. She had not surrendered to the temptation of sexual involvement with him despite Steve's ongoing efforts at seduction. As part of his efforts to please, Steve had his investigator spend many hours compiling a thorough report on Tommy's death. He was able to obtain access to the Coast Guard's file. The main pieces of information from this file that Molly felt supported her belief was a statement by the ship's captain. He testified that, based on Roy's demeanor, he strongly questioned the truthfulness of Roy's statement. The report also commented on Roy's statement of smelling alcohol when he met with Tommy. In questioning the shipmates who had seen Tommy that night, including the fellow card players, all of them said Tommy was not drinking immediately prior to his encounter with Roy. They said they would have been surprised if he drank after leaving them, considering they were all on watch because of the storm. The final and most powerful statement Molly felt proved Roy's guilt was his statement that Tommy had asked him to help check the hatches. Molly had reread Tommy's last letter so many times she could quote it from memory. She told Steve about Tommy writing that Roy had instigated the interaction when they went out to check the hatches.

Steve, who was planning a future political career, was well-connected politically and knew Congressman Blatnik who represented the Duluth area of Minnesota. He was lobbying the Congressman's office to keep pressure on the Coast Guard to continue the investigation of Roy and bring charges against him. To date these efforts had been futile.

Feeling very frustrated that nothing had happened for almost four years, Molly made the decision to take matters into her own hands. She called Tommy's brother, Si, and he agreed to take Molly to meet Arvin Berg and Hans Thompson. This was the first week they were home from the boats. Molly had with her the report of Steve's investigator and Tommy's last letter. She was hoping that one or both might remember something Roy had said or done the night of the storm, or even before or after, that would help incriminate him.

As Molly drove through Mora and saw the "McGrath - 26 miles" sign all her conflicting feelings, love for Tommy, the loneliness of being without him, the rage she was trying to suppress, and the growing, troubling desire for revenge overcame her. The strain of the conflict within her forced her to stop. She pulled over to the side of the road hoping to regain her composure. Instead, she cried uncontrollably for over five minutes as she resolved in her mind what she would do.

Si was waiting for Molly after she found her way to his house, half an hour late.

"Hi, I'm Molly," she smiled and hoped her crying jag had not done too much damage to the little make-up she was wearing.

Si looked dumbfounded at Molly for several moments.

"Tommy told me about his plan to leave Eleanor, but he never showed me a picture of you. Is there any way a brother could take his place?" Si laughed heartily.

"No one can take Tommy's place." Molly smiled at the warmth of Si's greeting. "But I really do need a friend, especially someone who was close to Tommy."

"I'll settle for that." Si reached out and took Molly by the hand. "Come in and meet my wife. Don't worry; she and Eleanor aren't close. She'll keep anything you say confidential. You look like you could use some coffee or something stronger."

"You're as perceptive as Tommy. He got me hooked on 7-7s." Molly walked into the house hand-in-hand with Si.

"Don't have any Seagram's, just Kessler's. I think you can use a straight shot with a beer chaser. This is the missus, Molly: Claudette." Si let go of Molly's hand and went into the kitchen to get the drinks.

"So, we were almost sisters-in-law. Tommy talked to us about you, and I was looking forward to that happening. Never got along with Eleanor. This was a sad household after we got the news of Tommy's accident. Worse for you I'm sure." Claudette embraced Molly.

"Don't believe it was an accident. That's why I want to meet with his shipmates." Molly, now crying, hugged Claudette hard. "I'm sure we would have been close."

"Si told me that it was your brother-in-law that was with Tommy. Do you think your husband put him up to knocking Tommy overboard?"

"I'm certain," Molly sobbed.

"I still talk to Eleanor. Maybe I can, without letting on I know you, suggest to her that she should go through his belongings she got from the Coast Guard to see if there is anything that might be a clue." Claudette patted Molly gently on the back.

"Well, looks like you two are getting along." Si came back with the drinks.

"How long can you stay? I told Hans and Arvin that we would be there around one. After you talk to them, we will come back here and have some dinner. But you can stay as long as you want." Si handed Molly her shot and a bottle of beer.

"Can't you offer our guest a glass to drink out of?" Claudette chided Si.

"No, that's fine. Tommy and I always drank from the bottle," Molly said with a look of pleasure as she recalled drinking beer with Tommy.

"Yaw, neither brother had any class," Claudette ribbed Si.

Si and Molly spent over two hours with Hans and Arvin. The conversation was mostly about Tommy and how everyone liked and respected him. The last hour was spent with the two shipmates reliving the final hours of Tommy's life. Hans told Molly about Tommy winning the final pot of the poker game with the Deadman's Hand. Molly showed them the report and the final letter. They both agreed with the captain's assessment of Roy's truthfulness and both were certain Tommy wasn't drinking. Neither one was surprised by Tommy saying Roy was the one who requested that Tommy help.

"If Tommy had believed that the hatch was coming loose, he would have notified the captain. Then, if he was instructed to verify his belief, he would've requested the help of a more experienced shipmate than Roy," Hans told Molly after reading the letter.

As Molly and Si were getting ready to leave Arvin said, "I've been trying to remember if anything else happened. What came to me just now was something that happened on the very first day of our first voyage. Hans, Tommy and I were standing at the rail waving to a small crowd as we passed Canal Park. Tommy seemed to be distracted, but if I was thinking about you, I would be distracted too." Arvin smiled at Molly. "Anyway, as we stood there Roy pushed his way in between Tommy and me. He said he wanted to get to know all of us better, but he mainly was talking to Tommy. I remember now that I had a very strange feeling about how Roy was trying to become our friend. I agree with your conviction that Roy planned to push Tommy overboard. Can you get anyone to act?"

"I have a lawyer working on it, but so far all the authorities say that without more evidence, or Roy confessing, the case is too weak," Molly answered. But her mind was thinking about Arvin's last statement. It was clear to her that Ray and Roy had planned the murder prior to the first voyage and Roy was waiting for the right opportunity. Anger and bitterness seethed through her. As Si drove towards his house they met an oncoming car.

"Here comes Tommy's son, Gordon. You probably never met him," Si said.

Molly, thinking quickly, said, "Can we stop him? Tommy brought me a load of wood once and Gordon was with him. Maybe Gordon is too young to cut wood, but if he does, I would like to buy a load from him.

That's what he's doing for spending money." Si made a U-turn and soon caught up to Gordon.

After Si and Molly talked to Gordon and Molly made arrangements for Gordon to deliver a load of wood, they returned to Si's house where Claudette had dinner waiting. After dinner Molly thanked both Claudette and Si and said, "I need to head back home. I have to work the morning shift at six." Then as Molly headed to the door she stopped and asked, "How far is Mille Lacs Lake from here? Is there a resort called Ole Johnson's Lakeside Resort?"

"If you go right and follow the road we took to Hans' place but go straight for another six miles instead of turning where we did, you will hit Highway 47. Take another right and go three more miles and then follow the signs into Ole's place. Something special about it?" Si gave Molly a quizzical look.

"Just curiosity. Ray ice fishes there." Molly went to her car.

After driving into Lakeside Resort, Molly turned around and drove south along the lake until she got to Isle, where the first building she saw was the Isle Liquor Store. Recalling how the straight shot that Si gave her relaxed her, she decided to have one more.

As she sat at the bar sipping her shot and drinking her beer chaser, a cocky, muscled, grimy twenty-something-year-old male came up to her and said, "Lordy! Lordy! Never, ever, expected to see a beauty queen alone in this dump. Buy you another drink?"

As Molly looked him over, an idea flashed in her brain. "You look like a tough sort of guy. If a girl wanted her boyfriend roughed up a little would you know anyone who might do the job?"

"Baby, you're talking to the man. Tell me who and where."

Molly got a pen out of her purse and grabbed a bar napkin. "I'm not sure what I want to do yet but give me a name and phone number."

"It's Virgil Larsen," he said as wrote on the bar napkin.

Molly put the napkin in her purse, finished her drink with one gulp, and said as she headed to the door, "When I decide, I may call."

The last 10 weeks of 1950 went by in a hurry. Gordon and his friend Melvin Smith delivered the load of wood in mid-November. Melvin unloaded most of the load while Molly took Gordon into the house to tell him about her love for his dad and the details surrounding Gordon's dad's death.

Molly had to work all New Year's weekend and when she got home late Wednesday afternoon, January 3, she had a message from Steve Mitchell for her to call his office ASAP.

When she called the next day, the receptionist got Steve out of a meeting to talk. "Molly, exciting news. We think there may be a break in the investigation of Roy. Apparently, Tommy's wife Eleanor, at the request of her sister-in-law Claudette, went through the items that were returned to her after Tommy's death. While she was going through Tommy's clothes, she found a half-empty pint bottle of Seagram's in Tommy's sport coat pocket. Eleanor immediately told Claudette that it was strange. For all the years Eleanor knew Tommy he always kept any whiskey bottle he had in a paper bag, but this bottle was not bagged."

Molly instantly replayed all the times she had seen Tommy drink, or pour whiskey from a bottle. She had a clear picture of the paper bag, as if Tommy believed that the bottle should always be concealed. "That's right. But what does that prove?"

"Claudette knew that if something was different from normal, it could be important. She had Eleanor leave the bottle in the sports coat and she called Tommy's friend, Hans. Hans got ahold of the investigator who had interviewed him. The investigator picked up the bottle and had it dusted for fingerprints."

Molly was beginning to realize the importance of the bottle. "Wow! Tell me, whose fingerprints?"

"Eleanor's were on the top of the bottle from when she took it out of the coat." Steve paused to emphasize the climactic information. "The rest were Roy's! Tommy hadn't touched the bottle."

"The bastard! The bastard! Killed him and then tried to make him look drunk. The bastard!" Molly was crying hard. "What now?"

"They are going to call Roy back in with this evidence. They also checked the detailed inventory of Tommy's room that was taken before the room was cleaned out. There was a small brown paper bag found on the floor. The police hope to break Roy," Steve answered.

"Thank you, thank you. I just can't express how much I appreciate all you have done for me," Molly said with love dripping off each word.

"Molly, for you, I'm only here to serve," Steve answered affectionately. "But I have to get back to my paying client. I'll keep you informed."

Molly looked at the phone before she hung it up. What was happening between Steve and her? Was it now possible Roy and Ray would be held accountable? That thought jolted Molly. She quickly found Ray's flight schedule. He was flying in this morning and most likely would be going straight up to his fish house on Mille Lacs. She then found Si's number, but no one answered when she called.

Molly slept for a few hours. After the kids came home from school, she fed them and got them ready for her sister to come and stay with them while she worked. Then she called Si again.

"Si, my attorney called and told me about what Claudette and Eleanor discovered," Molly said when Si answered. "Tell Claudette I'm really grateful for what she's done."

"That was pretty amazing. Boy, I would never have thought that the whiskey bottle was important." Si was in awe of his wife. "Did your attorney know what might happen now?"

"He thinks the police will try to get Roy to break and confess. But I'm calling because I have a favor to ask. Can you find Gordon and tell him to cancel the load of wood he was bringing this weekend? He'll know what I mean. It's important he gets the message as soon as possible." Molly's voice conveyed a sense of urgency.

"I will. Should I have him call you?" Si asked, a little puzzled by the message he was to convey.

"No, it's probably best he doesn't," Molly answered. Realizing her answer sounded strange she added. "I mean, I have to work tonight and I will be sleeping tomorrow."

Si called Eleanor who said Gordon wasn't home. He had left before supper acting stranger than normal. Si, sensing something was wrong, drove into McGrath looking for Gordon's car at the school or anywhere around town. He didn't find it. As he headed back home he met Larry and Ronnie, but Gordon was not with them.

"Have you seen Gordon tonight?" Si asked after he had stopped Larry.

"We're going to an ice skating party. We stopped to pick Gordon up but he was not home," Larry responded to Si's question. "Might be over at Melvin Smith's. Been going there a lot lately," Larry added.

Si drove past Melvin Smith's place but didn't see Gordon's car so he didn't stop. He then gave up looking for Gordon and went home.

The ringing phone woke up Sharon, Steven Mitchell's wife. It was 8:30 Sunday morning.

"Can I talk to Steve? This is Molly Kelseltz."

Sharon handed the phone to Steve who was also just waking up. "It's for you."

"Molly, is that you?" Steve said as Molly said hello. He sprang up into a sitting position in bed.

"Ray was found dead in his fish house last night. He'd been killed by someone using an ice pick." Molly's voice was a mixture of panic, fear and grief. "The Eagan Chief of Police was here when I got home from work. I told him I was too tired to talk to him this morning. I have to go down to the police station this afternoon. I want to hire you and have you go with me."

"Let's meet at my office in an hour," Steve said as he started getting out of bed and headed to the shower. "We have a lot to talk about."

Sharon was waiting for Steve as he came out of the bathroom.

"'Can I talk to Steve?', 'Molly, is that you?'" Sharon mocked the conversation that had just taken place.

"Since when do you have a new client with a sugar-sweet voice, calling you early Sunday morning, who is already on a first name basis with you? What happened to, 'Mr. Mitchell,' or, 'Who is this calling?' Apparently, it's someone you can't wait to get to the office to meet. How convenient. I assume there won't be anyone else in the office this early on Sunday morning."

Steve glared at Sharon. "What the hell are you talking about? Maybe you have forgotten I'm a criminal defense lawyer? Maybe you have forgotten how much money I make as a criminal defense lawyer? Maybe you have forgotten how much fucking money you spend at the Oval Room at Dayton's? If you don't want me to do my job, maybe you should find a good divorce lawyer. I know several I could recommend, but I know you wouldn't trust anyone I know."

Steve pulled on his slacks, found a U of M sweatshirt, grabbed his winter coat and gloves, and headed for the garage, realizing that for the first time in his marriage he had sworn at his wife.

Sharon quickly put on her robe and ran yelling, "Steve, I'm sorry. Steve, wait. Steve, don't go away mad." But as she got to the garage it was too late. The garage door was shutting and she saw Steve backing out of the driveway at a high rate of speed, squealing his tires.

Chapter 20
Summer 1951

On May 25th, the 1951 class of McGrath High School graduated. Larry, who had been competing with his cousin, Joanne, to finish second in the class standing, failed. He finished third behind Joanne and Bob, whose four years of straight A's and testing earned him a scholarship to MIT. Gordon finished fifteenth and Ronnie seventeenth out of the 23 graduates.

Since the state basketball tournament Larry and Ronnie had spent most of their nights out with Lois and Irene, going to dances and movies. Gordon, seeming to have an unspoken understanding that something had changed in the relationship between the three blind mice, spent most of his time with his two older drinking buddies, Melvin Smith and Joe Sandustski. Gordon never asked either Ronnie or Larry about what may have happened at the state tournament to prompt this change. He did, however, give them shit about their romances with Lois and Irene.

"You two assholes are acting like old married men. Are you allowed to drink a beer now and then?"

Larry and Ronnie for their part, struggled with the knowledge they had about Molly and Gordon's contact and Gordon's behavior the night at the fish house and since. Larry was especially upset whenever he considered the fate of the three guys from Isle who were still in jail, unable to raise their bail. Several times he considered either telling his dad or going to the sheriff, but he rationalized he didn't have any real evidence—only Gordon's fingerprints at the scene, which the sheriff also had, and his understanding of the relationship of Ray to Gordon's dad's death. Gordon was also his best friend.

After the graduation ceremony, Larry and Ronnie were leaving the school when Gordon caught up to them.

"Where're you headed? Maybe we can do a little beer drinking on the back roads like old times. We can talk about all our wonderful experiences at good old McGrath High."

"Sounds like fun," Ronnie said. "But Lois's parents are having a graduation party. Irene will be there. Larry and I are invited."

"I see." Gordon's expression went from excited to sullen. "Come on out with me, I parked next to Larry's car."

What was parked next to Larry's car was a brand-new Harley Davidson.

"Like it?" Gordon jumped on the bike and revved up the engine. "Sounds good, doesn't it?"

"What bank did you rob to buy this?" Ronnie was walking around in awe, admiring the bike.

Larry just stood and looked at the bike and Gordon. An immediate idea for the source of the money sprang into his mind. Larry opened his trunk and pulled out three beers from a cooler.

"On weekends, Melvin and I have been hauling the firewood I cut last winter to the Cities and we were very successful in selling everything I cut." Gordon made the bike roar one more time before turning it off as he took the beer from Larry. "I have another little surprise for you guys. When I played hooky from school last Monday I went up to Aitkin and enlisted in the army. Leaving in two weeks for Fort Leonard Wood in Missouri."

Larry walked over and gave Gordon a masculine hug. "Hey man, that's quick. When and why did you decide that?"

"I don't know. Things seemed to just be getting out of hand, the drinking with Melvin, my old lady ragging on me about that and getting a job now that I'm graduating. Also, you two are getting more serious with your girlfriends. The old gang is breaking up." Gordon took a big swallow of beer.

"So why did you buy the cycle? What are you going to do with it?" Ronnie was still looking the bike over.

"Well, my brother will ride it a little while I'm in basic training. The recruiter said after basic I can have the bike on base as long as I'm stateside. If you two want to ride it, I'll tell Dennis you can take it whenever. It's beautiful, isn't it?" Gordon petted the bike like it was a dog.

Ronnie and Larry nodded in agreement.

"Well, you two better get to your party. The girls are waiting." Gordon jumped back on his bike.

Before Gordon started the engine, Larry felt this would be a good time to see if Gordon had any recent contact with Molly.

"Say Goro, did we ever tell you who we met by chance when we were down at the state tournament?" Larry was watching Gordon's body language.

"You mean, ah, back in March?" Gordon tensed up.

Larry was sure Gordon had changed what he was going to say mid-sentence and had intended to say, "You mean Molly."

"Molly Kelseltz." Larry stopped to see Gordon's reaction.

"Molly who?" Gordon shifted his body like he needed to protect himself and started his Harley.

"The wife of the murdered fisherman," Larry answered.

"Oh," he said, as he quickly accelerated the Harley, throwing up gravel so Larry and Ronnie had to jump back, to avoid being hit.

They both stood and stared as Gordon disappeared around a street corner.

"I need another beer," Larry said as he looked at Ronnie. "Well?"

"I'm afraid what we don't want to believe is true," Ronnie continued to look down the street after Gordon.

On the Sunday afternoon following graduation Larry stopped at Gordon's house to tell him he was going to the Cities on Tuesday to start working with his older brother on construction. Larry, who was starting college at the University of Minnesota in September, didn't want to miss seeing Gordon before he left for the Army. He also wanted to see if Gordon would comment on his sudden need to leave when Molly's name was mentioned.

"When you think about the devil, he usually shows up," Gordon said. He was out polishing his Harley. "I was planning on riding over to your house to see if you were home. What're you doing a week from Saturday?"

"I stopped to tell you I start working with my brother on Tuesday. I'll be home on weekends. I guess nothing's going on that Saturday." Larry was touching the bike with admiration.

"Want to take it for spin?" Gordon motioned Larry to get on the bike. "I need to report to the National Guard Armory at 10 a.m. Then I and the rest of the recruits will be bussed to Minneapolis. There will be a whole train load of us going to Missouri."

"Sure." Larry jumped on the seat. His brother-in-law had given him a couple of lessons riding a motorcycle, but he was a little nervous driving one as big as the one he was on. He didn't let it show. "I'll take it easy. Just go a few miles and back."

But before Larry started, Gordon jumped on behind him. "Let's take it into McGrath and make a few runs on Main Street and some of the side streets. If I see any of those old gossip mouths who spread the lies about my dad, I'll give them one last middle finger before I leave."

Larry believed he knew what hard work was, given what he had done on the farm, but after working for two weeks tendering four block-layers building a twelve-inch block warehouse wall, he had a new definition. He had planned to go directly up to McGrath, after work the Friday night before Gordon was leaving and to pick up Ronnie and Gordon, for a final night together before Gordon left for the army. When the temperature hit 94 degrees at 2 o'clock in the afternoon and the job foreman refused to shut the job down despite requests from the block-layers, Larry was sure he would not survive until the 4:30 quitting time. He did, but instead of going to McGrath, he went to his brother's house on Mille Lacs Lake and ran right into the lake, wearing only his underwear. After staying in the lake for over an hour, Larry felt cool enough to go home. He was in bed by 9 and barely woke up in time to pick Gordon up to take him to Aitkin.

Larry met Gordon coming out of his house having seen Larry drive in. "Sorry I'm late. I overslept. I've never been so tired in my life as I was last night. Hopefully I won't have to work as hard as I did the last two weeks for the whole summer. If so, I'm not sure I will survive."

Gordon, wearing a white T-shirt, jeans, and an old pair of tennis shoes was carrying a paper bag. "Here's the deal. I'll be sworn in as soon as I get there and then will be issued a uniform. I'll put it on and give you what I'm wearing in this bag. You can bring it home. After that I'll be taken care of by my Uncle Sam." It was a quick trip as Larry drove over the speed limit all the way so Gordon wouldn't be late. Gordon kept trying to find news on the radio about Korea.

"I'm hoping that they get that settled over there by the time I'm done with my basic. Sounds like it's a stalemate now since the peace talks started. Don't want to go over there. If I do go and don't come back, I want you to take this." Gordon reached into the paper bag and pulled out a note he had written.

To All Concerned,   *June 9, 1951*

I have given the attached signed title certificate for my Harley Davidson motorcycle to Larry Oien. If for any reason I don't return from my tour of duty in the Army, Larry is to keep said Harley Davidson motorcycle. This is a gift from me for him being my one true friend.

                             Gordon Haas

Larry, pulled over to the side of the highway to read the note. As he felt tears coming down his face, he reached over clapped Gordon's arm and said, "Man, I appreciate the gesture, but I know it's meaningless. In two years, you'll be back and roaring around the whole country on your bike. Thanks anyway for the idea."

After dropping Gordon off and waiting until he had changed into his uniform, Larry took the bag of civilian clothes and gave Gordon another manly hug.

"Wow man, you sure look like a mean-ass soldier in that uniform. You have any idea when you will get your first leave?"

"No, no one tells you shit. They just gave me the uniform and said the bus leaves in 45 minutes. Man, this uniform is hot. I will write when I know something. Write back. Keep me posted. Don't run off and get married as soon as I leave." Gordon hugged Larry one more time and turned to go into the Armory to keep Larry from seeing his tears.

As Larry drove home, he was an emotional wreck. He had made a commitment to himself to confront Gordon about his connection, if any, to Molly or, if things went right, to ask him, point blank, if he murdered Ray. Now his two chances, the Friday night beer drinking party with Gordon and Ronnie, which didn't happen, and the trip to Aitkin, were gone. Not only had he not confronted Gordon, but Gordon's gesture with the Harley made any decision to disclose to the sheriff or anyone else the connection between Gordon and Ray more of an act of betrayal than it would have been before the trip to Aitkin.

"I have to write to Gordon at some point, but I guess nothing is happening with the investigation right now," He said out loud, rationalizing his inaction. Larry put the knowledge that Eddie Johansson, Irwin Moss and Virgil Larsen were sitting in jail out of his mind.

The summer passed quickly. Larry's construction jobs were much easier than the first warehouse job he worked on and in September he started at the University of Minnesota with a plan to obtain a journalism degree. He did exchange letters with Gordon. Gordon's letters were mostly about how he hated the military.

Man, I really got my ass ripped last night. I was walking back to the barracks and met a Second Lewy. It was just getting dark so I didn't recognize his rank in time to salute. This military sucks. I did bitch a little to my First Sargent the other day and he said I was becoming a soldier. He said he would rather have a platoon of men who speak up and bitch when they are pissed off, than a platoon of men who just compliantly take whatever shit that happens to them. They're the ones who will turn and run in battle and not have your back.

I haven't mentioned it before but my bunk mate, he did take the upper bunk because he thinks it's safer, is black. Woodrow Willis, from Muscle Shoals, Alabama. Hell, of a harmonica player. The next bunk to us has Tony Lazaro from Detroit and Merlyn Baker, a good ole boy from Oklahoma. The four of us hang together most of the time. I am the youngest. I think Woodrow and Merlyn are about twenty. Tony said the other day he is twenty-three. He was a Golden Glove boxing champion for the state of Michigan when he was eighteen. He proved it the other day when this real asshole from South Carolina was giving Tony, Merlyn and me shit about being nigger lovers for letting Woodrow hang with us. Tony told him it's better to be a nigger lover than being a dumb shit who walks around with his head up his ass. The South Carolina boy said, "Come outside and we see who has his head up his ass." His mistake. He took one swing which Tony easily blocked and then, with one quick right-handed jab, Tony coldcocked him. His buddies carried him off and put him in his bunk. He didn't come to for about five minutes and was still woozy the next morning. Hasn't bothered us since.

The other thing Gordon wrote about was how homesick he was and how he longed for the nights the three blind mice spent driving the back roads drinking beer or just hanging out.

For his part, Larry, when he wrote to Gordon, responded to Gordon's comments or filled Gordon in on his life and what was happening in McGrath.

> *After you are done with basic, hopefully you will be able to get some leave. You may have to get home for Ronnie's wedding. Nothing official yet, but when I get home on the weekends Ronnie is always tied up with Irene. Guess Irene's mom is now even excited about her prospective son-in-law. Probably helps that you and me are no longer influencing Ronnie. In your last letter, you asked about Lois. We agreed that we both had plans for the future that didn't include the other. Still good friends. She is taking a nursing course up in Duluth.*

Although he intended to do so every time he wrote, Larry never found the words to mention Ray's murder or Gordon's relationship to Molly. When he received a letter from Gordon stating that he would be home in late October in response to his comments about Ronnie and the possibility of a wedding, Larry put off bringing up the subject.

He would wait until Gordon's leave and confront him in person. Besides being reluctant to broach the matter, another reason he also decided to wait was Gordon said in his letter that he was upset because he was certain he would be sent to Korea after his leave. Larry didn't want to upset him further.

In late September, the urgency of confronting Gordon increased drastically. Larry was driving home to McGrath on a Friday night and had tuned-in the local Aitkin radio station as soon as he was within the signal range.

> "That was Lefty Frizzell singing about how he loves his Mommy and Pappi. Stay tuned for more great country music, but here is our news announcer with some breaking updates about the murder that happened just after New Year's Day.

Larry, who had been deep in thought about his Friday afternoon political science class, quickly turned up the volume.

"This is Phil Oberg, news director here at KMOJ. I have just returned from a press conference held by County Attorney Jim Ryan. He announced a major break in the prosecution's case of the murder of Ray Kelseltz. Mr. Kelseltz was found dead in his fish house last January 5th on Mille Lacs Lake in southern Aitkin County. In March, Eddie Johansson, Irwin Moss and Virgil Larsen were arrested and have been held since then on charges of second-degree murder pending a grand jury hearing. However today the county attorney disclosed that the defendant Virgil Larsen has agreed to plead to a count of robbery by breaking and entering the victim's pick-up truck and a count of second- degree manslaughter regarding the death of Mr. Kelseltz. In addition to the agreement to plead to these two counts, Mr. Larsen has agreed to testify that when he was breaking into the victim's truck, Mr. Johansson entered the victim's fish house, while Mr. Moss stood guard outside the house. Johansson found the victim sleeping, but during the process of stealing the victim's wallet he woke him up. Johansson then grabbed the victim's ice pick and hit him in the head, killing him instantly.

Based on this testimony, the county attorney will seek first-degree murder charges against Mr. Johansson and second- degree murder charges against Mr. Moss for aiding and abetting the crime. He stated he hopes to have this case go to trial during the spring calendar of the district court. That's it from the newsroom. Now back to DJ Jones and our good country music."

Larry wished he could hear the news report again as he tried to process what he had heard. Could it be true? Did Eddie actually do the killing? Was he wrong about Gordon? As all these thoughts raced around in his head, Larry saw a roadside rest area by a lake. He got out a blank notebook and sat down at a picnic table and started to write.

What do I know?

1. Gordon's fingerprints were the only ones in the fish house.
2. Ray's brother Roy was on the ore boat with Gordon's dad.
3. Ray's wife, Molly, and Gordon know each other, and are defensive about it.
4. The sheriff said that an FBI profiler believes that the killer was acting in a rage.
5. Gordon deliberately ran into the fish house the night we were guarding the house.
6. Gordon has been acting strange since the murder.
7. The fisherman from Wisconsin saw a person who looked like a bear walking away from Ray's fish house the night the murder most likely happened.

What do I believe is true?

1. Gordon's mom is very bitter at Ray's wife, Molly.
2. Eddie Johansson is not violent and would have run out of the fish house if he was caught stealing the wallet.
3. Vigil Larsen would sell his own mother to save his own skin.
4. Gordon did not sell enough firewood to afford his new Harley.

After completing the list, Larry sat and looked out across the lake. The truth was clear. So was his moral responsibility.

Chapter 21
October 1951

Gordon came home on October 23 for a ten-day leave with orders to report to Presidio Army Base, outside of San Francisco, at 15:00 hours on November 2. From there he would be debarking by ship for Korea. During this period, Larry was scheduled to take all his mid-quarter exams. Despite this, Larry made arrangements to pick Gordon up at the Milwaukee Road train depot in Minneapolis and drive him to McGrath on the Tuesday afternoon he was arriving. Larry had to be back to the University by 10 o'clock on Wednesday morning to take a test. During the drive the two just talked about Gordon's army experiences and Larry's college life. Larry didn't even tell Gordon about the developments with the murder case. Larry left Gordon with instructions to set up an all-weekend party with Ronnie.

"We'll have one last fling before you leave for Korea," Larry said as he dropped Gordon off at his house.

"So, what's the plans for tonight?" Larry asked as he met Ronnie and Gordon at Krisel's Bar and Restaurant in McGrath that Friday night.

"Let's just hit the back roads tonight and talk about old times," Ronnie said. "It's going to be a beautiful warm October afternoon tomorrow, so I thought we could have a little going away party for Gordon down at our favorite beach area on Pine Lake. Then we'll hit the Saturday night dance at Tony's. Gerald and George are home and they may join us. Irene's mom even trusts me enough that she can come, and Lois also wants to see both you and Gordon. Even Sandy wants to come."

"Sandy? Gordon's old girlfriend!" Larry laughed. "My recollection is that the last time you had her on a date and I was with, she yelled, 'I never want to see you again!' as she got out of the car and ran into her house."

"Time heals everything, as they say," Gordon smiled. "Maybe she wants to give me a little loving to remember her by when I'm in Korea."

Larry, who was driving, said as the three of them left McGrath, "For old times' sake, let's drive down to Ole Johnson's to buy some beer. I'm sure he will be happy to see us. Shouldn't be any problem since he has been selling to us for two years."

Larry then brought up the real reason he wanted to go to Ole Johnson's. "The last time we were down to Ole's it was the night after the murder. Did you hear about what has happened to the case since you've been gone?" Larry looked at Gordon to see his reaction to the question.

Gordon remained cool and collected and just responded, "No."

"Well, Virgil Larsen plead guilty to some lesser charges and is going to testify that Irving and Eddie went into the fish house to steal his wallet and then Eddie killed the fisherman with his own ice pick." Larry was driving slowly trying to see Gordon's facial expressions in the dark.

"So that ends that little mystery," Gordon said, hiding any sense of relief. "What comes around goes around. Those bastards tried to pin the theft of old Jake's batteries on me."

"It's hard for me to believe Eddie could kill someone like that. What I know about the facts of the whole case, that doesn't make sense," Larry said continuing to watch Gordon as he drove.

"What the hell! You've become Perry Mason while I've been gone! Who in the hell do you think did it?" Gordon was now agitated.

Larry fought the strong urge to say, "you" to avoid an immediate breakdown of communication with Gordon.

"I don't know, but Eddie is such a laid-back guy. Right Ronnie?" Larry looked into the rearview mirror hoping Ronnie might take over the questioning of Gordon.

"That's right. I can't see him as a killer," Ronnie responded without any other comment.

"All three of them were probably drunk on their ass. You both know some of the real stupid things we did when we were blind drunk," Gordon surmised.

"Yaw, like the time we ransacked Dr. Jones' cabin back in the woods south of McGrath and Goro stuffed the cigar into a mattress when we left. Then we heard the cabin burned down." Ronnie unwittingly supported Gordon's argument.

"That's right," Gordon quickly said. "All three of us could still be in reform school for arson."

Larry, trying to keep the discussion on the murder, asked Gordon, "Did you know the victim's brother was a shipmate of your dad's on the ore carrier he was washed off of?"

"Jesus Christ, how would I know that?" Gordon was sitting in a defensive posture like the night he rode away on his Harley after Larry mentioned seeing Molly during the basketball tournament.

"One night last spring when I was waiting for you to come home, I saw a book about the ship. There was a picture of the crew including both your dad and the brother. I thought maybe your mom may have mentioned it to you," Larry said as he got to the resort.

"She might have," Gordon said as he jumped out of the car. "Enough of this shit about the murder. Lets buy some beer."

Larry and Ronnie got to the beach area on Pine Lake first. It was a perfect party spot for several reasons. Although it was in Aitkin County, the half mile of road that went by the spot was never patrolled by the Aitkin County deputy sheriffs due to the way the lake shore curved. They followed the road that went on the other side of the lake shore line and did not go the half mile into Pine County. And since it was in Aitkin County, the Pine County deputy sheriffs never patrolled the area. Finally, there were no houses or cabins on the half mile of road.

While Ronnie and Larry were setting up a makeshift volleyball net and court in the sand and two horseshoe stakes, Gordon drove in on his Harley and swung a turn across the beach, throwing up sand. He pulled to a stop by the table. "You sure you got enough beer? Had Melvin buy a little hard stuff," Gordon said as he pulled two-quart bottles, one whiskey and one vodka, out of his saddle bags. "Where are the girls?"

"Lois is picking up Irene and Sandy. They are bringing some munchies. Plenty of beer," Ronnie answered.

"Don't worry. If we run out of beer, we're only a mile away from our favorite resort owner. Remember how he used to sell us beer when we were only sophomores?" Larry added.

The girls came, as did George and Gerald with their girlfriends, Judy and Phyllis, Gordon's brother, Dennis, and several other young people who had heard of the party. Lois set up her portable record player and played her collection of 45s, which consisted mainly of country western singers, but also included several big band dance records of Glenn Miller, Tommy Dorsey and Harry James.

The weather was great with a temperature in the upper 60s. With the music, dancing and Gordon telling tales about his army life and the rumors he had heard about Korea, the party rolled on.

Larry yelled, "Who's game for some volleyball?"

"Phyllis, Judy, George and I will take someone on." Gerald laid down a challenge.

Lois, who was keeping up with the boys' beer consumption in addition to her music-playing and dancing, quickly replied, "Sandy, Gordon, Larry and I will take you on."

Gerald then yelled as the teams were lining up, "One team should be shirts and one should be skins."

After exchanging a quick glance at Sandy, said, "We'll be skins." she pulled her sweater off. "Is that enough?"

"Take it off, take it off," chanted several of the boys who were watching the pending game.

As Lois reached around her back to unhook her bra, Larry looked at her and said, "Are you sure?"

Lois, as she flung her bra to the side, said with a sneering tone, "Why should you be the only one to enjoy such beauty?"

Sandy, after taking a drink of straight vodka from Gordon's bottle, followed Lois' lead and played topless.

Given that the skins were considerably ahead of the shirts in their degree of intoxication the volleyball match was not very competitive. But there were a lot of fun moments. Gordon and Sandy both dived for the ball to stop a spike by George, both missed the ball and ended up in an embrace on the sand. Sandy whispered something in Gordon's ear and Gordon smiled and nodded "yes." After the game ended and Lois and Sandy were putting their bras and tops back on, giggling as they did, Gordon started up his Harley.

"Going to give Sandy a little ride on this beautiful machine," Gordon said to anyone who was listening. "Back soon."

As Sandy jumped on behind Gordon, Irene yelled, "Don't have an accident on your ride or otherwise."

Sandy just laughed and waved without looking back.

During the hour Gordon and Sandy were gone the party kept going. Other players took over the volleyball area, but the girls stayed fully dressed. Ronnie and Irene took on anyone who wanted to throw horseshoes while Gerald and George started an arm-wrestling contest, which was won by Joey, a partier from Isle.

Then Lois asked Larry to help set up a makeshift table using some boards that had been discarded on the beach. They laid them across a couple of fallen trees. She used the table to set out several bowls of home-made fried chicken she and Irene had made. In addition, she put out several bowls of cut-up watermelon.

As Lois was setting out the food, she gave Larry a kiss on his cheek and said, "I'm sorry for that sharp retort to you. I would like for us to spend several hours alone after this party and before the dance. Not seeing you is harder than I thought."

"I love that idea. Let Ronnie and Irene take your car and you and I will find a nice romantic hide-away spot to be alone." Larry embraced Lois and as they were locked in a deep kiss, Gordon and Sandy roared back into the party.

"Just in time for chicken," Gordon shouted as he turned off the Harley.

"Everyone better come and get some chicken and watermelon before Gordon and Sandy eat it all. Looks like they worked up an appetite," Lois yelled.

Sandy, holding tight to Gordon, said, "That's right. I've got one appetite satisfied. Now I'm hungry for food." She kissed Gordon on his lips.

The sun was already starting to fade in the west and the last of the food was being consumed, when the great party atmosphere took a sudden and violent change. A simple statement by Lois changed everything in a flash. As she was eating one of the final pieces of chicken, she turned to Larry and asked, "Did you see what has happened with the murder case on Mille Lacs that you boys helped the sheriff with? I guess one of the guys from Isle did it during a robbery."

Larry, who once again had decided to put off confronting Gordon directly, quickly responded to Lois, "I don't think Eddie did it. The sheriff said an expert from the FBI believed the murder was an act of anger and hate, someone seeking revenge."

"Who do you think did—" Before she could finish the question, Gordon yelled! "Me!! My best friend thinks I'm a murderer!"

Half crying and full of rage Gordon charged and took a swing at Larry.

Larry, more agile and less drunk than Gordon, sidestepped the blow and Gordon fell over the makeshift table. But he quickly pushed himself up, grabbing a broken part of a tree branch for a club.

He charged again and swung the branch hard, but Larry jumped to the side. The blow missed his head, but a small twig grazed the side of his face and neck, causing a gash that started spurting blood.

Larry then bear-hugged Gordon trying to pin him to the ground. But Gordon, having a weight advantage, got on top of Larry and attempted to get his hands on his throat. Before he could, Gerald, using his football skills, hit Gordon with a flying block and knocked him off Larry. Then Ronnie, George and Joey held Gordon down. Gerald yelled to Lois, "Get Larry out of here."

Lois quickly pulled off her sweater again and used it to compress the bleeding wounds as she led Larry to his car. Turning to Irene she said, "You and Ronnie take my car after you clean up this place. The keys are in it."

After she got Larry propped up in the passenger seat, she put her top around the wound and got in the car to drive. The pile on the beach then let Gordon up.

He hurried to his Harley and yelled to Larry, "Get those papers I gave you on the way to Aitkin back to me before you leave for school." He jumped on the bike and peeled out onto the tar road.

As he left, all the women were crying, with Sandy crying the loudest.

Lois, holding herself together, turned to Larry and said "You're lucky I had training as a nurse. Baby, I'm going to nurse you tonight."

Larry drove into Gordon's yard with no small amount of trepidation. Both Gordon's car and bike were home, though the bike was lying on its side at a crazy angle in the driveway. Gordon came out of the door and walked slowly toward Larry looking hard at the small bandage on his face and larger dressings on the side of his neck.

Larry held out the papers Gordon had given him for the Harley.

"I'll be heading back to school after I stop to have Lois change my bandages. You said you wanted these back."

"No, you keep them. I can't tell you how sick I am about what happened. I was drunker than I realized, but that's no excuse. Had a nightmare that I'd hit you directly with the tree branch and your whole head exploded. How bad is your cut?" Gordon was crying.

"Not too bad. My nurse did a great job. Quite a scene at her house when we got there. We tried to sneak in through the back door, but her parents were home. Have you heard about television?"

"Yaw, there was a lot of talk about it especially after I got to Fort Chaffee after basic. Going to put radio out of business," Gordon answered.

"So Lois' dad was watching this set with a screen so small I would have a hard time seeing it and it was cloudy. Guess he was trying to watch a wrestling match. Anyway, he was a little distracted, but her mom wasn't. It was beautiful how Lois double-talked her way through why their daughter was coming home wearing only her bra and leading in her blood-covered boyfriend with her sweater wrapped around his neck. I don't remember what all she said, but it was about having this little going away party for you and then she and I decided to get away from the crowd. We went walking in the woods and I saw what I thought was a bear and ran to get a better look. While I was running I tripped over a dead log and a protruding branch cut me."

"Didn't either one of them blame you for getting their daughter drunk?" Gordon interjected. "She was drinking as much as we were."

"No, her dad kept watching the little box and her mom, after getting her daughter a blouse, helped her wash me off at the kitchen sink. A couple of times she wrinkled her nose, like she was smelling something, so I'm sure she knew. Didn't say anything, but they are really liberal. Already have 'Adlai for President' buttons. Signed picture of Hubert Humphrey on the wall. I think they wouldn't mind having me for a son-in-law."

"So why not? Lois has it all: good looking, outgoing, fun, not afraid to be herself." Gordon walked over and set his Harley back up. "Was drunk and disgusted when I got home last night. Just let the damn thing fall."

"Well, I told Lois about my dream of being a reporter for The New York Times and making it in the Big Apple. She wants to become a nurse and have a family of four or five kids in a town like Aitkin or Mora." Larry looked over the bike one more time. "We agreed to go our separate ways and continue to be friends. It's hard sometimes."

Gordon walked around the Harley and put his hand on Larry's shoulder. "O.K., let's talk about what we been avoiding since January. I will just say this for now. Bob may have gotten better grades than you, but you were clearly the smartest person in our class. When you figure out something you're usually 100% right, well maybe 99%." Gordon laughed. Then with a somber look Gordon said, "And that's true for what you figured out about what happened on the lake. Given that we have been friends since first grade and despite the fact I almost killed you I want you to do one more favor for me. I'm going to think hard during my ship ride to Korea on the best way for me to come clean. We were told one of the things we will get in the combat zone is access to chaplains. I hope to find one I can use for advice. So give me until you hear that Eddie's trial is about to start and if I haven't done anything, feel free to tell the sheriff everything you know including this conversation."

Larry was at a loss for words. He turned to walk to his car and everything that had been a distant remote possibility was now a flashing light of reality. The abstract was now a real burning ball of truth. What should he do? He remembered Eddie laughing and having fun the night they had played pool. He then looked at Gordon standing like a statue, waiting for an answer.

He turned to face Gordon, "I'll watch the schedule of court cases and as soon as I see that it's scheduled, I'll write to you. If I don't hear anything from you, I will go to the sheriff a week before the scheduled date." At least he had made a decision.

Larry felt he should give Gordon one last hug, or a shoulder bump, or at least a manly handshake, but he could not find the empathy to do anything. He backed his car around, waved at Gordon and as he drove out the driveway, he watched Gordon in his rearview mirror. Then it hit him. This might be the last time he would see him.

Chapter 22
October 1951

The Presidio was a beehive of activity. As Gordon rode on the bus from the front gate to the barracks for his predeparture three-day briefing, he saw several servicemen hugging and embracing wives or girlfriends, mothers and fathers or other family members. The corporal driving the bus said, "Those are returning soldiers. They have finished their tour of duty."

Gordon's mood darkened. Even if he survived the war, he faced a bleak future. Perhaps, with a good attorney, he could plead to a lesser count than first degree murder. He would work on a confession stating his rage as the cause and the giving reason for the rage, but for now he had a war to survive.

The first briefing was from an English-speaking South Korean major who talked about Korean culture, the history of the Korean Peninsula and how the peninsula was split after World War II. He expressed the appreciation of the South Korean people for the troops and their effort to maintain a democracy in their nation.

Then a U. S. army captain gave an extended lecture on the concept of the limited warfare being deployed while the peace talks were on-going. In addition, he talked about American troops being part of a United Nations force wherein the United States was joining with its allies in a collective effort for world security. He stressed the importance of all soldiers knowing the goal was not to obtain the unconditional surrender of the enemy in Korea. Rather, the goal was to stop the aggression of the enemy in a manner that would not escalate the conflict into a greater war. The understanding of this new kind of war was essential for maintaining morale. The captain also explained the rotation system now in place. Each soldier earned credit for duty in the active war zone or lesser credit for duty outside the active war zone. The number of credits determined the length of time before a soldier earned R & R time in Japan and also when the soldier would be rotated back home. Most soldiers were now earning this final rotation in less than a year.

The group Gordon was assigned to was taking the place of members of the Second Infantry Division of the Eighth Army. The captain stated, "This division is currently on bivouac near Kap'yong." He pointed to a map showing the positions of the United Nations forces and the enemy forces. "All soldiers will receive orders placing you in specific platoons as replacements for troops who have completed their rotation requirements and are coming home. During the remainder of the bivouac, you will receive additional small-unit tactics. Then the whole division will move up to this area on the map known as the Iron Triangle. Your sole mission will be to hold the current line until the final peace treaty is completed. Since the battle plan is to be completely defensive the goal is to minimize the number of casualties. The only military action that should take place would be small unit efforts to improve our position along the current line to obtain tactical advantages in holding the line. There will not be any attempt to push the enemy further north."

As Gordon was leaving the session, he heard a voice he immediately recognized calling his name. Woodrow Willis grabbed his hand.

"Yo, man. It's grand to see a 'whitey' I know. When I was sitting in the session I looked around and all I saw were white faces. Didn't know if I would find one I could trust. You know when we finished our basic training, I was assigned to an all-black company at Fort Hood. The plan was that the whole company would be shipped to Korea and fight intact. Then just before we were to disembark a new order came down, the army is now integrated. The whole company is now assigned individually to otherwise all white units. The big boys in Washington think we will fight harder. Do you know what company you will be in?" Woodrow checked his orders to verify his assignment.

"I'm in C Company, 2nd Platoon, 8th Battalion," Gordon said.

A huge wide smile formed on Woodrow's face. "Wow! If I had any friends here I would sit right down and start rolling dice. What kind of luck! I end up with the one whitey I know."

"Same platoon and company?" Gordon asked.

"Same platoon and company, man." Woodrow clasped Gordon's hand.

The voyage to Korea included a two-day layover in Honolulu. It took three days to make this leg of the journey. Gordon did not fare well as a first-time sailor. The first 60 hours he spent in his bunk or near the ship's rail so he could minimize the mess he made throwing up. His only solace was that he was not alone. When the ship's captain announced that the ship was docked in Honolulu the roar from the ship was loud enough to be heard in the downtown center of the city. A second roar rocked the ship when it was announced that all soldiers would be granted an 18-hour pass upon reporting to the ship's gangplank in proper uniform and carrying the proper papers.

Gordon, having spent the first night at sea barfing over the rail, turned and bumped into a soldier with "Olson" on his name tag.

"Must be from Minnesota with a name like that," Gordon said.

"You bet'cha, from Bird Island. Johnny is the first name. I think we are in the same sleeping quarters. Excuse me a minute," John Olson said as he barfed up his mess over the rail.

As Gordon was getting ready to go ashore, Johnny came up to him and said, "Us Minnesota boys better stick together when we go into the big city, don't you think?"

"Sounds like a plan to me," Gordon answered. "In our training they always stressed the buddy system. It's also nice to have someone who can carry his weight." Gordon joked as he looked at Johnny's six-foot six-inch frame and a body that must have been at least 255 pounds of pure muscle.

"Did you grow up working on a farm?" Gordon asked, shining his shoes.

"No, I lived in town, but I did work at the local grain elevator. Moved a lot of 100-pound sacks of grain." Johnny flexed his muscles.

After the two Minnesotans passed their inspection and were walking down the gang plank with their 18-hour passes, Woodrow yelled from the ship's rail, "Yo, whitey wait up for me."

"I've been watching for you at mess. Must feed the different sections of the ship at different times. How's your stomach liking the sea ride?" Woodrow asked when he caught up with Gordon.

"Well, the way I'll put it is that none of my food has got to my asshole yet," Gordon responded. "How about you?"

"When I was still in high school my daddy got me a summer job on a shrimp boat to help with the family finances. Rode out several storms. Got used to riding the waves," Woodrow said, sizing Johnny up.

"Oh, this is my bunkmate from basic training, Woodrow Willis. We called him Willy for short," Gordon said. "Willy, this is Johnny Olson, another whitey from Minnesota."

Willy smiled a big smile and stuck out his hand, "Are all you boys from Minnesota white? Do you have any of my bros up there? Probably too cold."

"None where I'm from. A few in the cities. Guess you are the first colored person I have met." Johnny shook Willy's hand.

"You must have played for—what's your team called, the Gophers?" Willy looked up at Johnny. "Are you in our company?"

"Naw, played a little high school ball, but that's all. I'm in C Company, 8th Battalion," Johnny quickly answered.

"You are?" Gordon said. "What platoon?"

"Second," Johnny said.

"What kind of odds is that? All three of us are in this together." Gordon threw his arms around both Willy's and Johnny's shoulders.

The three soldiers-in-arms caught a bus down to Pearl Harbor and spent a few hours sight-seeing until Gordon said, "It's time for some beer."

Willy hesitated as Gordon started for the door to the bar.

"What? Don't you drink?" Gordon questioned Willy.

"It's not that. I'm not sure I'll get served." Willy looked for a sign on the bar's window but didn't find one.

The bar was three-quarters full of soldiers and sailors along with a fair number of women working their trade. Gordon went up to a bartender to order.

"What's the best beer you got in this joint?" Gordon asked.

"A lot of good beer, but I can only sell you two. Your buddy there will have to wait outside." The bartender nodded toward Willy.

Gordon's face reddened and his body shifted so he was standing straight up. He stared at the bartender eye-to-eye. "What the hell! He's on his way to Korea to put his life on the line for you and everyone in here and he can't buy a beer?"

"Say buddy, I would advise all three of you to get your asses out of here before there is any trouble." The bartender reached under the bar and pulled out a nightstick, placing it on the bar.

The bar was suddenly silent and Gordon looked around. He judged that several of the customers were ready to come after them.

"Come on Gordon. We're leaving," Willy yelled back as he and Johnny headed to the door.

Gordon followed them but turned as he got to the door and yelled, "You're all assholes."

Upon leaving the bar Willy said, "Why don't I find a park bench and just cool my heels and play my harmonica for a while? You two can go have a few beers."

"No way, José. We find some place that will serve all three of us or, if they refuse, none of us," Gordon said while looking at his watch. "It's only noon, we have fifteen more hours to find a little fun."

"I love movies," Johnny said. "Maybe we can find a movie theater with a matinee showing?"

The theater they found was showing *A Streetcar Named Desire*. Upon leaving the theater they walked down the street, talking about the hot love scene between Marlon Brando and Kim Hunter.

"Makes you want to find a woman right now," Willy said as the trio passed a sign for the local USO. "Free entertainment, dancing, soda pop, and snacks. Cash bar. All military personnel welcome."

After having lunch at a sidewalk café, the trio got to the USO just after 4 p.m. Gordon finally got the beer he had been thirsting for all day. Willy was all excited since, in the crowd of about 100 soldiers, 20 or so were black.

Willy got another surprise. At 5 o'clock Lionel Hampton and his band took the stage as the featured entertainment for the night.

"Man, he's from my home state, Alabama. He's one of my role models. I'll need to do a little face-to-face with him on his break." Willy was excited.

The face-to-face got Willy an invite to sit in with the band and blow some blues on his harmonica. Mr. Hampton also gave him his card and promised to talk to him after Willy returned from Korea.

"Us getting kicked out of the bar this morning by the whities may be the best break of my life." Willy blew a few more notes on his harmonica.

After the final set by Lionel Hampton, a dance band took the stage and several dozen women came in to be dance partners for the soldiers and sailors.

Willy spent a lot of time on the dance floor, Gordon danced a few, but Johnny stayed at the table.

"Say Ole, you need to get out there and jive with some of these good-looking women. May be your last chance to see one unless you get shot up and have to be patched up by a nurse," Willy chided Johnny.

"Never really danced much." Johnny continued to nurse his third beer of the night.

When the next song, a slow waltz, started, Willy found a new dance partner. She was the tallest and heaviest woman of the group. After Willy talked to her briefly, he led her over to the table. She extended her hand to Johnny and, not knowing what else to do, he followed her out onto the dance floor. The couple danced three dances in a row, until the band broke out into a rumba.

Upon returning to their table, Johnny, a big grin on his face, said "Thank you."

His dance partner gave him a kiss on the cheek and said, "Thank you. You did well. It was fun."

Gordon, who was not feeling any pain now, walked over to Johnny and slapped him on his back, "Wow, you looked just like Arthur Murray out on the floor. Who said you can't dance?"

"Never have. Just followed my partner's lead," Johnny was responding when Willy returned to the table.

"Let's blow this pop stand." Willy was shaking and jiving. "Just talking to one of Hampton's band members and he told me that there's a bar about six blocks down toward the harbor where there will be a jazz jam session. He said it will be a mixed crowd so even you whities can come."

It was 9:15 when the trio found the Blue Note Café. It was swinging.

"Remember," Gordon said, "we have to be back to the ship by three."

"You be the time-keeper, man. I understand that there will be some real cool cats blowing and playing here. See if I can keep up with my 'piece' here." Willy held up his harmonica.

Willy kept up. He was the coolest cat on the band stand. Gordon was his main cheerleader. Standing up at their table right in front,

Gordon was yelling. "That's my man. Play the blues. Make that harmonica sing."

As Willy played, drinks started coming to the table. Willy was busy playing. Gordon was getting full, so Johnny began drinking the surplus. For the first time in his life he drank more than three beers.

As he got more drunk, he turned to Gordon. "Hey buddy, you know what I want to do? I want to get laid before I go to Korea and get killed. Dancing with that chick made me horny."

Gordon turned to him, "You're not a virgin, are you?"

"Well, yes, I was always too scared to ask any girl out. I always felt they thought I was just a big dumb jock," Johnny confessed.

"I bet there were a lot of girls in your school that were hoping for a chance to go out with the school's biggest jock. Probably talked in the girls' locker room about how well hung you were."

As Gordon finished talking, Willy took a break.

"Great job, Mr. Cool. Now that you proved that you're as good as anyone here, we have another little job to do before we go back abroad the ship. We have to get Johnny laid. We need to find a whore house." Gordon smiled at Johnny.

●●●●●●●●●●

The madam who unlocked the door of The House of the Setting Sun, was a 5-foot-9 brunette, wearing a bikini bottom and a large lei around her neck which semi-covered her firm D-cup breasts.

Gordon went right up to her and flashed a roll containing all the cash the trio had left, which totaled $119. "Say, madam, if that's your correct title, we're here to appeal to your patriotic spirit. Our friend here is on his way to Korea and he has never enjoyed the pleasure of being with a woman. This is the total amount of money the three of us have and we only have an hour and a half before we have to be aboard our troop ship. Do you have a girl available?"

The madam looked at Johnny and smiled. "You from the Midwest?"

"I'm from Bird Island, Minnesota, and proud of it," Johnny boldly announced. He was still high from the booze.

"I'll be happy to entertain a soldier from my home state. I grew up in north Minneapolis. My nickname is Goldie, like the gopher," the madam laughed.

"I assume you boys are going to wait here. Help yourself to our Hawaiian blend coffee. If you look on the shelf under the coffee pot, you'll find some cream." Goldie took Johnny by the hand and led him into a back room.

Gordon and Willy, who were starting to feel exhausted from the excitement and heavy drinking of the day, sprawled out on the two big easy chairs in the waiting area.

"I'm ready to hit the rock they gave us for a pillow on the ship," Gordon said. "Maybe Goldie will pleasure Johnny quick. He will be plenty excited."

"I'm with you there, whitey. Think I'll give all the lovers a little romantic music." Willy began to blow some more blues.

Johnny did not make a quick exit. While Gordon was keeping awake only because of Willy's music, two johns left and the girls asked if the two of them were waiting for sex. Gordon replied, "No, we're broke. Gave all our money to our friend so he could screw Goldie."

The two girls looked at each other in disbelief.

After 45 minutes Gordon got up. "May as well try the coffee." After pouring a cup he looked under the coffee pot and pulled a pint of Jack Daniel's out from the shelf.

"I found the cream," Gordon shouted at Willy.

"I'll just have a shot of the cream." Willy got up and walked over to Gordon.

"It's almost two," Gordon looked at his watch. "Think we should check on them. We have to be back in an hour."

"Can't do that. We'll walk in just when the big bang is happening." Willy took a healthy swig of cream.

Gordon sat back down with his cup of half coffee and half cream.

Fifteen minutes later Johnny walked out with a smile as wide as his whole face, wearing Goldie's lei around his neck. Goldie was hanging tight against him wearing only a towel in place of her bikini bottom.

"I want to thank you boys for the gift you gave Johnny. It was really a gift to me. I told Johnny if he comes through Honolulu on his way home to stop in for a night on the house. If you boys are with him, you're welcome too. That music you were playing out here, Willy, . . . is the name, right? . . . really added to the mood. Think I'll get some good blues records and play them for my customers. Felt like I was twenty years old again. I remember the first time I made love some jazz was playing." Goldie turned and gave Johnny one more, long deep kiss.

"I just can't tell you two how great that was. Night I will never forget, if I make it to a hundred. Got to figure out a way to really thank you two." Johnny spoke as the trio ran down the dark streets toward the harbor and the ship.

"You can thank us by describing every move Goldie made some night when we are in our bunks so we can share the ecstasy. Now we got to move our asses so we are not late or we will get busted a grade," Willy said on the run.

The trio made the gate leading to the secured area in front of the gang plank at 2:53 hours.

"Show your papers to the guard post. You will be stamped in and then you can go into the secured area and up into the ship at your leisure." The announcement played over and over on the loudspeaker.

Gordon and Willy went through the line first and were stamped in. Then they heard Johnny yelling behind them, "I don't have my papers! I don't have my papers! I left them by Goldie's bed."

"M.P.'s! Take this soldier and put him in the holding pen with the rest of the soldiers who don't have enough discipline to keep track of their papers," the guard post commander yelled out orders to the several M.P.'s on duty at the gate.

Gordon and Willy turned to see Johnny being taken by two M.P.'s to a fenced off area where about a dozen other soldiers were being held.

Chapter 23
November 1951

The troop ship docked at Pusan on November 5, 1951. Johnny, who was back to being a private after being busted one rank and losing three months of time before he could start earning credits toward his rotation time because of losing his papers, said to Gordon, "We are in a war zone. All the make-believe shit is over."

"That's right, buddy," Gordon said. "From now on if someone is shooting at you, he is shooting real bullets."

The first two days in Pusan were spent waiting in lines; a long line to get clearance to enter the secured area housing the troops until they were to be transported to the combat area, another long line to be issued their weapons, military clothing, c-rations, sleeping bags, blankets, pup tents and other supplies, and another long line to have their orders reviewed and be assigned to the correct platoon. Finally, there was a long line to board the train to the correct destination.

It was not until this last line that Willy was able to join up with Gordon and Johnny.

"Man, with all these troops we should be able to end this war as quick as it takes a bull to find a cow in heat." Willy raised his bent arm and muscled up with Gordon and then with Johnny.

"You must have slept through that session back in Frisco where the brass told us this is not a war, but just a police action. He also told us that for each of us there will be three North Koreans and seven Chinese soldiers," Gordon jived Willy.

A loudspeaker blasted out warnings to the troops that during the fifteen-hour ride to the combat area they were to be in full combat gear and in possession of their weapons. Although the area the train was passing through was controlled by the South Korean Army, North Korean soldiers who had been left behind when their forces were pushed back north had taken on civilian identities and were operating as guerillas, mainly attacking troop trains.

"Great," Willy said, "we haven't been here long enough to even say hello to our platoon commander and we may become moving targets."

After leaving Pusan, the train traveled through hilly and wooded terrain. Just after 14:00 hours clouds moved over the train and the rain started. Half an hour later the shooting began. Several bursts of gunfire from a Russian AR 47 automatic rifle hit the train. The troops all quickly hit the floor wherever they could find any space. Willy sprawled in the center aisle, Johnny slumped down between the seats, and Gordon crouched down next to the train wall. Willy, looking back down the aisle, could see three young soldiers who had been hit. Gordon looked out and got a clear view of a young Korean man running, in the rain, along the top of a long hill which the train was passing. Gordon raised his rifle, took aim and fired several rounds. The shooter fell and rolled down the hill toward the train. Apparently, he was a lone gunman, as the shooting stopped.

The train came to a stop half a mile down the track besides a clear flat meadow. As soon as the train stopped three U.S. Army helicopters landed. From the largest copter, a squad of marines quickly descended and formed a defensive perimeter around the clearing. From the other two copters three teams of medics rushed to the train, followed by several army officers.

The three hit soldiers were the only casualties. Two of the three were wounded, but the third had been hit in the head and died instantly. Willy went down to look as the medics were working. He recognized the dead soldier.

He returned to where Gordon and Johnny were standing outside the train, clearly in shock, looking as ghostly white as a black man could. "It's not fair, just not fair. Aaron was a fellow Alabamian, from Huntsville. He was in my part of the ship on the way over. Came right up to me, even though he was with some other southern white boys and shook my hand. Said he was glad the Army had decided to integrate. Time for the races to learn to live together, especially in our home state. He wanted to go to Auburn and become a lawyer but had to work for a year to earn some money. Then got drafted. Now he's dead." Willy took out his trusty harmonica and blew a few sad notes.

"Some shooting," Johnny said, grabbing hold of Gordon's arm. He also felt weak from the emotional excitement of being attacked. "So now you have killed another person."

"Yes, I have killed another man." Gordon stood with a somber look, staring off in the distance, staring like he could see Mille Lacs Lake.

"Who's the sharpshooter who killed that gook?" a major bellowed as he approached the trio.

The three of them, taken by surprise, jumped to attention and started to salute.

"At ease," the major barked.

Willy pointed to Gordon.

"So, it's Private first-class Haas," the major said.

"Right sir," Gordon replied.

"Wrong, soldier. It's Corporal Haas now." The Major reached out and ripped the Private first-class patch off Gordon's fatigue. "The paper work and new uniform will be waiting for you when you report to your unit. Good to have another soldier here who can respond in a crisis."

The trio reported to the platoon HQ tent together at 15:22. The company's First Sergeant, Earl Hawes; the Platoon Sergeant, Bill Evans; and the Platoon commanding Officer, First Lieutenant Howard Smith, were waiting for them.

"Welcome to our humble surroundings. Given it will be your home for a while make yourselves comfortable the best you can. We will be on bivouac for another three weeks before we will be moving up to the front." Lt. Smith did the talking for the group. "The whole company is out on some maneuvers now but will be back at 20:00 hours for mess. After we are done here with the paper work Sergeant Evans will take you to your tent and you can get settled in and then join your squad for mess."

"Now for some personal comments," the lieutenant continued as he talked directly to Gordon. "Here are your new fatigue tops with your new rank. Not too often we have a field promotion on the train ride from Pusan. Great job of being alert and reacting. All three of you will be assigned to squad three. The corporal for that squad will be rotating home next Monday so having a new corporal in our platoon works out well."

"Private Willis, I'm proud to have you in our platoon. I know my men and don't foresee any trouble. If there is some you come directly to me."

"Private Olson, saw about your little problem in Honolulu. Work hard and I'll see if I can't get the rank back and you can start earning rotation points."

"Any questions for me?" the lieutenant concluded.

"Just one," Gordon said. "Who is the company chaplain? Do I need an appointment to see him?"

"Chaplain Delaney is around the area practically all the time. Good man. When you see him, you can ask him when he has time to meet you in private. Do you need some counseling about killing another human?" the lieutenant asked.

"Yes, I do," Gordon responded.

The trio had mess with their squad. Second Lieutenant Mike Rogers, the squad leader and Squad Sergeant Stanley Harp both embraced Willy as a show of unity and introduced Gordon as the new squad corporal. After mess, the platoon's makeshift beer tent was opened and the trio had the opportunity to mix with the whole platoon.

During the remainder of the bivouac the troops worked on small unit attack drills using coordinated artillery, mortar and air support. There was very little down time except for Sundays, the day Chaplain Delaney was busy conducting services, so Gordon did not have any extended conversation with him.

"I tell you now, my son, that when we go back on the battle line, you're going to find that you will have a lot of idle time. We will be waiting around for orders, or for something to happen at the peace talks, or for the enemy to try to take back some hill we have taken from them. So, we will have time to talk and I will be looking forward to our conversations." Chaplain Delaney was very comforting when he spoke.

The whole division moved the thirty miles from the bivouac area back to the area along the front known as the Iron Triangle. The area, which was being temporarily held by a French division, was a wedge-shape indentation in the enemy's line, allowing the United Nations forces to control both a major highway and river, thereby they prevented the enemy from moving troops and supplies across that section of the peninsula and required this movement be made 40 miles further north.

The problem with this placement was that the enemy controlled the hills on both sides of the triangle. It was from these hills that a periodic artillery barrage would be launched. To prepare for these barrages the troops had to work on digging foxholes, reinforcing existing bunkers, and drilling on quickly getting dressed in full battle gear to move to assigned positions while surviving the barrage. This kept the trio busy, but little else was happening except for this activity.

"If this is all there is to war this year won't be so bad," Willy said to Gordon as the two sat and cleaned their rifles.

Sergeant Harp overheard Willy's comment as he was walking past. He quickly stopped, turned to Willy and said, "Soldier, don't be fooled by this lull. Both sides agreed to a 30-day cease-fire period. The gooks always use these periods to reinforce their position. As soon as the 30 days are over, I expect all hell to break loose."

Two days later at 04:00 hours the air raid sirens awoke all units and the loudspeakers blared, "Incoming artillery, assume defensive positions."

Willy, who slept soundly, hardly moved until Gordon kicked over his cot. "Wake up man. This is the real war," Gordon shouted.

Johnny was already fully dressed. Willy moving quickly, got dressed, grabbed his harmonica and slipped it in his pants pocket. "If I die man, I want my piece with me."

Gordon, carrying out his duties as the squad corporal, directed everyone to their assigned locations and then assumed his position in a bunker to record the incoming volleys. The barrage lasted for over three hours. After it was over Gordon assisted in the damage assessment. Due to the main barrage being directed at an area south of where his squad was quartered and the North Koreans also not being very accurate at firing artillery, there weren't any casualties, injuries, or significant damage.

Over the next month the division maintained its position with no attempt to expand the area it controlled. Other than surviving occasional artillery barrage, the squad had little to do. This allowed Gordon to start his dialogue with Chaplain Delaney.

"Your first name is Gordon, isn't it, Corporal? Can I use it so we are more informal? My name is Robert. You can call me Bob if you like," the chaplain started the session. "I understand you shot an enemy soldier the first day you were in Korea. Is that what you want to talk about in these sessions?"

"Well, first of all, I would like to make sure what I tell you will be completely confidential. Isn't there something about what a person tells a clergy being privileged?" Gordon didn't know if it really mattered, but he knew he would be more honest if it was true.

"That's right. What that means is that I cannot be forced to disclose what you tell me to the police or courts. The only exception is if you tell me about a crime you are going to commit in the future, I am required to report that to the proper authorities," Bob answered Gordon.

"Good, however I'm not here to talk about the soldier I shot from the train. I'm here to talk about the first man I killed. I murdered a man back in Minnesota."

Chaplin Delaney, who had served with Patton's Army in World War II all the way from North Africa up to Germany, had heard many confessions, but never a confession to murder. He immediately put his hand on Gordon's shoulder and said, "Before we go further, let's pray."

Heavenly Father, on behalf of your servant, Gordon, I ask you to hear his confession and to forgive the sins he is confessing. Although mortal man may view the sin of murder as a greater sin and require greater punishment for such sin, you, as proclaimed by your son Jesus, don't judge one sin greater than another. With great obedience, I pray that Gordon be granted the same forgiveness that you granted to the sinner Saul that transformed him into your servant Paul. Amen.

So, Gordon, feeling like a 500-hundred-pound weight had been lifted from his shoulders, started telling his story. Over several sessions he told Chaplain Delaney about how, after his dad was reported to have accidentally been washed overboard from the ore carrier, he grieved alone, since, for a reason he would later understand, his mother did not share in the grieving.

"I was always the closest son to my dad. I was the one who helped him cut firewood. I would hunt with him and listen to his stories about how hard it was growing up during the Depression. My older brother was always doing his own thing with his friends and my other brother was too young."

Gordon continued talking about how he started to hear rumors that his dad had jumped ship in Detroit to abandon his family just when he was getting over the grieving process.

"It was like being stabbed twice. I was sure my dad would not do that to the family, especially me. Yet I knew my dad's plan to divorce my mom. A lingering doubt crept into my head. Did he not have the nerve to go through with the divorce and had taken the cowardly way out? As soon as I got my driver's license, I drove the 100 miles down to a suburb of Minneapolis and found the house of my dad's lover. I had been there one time with my dad delivering firewood. I watched the house for two days and saw that the woman my dad was in love with was still living with her husband. I knew that my dad had not abandoned me and must have been washed overboard. Last October, Molly, his lover, came up to my home town to visit my uncle. She stopped me on the road and asked me if I had firewood for sale, if so, she wanted to arrange for a load to be delivered. She also asked, if possible, that I would come with the person making the delivery. I made arrangements for my friend Melvin and I to deliver a load of wood I had cut. We made the delivery on a weekend date when her husband, who was a pilot, was flying. After we had unloaded the wood Molly fed us supper along with some beer. After we ate, she asked Melvin if he could wait in the truck while she talked to me in private. She broke down and started crying as soon as Melvin walked out the door. She told me how deeply she loved my dad. Then she told me the whole story about her brother-in-law being a shipmate of my dad and how she was certain he and her husband had murdered my dad. She said she had a lawyer investigating the case to try to prove her husband was guilty."

As Gordon was telling about his meeting with Molly, Chaplin Delaney stopped him and said, "I probably should interject at this point that if you implicate any other person in a crime, the privilege you are afforded may not apply to the other person. I can't be required to disclose what you told me, but if I am asked if I know if someone else committed a crime I would have to answer truthfully."

"I have nothing incriminating to say about Molly. I know my dad loved her and she loved him. I know how hard it was growing up in a home where there wasn't love between my parents, two people living together out of necessity. I did see Molly about five weeks before I killed her husband, but all she did was tell me about him spending a lot of his free time in the winter ice fishing at the resort where I killed him."

Gordon's voice broke as he twice mentioned killing Ray. For the first time in his meeting with Chaplin Delaney he looked away from him as he was talking.

The chaplain sensed Gordon was stressed out and put his hand on Gordon. "I believe we have talked enough for today. You can tell me more at our next session." As Gordon left, the chaplain intuitively knew that for the first time in their talks Gordon was not fully truthful.

At their final formal session Gordon talked about the actual details of the murder. "After the start of the ice fishing season, which in Minnesota is December 1, I started looking for Ray's fish house. On my second trip out on the ice looking, I found the house with Ray's name on it. It was a Sunday afternoon in mid-December and I almost stopped to confront Ray. I took one drive by the house and I saw Ray Jr., his son, standing outside. Since Junior knew me from the times I had delivered wood, I didn't stop."

"As I drove off the lake I realized that Ray would just deny being involved in my dad's death unless I could scare him into confessing. Also, I realized that I shouldn't just drive and park in front of his fish house in case something went wrong. That's when I made my plan. I found what appeared to be just a private, summer house, where the driveway and a road out onto the lake were plowed. Then, the night of the murder, I drove onto the lake and parked a half mile away from Ray's fish house. I put on a full ski face mask, my heaviest parka, and some winter gloves. I got a switchblade out of my glove compartment and put it in my parka pocket. It was the weapon I planned to use to scare him. As I walked the half mile I kept getting hotter and hotter even though it was 22 below zero. All I could think about were recollections of the good times I had had with my dad, of working with him cutting wood, of hunting together, of him telling me about falling in love with Molly and his plan of getting divorced and marrying her. He promised me that he would get the court to allow me to live with him and Molly. The closer I got the angrier I got."

"Perhaps you want to take a break?" the chaplain said. "I can see you are reliving that half mile walk. Is your rage building again?"

"I have relived that whole night often—sleepless nights, nightmares, heavy drinking bouts, alienation from my two best friends. Let me finish the final moments of that night. Maybe then I can find a small amount of peace," Gordon answered.

"When I got to the fish house the door was unlocked. I barged in with my knife out and open. Ray had his back to me clearing his fish hole with his ice pick. He turned, and although he was wobbly, without saying a word, he threw his ice pick at me. It was wide of me and I easily caught the pick as I dropped my knife. His act of trying to hit me with the pick released a floodgate of hate. I moved across the fish house in one quick lunge with the ice pick held as far back behind my head as possible. Then I swung the pick forward with all my strength and buried it into the side of Ray's head halfway between his forehead and his upper earlobe. Ray did not make a sound, but from somewhere in my body a primeval warrior's chant erupted. That chant sounded so loud to me, I was sure it would be heard across the whole lake. Then I stood, stunned. The enormity of my act hit me with its full weight. I turned to leave the fish house and saw my knife. In a state of shock and without any forethought I pulled off my glove, picked up my knife and opened the door. I looked for anyone nearby. Tuning my flashlight off and on, I got to my car as quickly as possible and left the lake." Gordon, upon finishing this confession, fell to the floor and cried in anguish, "God forgive me. God forgive me."

It was two days before Christmas when Gordon finished his final session with Chaplin Delaney. On Christmas Day, the colonel commanding the division ordered that all platoons have a full Christmas menu mess. Second Lt. Rogers, wearing a Santa stocking cap, helped the cooks dish up the turkey and mashed potatoes while singing "I'll Be Home for Christmas." Upon being asked about the song, the lieutenant smiled and said, "I won't be home for Christmas, but I will be home for Valentine's Day. Rotate out in 30 days."

As Gordon's squad was just finishing its meal, the first sirens sounded and the loudspeakers again blared, "Incoming artillery, assume defensive positions."

Boom! The first round hit 400 yards behind the mess tent. Second Lt. Rogers yelled, "Move quickly, men. Looks like the commies are getting a little more accurate."

Gordon responded quickly and yelled out orders to his squad members as to which shelter they were assigned. As everyone was taking cover a second incoming round landed 200 yards in front of the squad. A soldier from another squad was hit with flying debris and went down. Second Lt. Rogers instantly rushed out and picked up the downed soldier in a shoulder carry to get him to the bunker, yelling on the way, "Sergeant, get a medic over here."

Kaboom, kaboom, boom, boom! The bombardment lasted for 45 minutes. Nothing incoming hit the defensive positions directly, but the rounds were more accurate than the prior attacks. The squad area was littered with spent shells and the resulting debris.

Soon after the bombardment started, the division's artillery, which had been moved into place since the last attack, started firing. From their holes in the ground the squad members could see plumes of smoke and occasional balls of flames rising from behind the hills being held by the enemy.

"Looks like we're hitting back. I believe our boys are a little bit better shooter," the second lieutenant. yelled.

The whole platoon cheered.

The next day the orders came down from the division command.

> *Those bastards raining artillery on our Christmas dinner need to be taught a lesson. Although we are in a defensive holding pattern we are not going to sit and be targets while their artillery units become better shooters. Prepare all units for offensive actions to move the enemy off hill 836, hill 839 and hill 841. The objective still remains to minimize casualties while achieving this outcome. All officers are to report to division HQ at 13:00 hours today, December 26, 1951, to receive and review the overall battle plan.*
>
> *Colonel HP Farris*
> *Commander Second Infantry Division*

Chapter 24
Winter 1952

The first action assigned to Second Lt. Rogers' squad was to serve as an advance scouting unit to pinpoint the enemy's position on Hill 839. The platoon moved out at 5:00 hours to avoid being detected before they had the cover of the tree line at the bottom of the steep rocky hill. The plan was to find a pathway up to the middle of the hill, which was more of a small mountain rising over 800 feet, with a 30-degree rise. From that location the squad would dig in and send two man scouting parties further up the hill to identify the enemy's positions. The plan failed. A sentry posted near the bottom of the hill spotted the squad just after daylight and soon mortar rounds were falling near the squad. Rogers ordered a retreat and called into the company's command post for air cover to protect the squad. A mortar round then hit a squad member and Rogers moved quickly to his aid. As he tried to pick up the wounded soldier another mortar hit both of them directly. The squad froze for a moment realizing they had lost their commander and a fellow squad member.

Sgt. Harp yelled, "Double time down the hill. If we don't get the hell out of here, we're all dead."

As he was giving the order, three helicopter gunships flew over the squad's head firing at the enemy troops on the hilltop. The squad moved quickly back toward the safety of the base while still watching the air cover.

Suddenly, as the helicopters circled to make another pass at the enemy, a ball of flame lit up the hilltop. The middle helicopter was spinning around on fire. It crashed within 100 yards of Rogers and the other squad member's bodies.

An armored unit was dispatched to pick up the bodies of Rogers, the squad member, and the three helicopter crewmen. Two days later the replacements for Second Lt. Rogers and the deceased squad member joined the squad.

"I have read the report on how this platoon fucked up their first real fighting assignment," Second Lt. Masters, Rogers' replacement, addressed the troops of his first command in his strong southern voice. Masters, who had graduated from the Citadel prior to his officer training, continued, "Looking at the manner that some of you are dressed and around at this platoon's area I suspect that your last commanding officer may have been a little easy on enforcing military discipline." The area had not been policed since the Christmas day bombardment. "Well, that will now change. This unit will now dress, act and carry on in a military manner at all times. Is that understood?"

The troops mumbled, "Yes, sir."

"What did I hear? Did I hear an enthusiastic response? NO. I'll try it one more time. If I don't hear the response I want this whole unit will do a two-mile jog in full combat dress around this whole division. Now, is that understood?"

"Yes, sir," was yelled loud enough to satisfy Masters, although some of the troops, including Gordon, stood mute.

"Private Willis, where are you from?" Masters called out Willy.

"Muscle Shoals, Alabama, Sir," Willy answered.

"A southern boy, huh. Well, I want to make clear that just because you're allowed to serve with a real army unit, doesn't mean you won't have to carry your own weight. Is that clear, boy?"

Willy responded, "Yes, sir," with a clear look of contempt on his face.

"I hope that wasn't a look of disrespect on your face, because if it was you and I won't get along. That will not be good for you," Masters said. "Now I want this area policed up, right now, before we have mess. Troops dismissed."

Masters proceeded to work the squad hard with practice drills for artillery attacks and other basic training exercises. He also gave Willy various make-work jobs and, upon finding out Gordon and Johnny were close friends with Willy, he started to give them the same kinds of jobs.

"I see you were made a corporal just because you shot an enemy on your first day in Korea. Then I saw some notes that you had to spend a lot of hours with the chaplain to get over the trauma of killing a man. You better show me you have a right to that rank or I will bust you fast," Masters chided Gordon after summoning him for a one-on-one talk.

The morale of the platoon decreased daily. Sgt. Harp talked about going to the company commander with a formal complaint, but with twenty years of army experience he knew that a non-commissioned soldier had to be careful when filing a grievance against a superior officer. Often nothing was done. The superior officer would be informed and thereafter make life miserable for the complainer.

For two weeks the squad wasn't involved in any additional action. Besides Masters' busy work and excess drills, Gordon had little to do. He took this time to write the letter to Larry containing the detailed confession that he had made to the chaplain. Since he had not received any letter from Larry about the trial date for Eddie Johansson and knowing the letter would be inspected before it would be cleared for mailing, he delayed mailing it. However, he did give the letter to the chaplain with instructions for him to mail it if he was killed in battle.

Due to the casualties suffered during the first mission, a new battle plan was implemented by the battalion command. Instead of using the infantry division to reclaim the three hills, two marine platoons were flown in by helicopter after Air Force fighter planes had sprayed the enemy's position with machine gun and rocket fire for two straight days. In addition, armored and field artillery units moved around the hills to provide additional bombardment. Once a hill was secured by the marines, the infantry units were to then move on the hill and dig in to hold the hills. Each hill was small enough in size so that only one platoon could occupy the hill without causing it to be overcrowded with troops in each other's line of fire. Underlying the battle plan was a final directive. In the event the North Korean and Chinese forces attacked the hills with superior force, all units were to evacuate to minimize casualties.

On the seventeenth day after the failed scouting mission the platoon was ordered back in action, moving on to hill 839 which had been secured by the marines.

"We are moving up to occupy Hill 839. Squad three has been assigned to defend the north quarter section of the hill." Masters pointed to a map of the hill. "This squad should be ashamed that the marines had to be brought in to do our job. Now that the hill has been reclaimed let's make damn sure we hold on to it."

The platoon moved up to the top of the hill without incident. The first several days the troops were kept busy building defensive bunkers and removing the gun placements and artillery pads that had been left in place by the enemy making a quick retreat after the marines had landed.

On the second day of this duty Gordon and Johnny were working on digging out rocks to build another defensive bunker. They were building it near a ravine that could also be used for protection during an enemy shelling of the hill. As Johnny was lifting a large rock into place a young Chinese soldier, who apparently had been trapped in the ravine as the marines had taken control of the hill, leapt out of the ravine holding his rifle with its bayonet attached. As he ran toward Johnny, Gordon yelled. Johnny turned quickly and dropped the rock between him and the oncoming assailant, causing the Chinese soldier to trip. Gordon, who had taken his rifle off his shoulder, yelled at the Chinese boy, who had to be younger than he was. Knowing that the kid had to be out of ammunition, Gordon didn't shoot until the Chinese soldier charged at him. He then fired four times, moving back from the bayonet. As the dead soldier lay in front of him, Gordon wondered, "What is the purpose of this?"

After the digging-in process was completed, the troops had little to do except try to keep warm. The mid-January temperatures dropped below zero at night with the wind buffeting the hill increasing to 30 miles plus per hour at times.

"I suppose this is like summertime to you boys from Minnesota," Willy joked as he and Stephan, the private who had transferred in at the same time Masters had, joined Gordon and Johnny in Gordon's pup tent. Being crowded together in the tent generated a lot of body heat.

"Expected I might get shot while I was here but never thought I would freeze to death," Stephan, who was from Little Rock, Arkansas, added.

"If you don't bitch about it all the time, you won't be so cold. Cold is a state of mind," Gordon countered. "At home we used to ice skate bareheaded at 20 below."

"One good thing about the cold, it keeps Masters off our backs. I doubt he has left his pup tent with his propane heater for more than five minutes a day," Johnny said. "He told the sergeant he didn't know war would be so cold."

"I should go and join him next to the heater and tell him us southern boys need to stick together," Willy laughed.

During the down time Gordon wrote to his mom, Larry and Molly.

After spending 37 days on the hill the platoon received orders that they would be rotated off in 13 days. Two days later all hell broke loose. At 04:00 hours the artillery barrage started. The troops deployed to their defensive positions. Three hours later the mortar fire started. Overhead army helicopters and air force fighters attacked the advancing North Korean and Chinese troops.

At 10:00 hours an advance unit of the enemy attacked. After a three hour battle the attack was repelled. The platoon suffered three casualties, but none in squad three.

Just as Masters was marching around in a Napoleonesque manner, basking in what he deemed to be his first great victory as an officer, the order to evacuate the hill came down from the division commander. Intelligence reports showed that a very large enemy force was moving forward to retake the hill.

"All squad leaders report to the headquarters tent," First Sergeant Hawes announced over the loudspeaker.

"Sir, I believe my troops are ready to repel another attack no matter how large a force the enemy has," Masters said to Lt. Smith after he had relayed the order.

"Masters, this is not the Alamo," Smith quickly responded.

"But, sir, my men have really prepared—," Masters said before Smith cut him off.

After walking up to him and looking directly into his face Smith said, "Masters, I don't know what army you got your training in but in this man's army when a soldier gets an order from a superior officer he doesn't debate if it should be followed. Now get your ass out of this tent and have your squad ready to move by 15:00 hours."

Masters, smarting from the strong rebuke, took his time informing his squad and just told them to prepare to evacuate without stating the urgency.

At 15:00 hours the rest of the platoon was moving, but Lt. Smith, looking back through his field glasses, didn't see any real movement from squad three.

He called Masters on his walkie-talkie and said, "If, in five minutes, your squad isn't moving at double time to catch up with the rest of this platoon your career in the military will be in severe jeopardy. To put it more bluntly, I'll court-martial your ass."

Squad three did move quickly after that as most of the squad heard Smith's comment as it played on Masters' walkie-talkie. It was not fast enough. As they started their descent down the main trail off the hill the two squad members who were serving as rear sentinels failed to see the Chinese soldier. He had survived in a cave on the side of the hill for the entire time the platoon had occupied the hill. He not only had managed to store enough food and water to survive in his cave, but he also had stored hundreds of rounds of ammunition for his AK-47 Russian automatic rifle.

As the sentinels started their descent, the Chinese soldier moved with the rifle and as much ammunition as he could carry to a location on the cliff overlooking the trail. He arranged some of the rocks into a tripod for his rifle. Then he started shooting.

The two sentinels were killed. Sgt. Harp acted instinctively. He saw a 100-yard indentation in the side of the hill and yelled, "Squad sharp right."

The squad immediately saw the shelter they were being directed to and hustled up into the indentation as the gunner's bullets hit the trail they had been on.

"Sgt. Harp, I need to remind you I am in command of this squad and I give the orders," Masters said as he sat tight against the wall of the overhang protecting them.

"I'm just glad you are alive to worry about protocol," Sgt. Harp snapped back. "I should think you would be contacting division headquarters to see how they can get us out of this mess that we're in." He didn't add what he was thinking, "that you have got us in."

The squad was able to establish radio contact with the division HQ. The extent of their dire position was disclosed. The enemy's main force would be overrunning the hill within an hour. The wind gusts on the hill had picked up to over 50 miles per hour eliminating use of helicopters or paratroopers to dislodge the shooter. A plan to try to attack the shooter without a direct frontal attack in the face of the machine gun was being worked out. There were few options. The use of mortar or bombs would risk causing the overhang to cave in on the squad.

As Masters listened to the problems of resolving the squad's situation, he became distraught. "I don't want to die! I don't want to die!" he yelled.

Masters walked to the edge of the indentation causing a hail of bullets to land in front of where he was standing.

"Private Olson, you are the strongest soldier in the squad. Get a couple of hand grenades ready and I will throw some rocks out in front of us. While he is shooting at the rocks, jump out and lob them up at him," Masters ordered.

"Don't do it!" Gordon yelled.

Masters unbuckled the holster holding his 45mm pistol and said to Gordon, "Disobeying a commandeering officer's order in combat is treason and I can legally shoot you. I'm now ordering you to shut up."

"Olson, you heard my order."

Johnny, shaking as he got out two grenades, stepped to the front of the indentation and waited for Masters to throw the rocks. He did. Johnny jumped out and with a mighty heave threw the first grenade up at the shooter. Before he could throw the second one his body was torn apart by 20 bullets.

The grenade exploded, causing debris and rocks to fall from the cliff. Some of it fell into the indentation causing the squad members to jump out of the way to avoid being hit.

Willy, who had been watching the whole incident in silence, yelled "Ole, Ole," as he ran out to try to retrieve Johnny's body. The gunner, who had not been hit by the grenade, fired again.

Gordon sat stone-faced as he looked at the bodies of his two best buddies lying in an ever-increasing pool of blood. The memory of the three of them leaving the House of the Setting Sun in Honolulu flashed in his mind. He clearly saw Goldie standing holding on to Johnny and saying, "If the three of you come back through Honolulu together, I will give all three of you a night on the house." Again and again, *all three of you,* raced through his mind. He wished he could go out and retrieve Willy's harmonica.

Gordon put his hand on his holster and looked at Masters. "No, it wouldn't help," he said to himself. Instead, he looked up to the cliff where the gunner was shooting and then he leaned over to Stephan and whispered a plan.

Gordon slipped out from under the overhang between bursts of gunfire. Stephan then started throwing whatever he could get his hands on out into the open area in front of their position. The gunner fired over Gordon as he ran to the base of the cliff. He backed up tight against the wall, knowing the gunner could not see him. Now, all he had to do was climb the wall. He moved a few yards over to where the cliff was not so steep, hoping he was still out of sight. He hung his M-1 over his shoulder, pushed it back, unsnapped the holster holding his 45mm pistol, and slowly started his climb. His climb took an eternity of three minutes. He expected at any moment to look up and see the gunner poised to shoot him. As he reached a point just below the gunner, he discovered a slight, level indentation in the cliff on which he could get his whole-body level. He could then spring up and get some shots off at the gunner. As he pushed his body one last time to get up on the level area he felt the strap of his M-1 slipping off his shoulder. He could not grab it without the risk of falling down the cliff. Luck was on his side as the gunner started firing again, covering the sound of his rifle falling.

Gordon took a deep breath, pulled out his 45mm pistol and said to himself, addressing the gun, "You're its baby. You got a job to do." He allowed himself a half-smile as he recalled the comments of the second lewy who gave the class in basic training on using the pistol. "This is the standard issue pistol. You can trust it to be accurate for about the amount of distance you can throw it. Other than that, don't rely on it for much else."

A new wave of adrenalin flowed through Gordon's body. Again, to himself, "It's show time. Time to get the job done."

He pushed himself up and sprang up the last 10 yards to the gunner's tripod. Suddenly, he was standing face-to-face with a Chinese boy about the same age as him, who jumped out from behind his gun and drew his pistol. For an instant that would be, a lifetime, the two teenagers placed together by powers much higher than themselves, carrying out the archaic and idiotic practice called war, looked into each other's eyes. The look was not fear, but of respect for a fellow warrior and compassion for what they were required to do. Both of them fired their pistols at the same time.

Chapter 25
February 1952

Larry left school early on leap year day, February 29. It was a Friday, and he had only one humanities class after lunch so he was in McGrath by 2 o'clock that afternoon. He had not heard from Gordon except for a letter in early December. In that letter he talked about shooting a North Korean soldier from the troop train which had probably saved several soldiers' lives. That got him a promotion to the rank of corporal. He also wrote how everything was in a holding pattern pending the outcome of the peace talks and that he was meeting with a chaplain about confessing to Ray's murder. However, Gordon had not included any direct statements that Larry could take to the county attorney to convince him to drop the charges against Eddie Johansson.

The trial was scheduled for April 2 so Larry was feeling the pressure to get something done. He decided not to wait any longer for Gordon's letter of confession.

As he thought about what needed to be done, he realized that he should tell Gordon's mother about Gordon's crime before he talked to the authorities. He didn't want her to find out from the newspapers.

Hello, stranger, this is a surprise. I didn't think you would stop and visit me with Gordon gone," Eleanor said as she invited Larry into the house. Then she stopped and with an apprehensive look on her face asked, "You haven't heard anything bad about him from Korea, have you? I worry every day that I will get some bad news. I think if Gordon did get killed, I would just give up, with Tommy's death and all."

"No, I haven't. Gordon wrote to me before Christmas. Maybe he wrote to you about being promoted to corporal?" Larry answered.

"Yaw, he shot that chink from the troop train. He always was a good shot when he hunted with his dad." Eleanor had to choke back the tears at the mention of Tommy. "Still drink coffee now that you are a hot shot college student?"

"More than before. Lot of late-night reading and cramming for tests," Larry said as he was thinking on how he could bring up the murder Gordon had committed.

Eleanor went into the kitchen and returned with a cup of coffee, a piece of cherry pie and a newspaper. "I made two pies from some canned cherry filling, but the kids don't like the taste. Hopefully, you will. If you do, I can send one home with you. I'm done with this Aitkin paper. Your folks may have one, but if you want this one to read on your own you can have it."

Larry tasted the pie and said, "Love this pie. Like the tart taste. Gladly take the extra one."

While taking a drink of coffee, he noticed the headline article in the paper.

MURDER TRIAL SET TO START ON APRIL SECOND

Without reading the article he was sure it was about Eddie Johansson's trial. As he pointed to the headline, Larry said, "Been following this murder trial? It's about the fisherman who got killed in his fish house on Mille Lacs."

Eleanor, who had just sat down with her coffee, quickly changed her posture. Her shoulders hunched forward, the rest of her body tightened and the look on her face changed from pleasant to a hard, angry look.

"No, not really. From what I read I always thought the wife did it."

Larry, at first taken aback by the sudden change in Eleanor's demeanor, then realized she knew about Tommy's plans to leave her for Molly. He also remembered that when he had seen the picture of Tommy's shipmates and recognized Roy Kelseltz's name, Eleanor had associated it with Molly. She had then figured out that Ray was Molly's husband.

Despite Eleanor's distress, Larry decided this was the time to tell her about Gordon. He may as well be direct.

"Mrs. Hass, neither Eddie Johansson nor Mrs. Kelseltz killed the fisherman. Gordon has confessed to me that he is the murderer.

Two minutes of total silence blanketed the room, which to Larry seemed like an hour. Eleanor stood, her whole body trembling and her face reddened, as she just stared at Larry.

"You liar, you damn liar! I was wondering why you stopped here in the middle of the afternoon. What? Just to tell me some crazy, outlandish, bizarre story about my son. What's the reason? Oh, I know.

You want to keep that motorcycle he gave you to keep while he is in Korea. Get the hell out of my house! Get the hell out of my house, you bastard! How many times have you sat at that table and ate supper here? Get out. Get out." The last few words Eleanor spoke were hardly audible due to her crying.

Larry had planned out just what he was going to say to Eleanor about how he had figured out Gordon was guilty. He also was going to tell her what Gordon had told him that last Sunday before he left for Korea. Now he didn't know what to say or do. Maybe he should leave. As he was deciding, he saw the brown sedan driving up the driveway through the window, a brown sedan with "U.S. Army" printed on the door.

Larry froze. His brain knew there was only one reason an Army staff car would be coming to Eleanor's house, but his would not allow him to process the truth. He watched as the driver, a staff sergeant and the captain, holding an envelope in his hand, exited the car. Larry turned and walked over to Eleanor who had ended her tirade and was now wailing loudly.

As he put his arms around her, he said, "Mrs. Haas, I am deeply sorry for telling you what I have just said. But I'm afraid you and I are about to receive the worst news possible."

Before Larry could say anything more, the captain knocked on the front door. Larry yelled, "Come in."

"Mrs. Haas, I'm Captain Harrison. I and Staff Sergeant McGuire are stationed at the Fort Snelling Army Reserve base in Minneapolis. We have the unfortunate duty of delivering this letter from President Truman." As he handed the letter to Eleanor the captain looked at Larry. "Are you Gordon's brother?"

"No, I am Gordon's best friend. I was just visiting Mrs. Haas when I saw you drive up. I assumed the worst and was trying to give Eleanor a little warning," Larry answered.

Eleanor was standing mute as she took the letter from the captain. She softly tossed the letter onto the dining room table without opening it. With a completely blank expression on her face she said, "Would you two officers care for any coffee and pie?" Without waiting for an answer, she turned and walked into her kitchen. The heart piercing screams then began.

"Is there any other family member home?" the captain asked Larry.

"No, I think Gordon's older brother is working in the Cities." Larry looked at his watch. "And I think his younger brother and sister will be home from school pretty soon."

"Are there any close relatives or a family minister we can call? I believe Mrs. Haas is in shock," the captain continued.

"Her brother-in-law lives a mile away. I'll call him," Larry said as he went to the phone. "I'm correct? That letter said Gordon was killed in Korea?"

The captain nodded his head yes.

After dialing one long ring for the local operator, who answered immediately, Larry said, "This is Larry Oien. Can you connect me to Si Haas, please?"

Within a minute Si answered, "Si here."

"Si, this is Larry Oien. I am at Eleanor's house. Can you come over as soon as possible? Two army officers are here. Gordon has been killed in Korea. Eleanor is in a state of shock."

"Claudette and I will be right over."

Luckily, they arrived before the two kids came home from school. Eleanor was moving around like a zombie. She had set out four cups of cold coffee and the whole pie on the table without any silverware or plates.

Claudette took over. She got Eleanor to sit down, made a pot of fresh coffee and set the table with plates and silverware. She met Lee and Linda, Gordon's two young siblings, at the door, gave them a strong hug and gently told them the sad news.

After everyone was gathered at the table Si picked up the letter and asked Eleanor permission to read it out loud.

Dear Mrs. Thomas Haas:

On behalf of all the citizens of the United States of America, I as President, herein extend sincere condolences to you, the mother of Corporal Gordon T. Haas. On February 23, 1952, Corporal Haas made the supreme sacrifice to his country when he was killed in combat in Korea. I personally, and all the freedom-loving citizens of this country, express our sincere condolences.

Harry S. Truman
President of the United States

As Si was reading, Larry was fighting hard to keep from breaking down and crying. When Si read, "*Was killed in combat,*" he lost the fight. Wailing loudly, with tears flowing, Larry put his head on the table as Claudette came to hug him. Si, upon finishing the letter, came and put his hand on Larry's shoulder. Larry's breakdown triggered hard crying from both Lee and Linda. Eleanor sat, stoically. No one spoke for several minutes.

"Gordon was a murderer," Eleanor broke the silence. Her blank look and stoic disposition did not change as she spoke. The words that were coming from her mouth sounded more like a prerecorded message from a tape within her body than words being spoken by a human person.

"Gordon was a murderer," Eleanor repeated.

"Mrs. Haas," Captain Harrison rose and took Eleanor's hand, "your son did kill three enemy soldiers during his brief time in Korea. All three of those instances saved the lives of fellow soldiers. The killings were an act of war and not murder."

The blank look on Eleanor's face hardened as she stared at the captain.

"I'm not talking about what happened in Korea."

Larry raised his head from the table and choking back his crying long enough to speak, said, "Mrs. Haas is talking about something she and I were discussing when you arrived. I believe it's best we don't talk about it anymore at this time."

As Si and Claudette exchanged looks of puzzlement, the captain said, "I believe that is a good idea. Sergeant McGuire and I need to return to our base. However, I do have additional information for the family. Sergeant McGuire, why don't you give Si the letter you have prepared with this information. Briefly what the letter says is that Corporal Haas' remains will be arriving at our base within seven to ten days. Sergeant McGuire will need to be notified as to which funeral home the family wants the remains to be delivered for preparation for burial. I have been informed that Sergeant Harp, who was Gordon's squad sergeant, will be accompanying the remains and will want to speak at the service. Of course, an honor guard unit from our command will be available if you decide to have a full military service. Sergeant Harp will provide you full details on Gordon's actions that resulted in his death. They were very heroic and saved the lives of his squad members.

After the captain and sergeant departed, Larry said, "I should go. So, I can help my dad with the evening milking."

He gave Eleanor a hug before he left. Her disposition changed as she warmly returned Larry's hug.

She whispered, "Thank you for being here. I wouldn't have been able to handle the news if I had been alone. I'm sorry for what I yelled just before the army officers came. Call it mother's intuition, but I have suspected that Gordon was the murderer for quite a while, the way he started drinking so hard with Melvin Smith. Also, I heard him planning with Melvin about hauling the firewood down to that bitch, Molly, who took both my husband and my son from me. I just refused to admit it to myself and didn't want to hear the truth when you told me."

Si walked Larry to his car. "O.K., tell me what that was all about?"

Larry looked at Si and said, "Please keep this completely confidential. For various reasons I suspected Gordon murdered the fisherman that was killed on Mille Lacs. The last day I saw Gordon before he left for Korea, he told me I was right."

"His name was Kelseltz, right? I didn't pay that much attention to the details of the murder, but was his wife Molly?"

Larry nodded his head, "Yes, did you know Tommy was planning on leaving Eleanor to marry her?"

"I did. Matter of fact, Molly came up to see me the fall before the murder. She was sure her brother-in-law had caused Tommy to go overboard. Took her over to see Arvin Berg and Hans Thompson. Just remembered, we met Gordon on the way. We stopped, and she asked him to bring her a load of firewood. Do you think she put Gordon up to the killing?"

"Don't know," Larry answered. "That will be up to the police to figure out.

Larry's mom was kneading bread dough when he got home. Without looking up she said, "You made good time coming home this weekend. Wasn't sure if you'd be home at all. When do your final tests start?"

"Finals are in two weeks. I skipped my Friday afternoon class. I had to talk to Gordon's mom about something important."

"You look terrible. Is there something wrong?" Larry's mom looked up at Larry for the first time since he had walked in the door.

"Gordon was killed last week in Korea." Larry started to cry again, as his mother came and embraced him.

"Terrible, terrible news," his mom said as she held his head on her shoulder. "Do you remember when your dog, Tricky, got killed chasing a car? You didn't believe you would ever get over her death. Time heals. Did you hear about it before you came home? Is that why you stopped at Eleanor's house?"

"No, I have something important to talk to you and Pa about. I have known since the day Gordon left for Korea that he killed the fisherman on Mille Lacs. Gordon was going to write a letter to me with a full confession, but since I haven't received it yet, I plan on talking to the sheriff this weekend. I decided to stop and tell his mom about it first. While I was talking to her two army officers came with a letter from President Truman. Eleanor went into a state of shock. I called Si. He and Claudette came over."

"Pa is out in the barn. He starts the milking early now that he is alone." Larry's mom stepped back. "You have been carrying this burden for a long time, haven't you?"

Larry broke down again as his mom got a kitchen wash cloth for him to use to wipe away his tears. "Yes, I have. I keep thinking about the three guys from Isle sitting in jail. I had rationalized I needed something stronger than just my word. That's why I waited for Gordon's written confession."

"He was your best friend." Larry's mom, for the first time since he was eight years old and got slightly hurt falling out of a tree, kissed him on the cheek.

"I'll change clothes and go to the barn. I'll talk to Pa about this while I help finish the milking." Larry wiped away some final tears.

Sheriff Hewitt arrived at Oien's farm at 11 o'clock, Saturday morning. Larry's dad had called him as soon as he heard Larry's story.

"Smells just like a bakery in here." All of Larry's sisters were gone this Saturday so his mom was baking alone. She had six loaves of bread and two trays of biscuits made.

"Sit up at the dining room table. I have hot biscuits, blueberry jam and coffee for you while Larry tells you, his story. If you have time, I will be making venison steak, corn, mashed potatoes and gravy for dinner," Larry's mom said.

"Barring any triple murder in the county, I'll have time." The sheriff took in another whiff of the aroma.

"Sheriff, my son has a story to tell you about Gordon Haas. Unfortunately, Gordon was killed in Korea last week," Albert said.

"I'm sorry to hear that. You and Gordon were really close, weren't you?" The sheriff turned to Larry.

"Yes, we were," Larry answered.

"You said on the phone that you had information that would clear the three current defendants. I'll be glad to hear that information. I have never felt we had any good evidence they committed the murder. Of course, Virgil Larsen's testimony as part of his plea bargain may carry a lot of weight with the right jury. The county attorney is adamant he will get a conviction. He wants it bad. He is up for reelection." The sheriff finished his first biscuit.

Larry started with the suspicions that first arose from Gordon entering the fish house the night they were on the lake as well as from the black fisherman's description of someone walking away from the fish house that looked like a bear. Next, he described looking at Tommy Haas' book about the Johnathan Stevenson and seeing that Roy Kelseltz was a shipmate of Tommy, along with Mrs. Haas' reaction when he mentioned that it was the same last name as the victim. He told the sheriff about him and Ronnie meeting with Molly during the state basketball tournament and her reaction when they told her they were friends of Gordon. Then he talked about Gordon's heavy drinking since the night of the murder and the way Gordon attacked him at his going away party. Finally, he recounted Gordon's last words to him, telling him he was right about his suspicions and that he would send a letter with a written confession.

The sheriff finished his second biscuit. "Well, I guess we know who the killer was. You said Gordon was going to mail you a letter with a written confession. Do you have it?"

"No, I don't. I have a letter where he wrote that he was meeting a chaplain and was confessing to him," Larry answered.

"Do you think Gordon may have written one before he got killed?" The sheriff licked jelly off his fingers.

"Don't know. There's usually a three-week time gap between the date his letters were written and when they're delivered. I guess they're inspected or something." As Larry answered the sheriff, the realization he may have received the last letter ever from Gordon jarred his composure. "Excuse me, sheriff, I need a little break."

Larry went upstairs to his room and found the last letter in his carrying case. He took it out and held onto it for a few minutes. Then he got up to take it down to show the sheriff. As he was about to leave his room he saw a picture from his high school yearbook. It was a picture of Ronnie, Gordon and him, clearly intoxicated, with their arms around each other's shoulders. Below the picture was the inscription "The Three Blind Mice." Larry lost it. He fell on his bed facedown, crying uncontrollably.

When Larry didn't return, his dad went up to his room to check on him. As he was being comforted by his dad, Larry talked about Gordon giving him the bike, again recalling when Gordon attacked him at the going away party, and the conversation the next day. He told his dad about how he looked back in his rearview mirror and had the thought that he may never see Gordon again. Talking about all these memories helped Larry regain his composure.

"Here is the last letter from Gordon." Larry held the letter up for his dad. "We shouldn't keep the sheriff waiting any longer."

The sheriff wasn't waiting impatiently. Larry's mom had set out the food for dinner and told the sheriff not to wait for Larry and his dad. The sheriff did what he was told. He was working on his second helping of venison steak and of mashed potatoes when the two came down from Larry's room.

Larry handed him the letter and said, "This is the letter where Gordon wrote about confessing to the chaplain."

"Well, it's clear to me Gordon was the one who killed the fisherman. But I should warn you. The county attorney, Ryan, may try to dispute this evidence. Not indicting the right suspect makes both him and me look bad to the voters. As I told you before I'm retiring, so I'm not worried what the voters think about my performance. Ryan will worry and he might try to put the blame on you for not coming forward sooner. Your dad and I talked about whether or not you'll be in trouble because you didn't. I told him I am the one who would recommend bringing any charges against you, and I won't. It's clear to me that all you had were suspicions."

While Larry was listening to the sheriff, he began thinking about how the news of Gordon being a murderer would affect his chances of being recognized as a war hero. Upon hearing how County Attorney Ryan worried about bad publicity, Larry started to form a plan in his head.

"Sheriff, when do you plan to talk to the county attorney about Gordon?" Larry asked.

"Sometime this week. I know he is trying a bank robbery case. The defendant is the main suspect in the robbery of the Hill City State Bank. Why do you ask?"

"Well, I would like to join you when you talk to him. I have one more week of classes and then it is finals week. All my tests are at the end of the week so I could come up to Aitkin a week from Monday. Maybe Gordon's letter of confession will come before then," Larry said.

Chapter 26
March 1952

Before going back to school Larry stopped at Si's house to give Si his phone number and ask him to call when he found out the date Gordon's remains would arrive.

On Tuesday night Larry received the call from Si. The body was going to be delivered to the Mora funeral home on Friday morning and the family was meeting at 2 o'clock that afternoon. Larry met with his humanities class professor and told him about his best friend being killed and explaining that why he missed his last class and would miss the final class.

The professor said, "It's a shame so many of our young men are dying because of the war. I will not only excuse you from the last class, but will let you miss the final test, if you write a paper on how the tragedy affected you, your friend's family and anyone else you feel should be included. Turn the paper in when you return from the quarter break."

Larry arrived at the funeral home just after 1:30. Sgt. Harp was sitting alone with the open casket reading some notes he had made on what he wanted to tell the family.

"Hello, I'm Larry Oien. I've been Gordon's best friend since we were in fifth grade. The family hasn't arrived yet?" Larry walked up to the casket. Gordon was attired in his army dress uniform with his name tag, reading Corporal Gordon Haas, on his chest.

As Larry began to cry, Sgt. Harp walked up to him, placed a hand on his shoulder and said, "Go ahead and cry for the loss of your friend, but know you are also crying for the loss of a real hero. If he had not sacrificed his life, I and eleven other members of our squad would also have been brought home in a casket. After the family arrives and has a chance to mourn, I will tell all of you the whole story. If you want to be alone with your friend for a little while I can step out of the room."

"No, I'm glad you are here with me. I'm sure I would break down entirely if I was alone." Larry reached into the casket and placed his hand on Gordon's hand.

"While we are alone, I will give you this letter Gordon wrote to you while we were holding the hill on which Gordon was killed. He didn't get a chance to mail it and when it was determined that I would be allowed to accompany him home, our commanding officer gave me permission to bring it in person. I also have a letter for Mrs. Eleanor Haas. I assume she is his mother. Then I have a letter for a Mrs. Molly Kelseltz. Will she be attending the services this week?"

"No," Larry said quickly. "I'm glad you mentioned that before Gordon's mom came. It would have upset her to know Gordon wrote to Molly. She won't be here this week, so if it is not any trouble for you, can you mail it to her?"

"Sure," Sgt. Harp said. "Oh, I almost forgot. I also have this letter to you from Gordon which he had given to our chaplain to hold in the event he was killed." Sgt. Harp took the letter out of his carrying case.

Before Larry could open the letters, Eleanor, all of Gordon's siblings, Si and Claudette and their two sons joined Larry and Sgt. Harp. Larry and the sergeant stepped back to allow the family a chance to view the casket and grieve.

After the group left the funeral home they went to the Main Street Café, where they got a table in the back banquet room. Sgt. Harp described how the squad was pinned down by the gunner and would have been destroyed by the enemy assault which started half an hour after Gordon killed the gunner. In detail, he recounted the events before Gordon scaled the hill and how the squad had watched in awe at his superhuman effort to climb the hill. He explained since that, the pistol shots happened simultaneously the squad members were not sure who had been shot.

"I and several other squad members started throwing rocks and some of our equipment out onto the trail in the gunner's line of fire. When this didn't bring any more firing we were sure Gordon had killed the gunner and would be coming back down the hill, maybe carrying the automatic rifle. I took a chance and stepped out from under the overhang. With no one shooting at me I ordered the squad to evacuate, called in the force that had been assembled at the bottom of the hill to attempt an assault on the gunner and rushed up to find Gordon. I found his body lying face down next to the body of the gunner with their pistols on the ground in front of them. The assault force moved quickly up the hill and recovered Gordon's and the other four dead soldiers' bodies. Only moments after everyone was out of harm's way, the mortar fire from the oncoming enemy assault started raking the hill, hitting the overhang that was our shelter." Sgt. Harp was crying as he finished his account of Gordon's heroism.

"What was Lt. Masters doing after Gordon scaled the hill?" Si asked. "It sounds like you were making all the decisions."

Masters had a complete mental breakdown after he saw Johnny and Willy get shot. He was taken away as soon as we were back in our area. I suspect he will get treatment and then will be given a medical discharge," Harp replied.

"Will Gordon receive any medals for his action?" Dennis, Gordon's older brother, asked.

"The battalion commander has interviewed everyone involved with the action—well, of course besides Masters, and is preparing a recommendation he that receive the Congressional Medal of Honor. Of course, I supported that recommendation in the strongest possible terms." Sgt. Harp answered Dennis but he looked at Eleanor. "You had a very brave son, Mrs. Haas. He saved my life."

How long will you be staying with us?" Si asked the sergeant.

"I was going to ask if you have scheduled a memorial service, yet? I certainly want to have an opportunity to give a eulogy at the service. I was scheduled to rotate out of Korea at the end of this month, but when this happened, I requested approval to serve as the honor guard for Gordon. I will have put my 20 years in with the army in May so I am planning to retire then."

"Well, we have an extra room and you can stay with us for as long as you like. We were talking on the way down about a date for the service, probably a week from tomorrow. We are planning to try to have it at the school. We certainly want you to speak," Si told the sergeant.

"That will be good. I have an old army buddy who lives in Duluth. We were together from Normandy to the Battle of the Bulge. I hope to spend a few days with him before the service."

"Sergeant, I would like to meet with you for a while tomorrow," Larry said. "I have a meeting on Monday concerning Gordon. I'll explain tomorrow why I would like you to come with me to this meeting."

"Sure, my time is your time," the sergeant answered.

When Larry got to his car, he opened the letter Gordon had written from the hill. It told about how he had shot the young Chinese boy who had charged him with the bayonet, how cold it was on the hill, his ever-increasing companionship with Willy and Johnny, and the stupidity of Masters. Larry then opened the letter Gordon had left with the chaplain. It was a full confession setting forth the details of the night of the murder, as well as how Gordon had gone back into the fish house the night the sheriff had left the boys on guard duty, knowing his fingerprints were in the house. The letter also detailed the background of how he had learned that Ray Kelseltz may have been responsible for his dad's death. Gordon reiterated that he went to the fish house to confront Ray and to find out if what he had heard was true, but when Ray threw the ice pick at him he lost all control. Again, Gordon didn't implicate Molly. He only stated she told him about her conviction that Roy and Ray had planned the killing of Tommy and the location of Ray's fish house.

On Sunday Larry met with Sgt. Harp and had him read Gordon's confession letter. He explained the history of the murder including that three innocent men were in jail for the crime Gordon committed. He then outlined his plan for having the county attorney drop the charges against the three-current suspects without publicizing Gordon's confession.

"Mr. Oien," County Attorney Ryan said to Larry's dad, "I guess we haven't actually met, but I have seen your picture on the courthouse wall from when you were a county commissioner. I know my dad did legal work for you and spoke highly of you. I also know the Sheriff and you are old friends. He said you are the reason he gets 85% of the vote from the southern part of the county. I've been planning to ask for your support in the election this fall. Who are the other two gentlemen with you? Is this one your son?" Ryan nodded toward Larry.

"Glad to meet you," Albert shook Ryan's hand. "Yes, this is my son Larry. He is a freshman at the 'U'. This is Sergeant Harp. He's from Frankfort, Kentucky. My son will explain why he is here in Minnesota."

"I understand this is in relation to the murder case on Mille Lacs?" Ryan said with a puzzled look

"That's right," Larry took over the meeting. "I think I have sufficient information for you to drop the charges against the three suspects you have in custody. However, before I provide you that information, I want to get your assurance that the identity of the actual guilty party will not be disclosed, at least not for several years. That's where Sergeant Harp comes in. He is here to tell you how the guilty party is now a deceased war hero."

Sgt. Harp proceeded to tell, in a few less details, the same story about Gordon's heroics he had told the family.

After he finished, Ryan looked at Larry and said, "I assume that the information you have will implicate Gordon. I don't know how this war story relates to the information, but just to warn you, the information will have to be really strong. I just interviewed Virgil Larsen again this weekend and I believe his testimony is solid. I feel pretty confident about getting a conviction."

"Virgil Larsen is a 'no-good save-my-own-ass liar.' I would think the defense lawyer has lined up several witnesses to testify to that fact." Larry was forceful.

Ryan's face reddened as he was taken aback by Larry's assessment of his star witness. "O.K., let me see your evidence."

Larry handed him the letter of confession.

"How long have you had this letter?" Ryan asked.

"Sgt. Harp brought it with him from Korea. He gave it to me Friday," Larry answered.

"Is this the first you knew that Gordon might be the murderer?" Ryan was still looking at the letter.

"No, I had my suspicions for a while. In November, the week before Gordon left for Korea, Gordon tried to beat me up at his going away party because he knew I suspected him. The next day he told me I was right but he would send this confession letter." Larry was ready to defend his actions.

"So, you withheld evidence for three months?" Ryan knew he had made a mistake and was looking for a scapegoat.

"Sir, I would like to point out that the only evidence I had was something you have had since the murder. I did figure out the relationship between the victim and Gordon's dad, something maybe you would have figured out if you had investigated the case a little harder, instead of rushing to judgement about Eddie Johansson." Larry responded.

"I guess Larry's referring to Gordon's fingerprints being the only ones in the fish house besides the victims," the sheriff interjected. "You can blame me for that mistake. If my ass hadn't been so cold, I wouldn't have left you three boys to watch the fish house. Of course, none of us knew at the time we had the murderer right at the crime scene."

"I, for one, am glad no one figured out Gordon's guilt before he left for Korea," Sgt. Harp said. "I and at least 10 other soldiers would probably be dead today if he had been arrested."

"Well, I suppose we can sit here all day and talk about what would have happened if something else would have happened, but let's talk about how we are going to proceed from here. Now tell me—Mr. Smart Ass—how I can dismiss charges against three men and say I know who the murderer is without identifying the murderer." Ryan was clearly smarting from Larry pointing out the inadequacy of his investigation.

"Two people," Larry said, "Virgil Larsen and Molly Kelseltz, are the key. You can issue a press release stating you have verifiable information that Virgil Larsen was lying under oath and, based on this information, you have made a motion to the court to dismiss all charges against Eddie Johansson and Irving Moss. You should charge Virgil with perjury. Then you can say there is an ongoing investigation of the spouse of the victim and her brother-in-law regarding their role in the events leading up to the murder. Therefore, you cannot disclose the name of the deceased's actual killer without affecting the investigation. Matter of fact, since I'm studying journalism, I have prepared a proposed press release." Larry took a typed sheet from his notebook and gave it to Attorney Ryan.

PRESS RELEASE: 11:00 AM, March 8, 1952

Today I am filing several motions with the district court to dismiss all charges now pending against Edward Johansson and Irving Moss in regard to the murder of Raymond Kelseltz on January 5th 1951. In addition, I am dismissing the one count of second degree manslaughter and filing one count of perjury by lying under oath, in addition to the current count of robbery by breaking and entering, against Virgil Larsen.

These motions are based on information received by this office this morning including a detailed confession by the deceased assailant who attacked the victim in a rage resulting in the victim's death. Due to an investigation into the possibility other persons may have assisted or hired the assailant and into the possible relationship of this crime to another crime, the identity of the deceased assailant cannot be disclosed at this time.

The new charge of perjury being filed against Virgil Larsen is for his statements, under oath, given when he was arranging a plea bargain with this office. These statements, which are known to be false statements based on the information received this morning, were the basis for the indictment and charges filed against both Edward Johansson and Irving Moss. Without these false statements, these two individuals would not have been charged and the investigation would have continued leading to information received this morning being discovered at an earlier date.

Aitkin County Attorney's Office
James A Ryan, County Attorney

"Beautiful, just beautiful. I apologize for calling you a smart ass. You're just smart. You should consider law school after you are done with your undergraduate degree." Ryan buzzed his secretary and said "Type this press release on our letterhead and try to get all three defense attorneys on the phone. If possible, set up a conference call." As the group got up to leave, Ryan said, "Sheriff, can you stay for a few minutes? Sgt. Harp, thank you for being here and thank you for your service. I am sure you are a war hero in your own right. Mr. Oien, I'm sure you know this, but you should be very proud of your son."

Then he turned to Larry. "I'm sure you had a real moral decision to make about whether to come forth with what you knew or not. You would have been turning in your best friend. I would like to know what you would have done if Gordon hadn't been killed?"

"I was at Gordon's mother's house the day she got the news about his death. I had just told her that I knew Gordon was the murderer and was planning on coming to discuss this with you. If Gordon hadn't been killed, I would have been here last Monday without the letter of confession. By the way, you mentioned meeting the voters in south Aitkin County. Gordon's memorial service is a week from this Saturday. Maybe you and Sheriff Hewitt would come as representatives of the county. Being supportive of a war hero is always a good political move."

Ryan slapped Larry on the back. "You better get a law degree and go into politics."

Plans for the service had been completed, but on the Thursday before the Saturday service, one of the fabled state tournament storms dumped thirteen inches of snow on McGrath. On Friday a massive effort by the state and county highway departments cleared all of the roads leading to McGrath and the VFW membership cleared the high school parking lot and the cemetery lot as well as the driveways and burial site.

The final arrangements were for the memorial service to be held at the school. An honor guard from the Army Reserve in Minneapolis, led by Sgt. Harp would escort the coffin into the service, followed by the family, including Ronnie and Larry at the request of Eleanor, then Howard Hanson, the state senator for McGrath, Sheriff Hewitt, County Attorney Ryan, and the entire VFW membership would make up the official procession.

After the invocation by the minister, Carl Peterson, who was a decorated wounded veteran from World War II and now the commanding officer of the VFW post, would lead into a brief ceremony by the VFW honoring a fallen comrade. Then Sgt. Harp would speak, followed by Larry, giving the final reflections, at the request of Eleanor.

Larry walked to the podium, and as he looked out at the full gymnasium, he realized this was the first time he had ever given a speech.

He took a deep breath and remembered all the crazy things Gordon and he had done without worrying about the outcome. He started his speech.

Senator Hanson, County Attorney Ryan, Sheriff Hewitt, Commander Peterson, Sgt. Harp, Ronnie, Eleanor and family, and all the rest of you who have come to honor a war hero: It is very difficult for me to talk about Gordon as a deceased war hero. The fact he died saving the lives of 12 of his comrades does make him a hero. However, it does not ease the pain of the fact that he died. He will never be here for me to talk to. He, Ronnie and I will never ride around the backroads listening to the radio, making sarcastic but friendly remarks about each other, talking about or sometimes actually having female companions with us, and doing things which may have been beyond what the law allowed.

As most of you know, I have seven biological brothers. For the last four years, I also had two soul brothers. Gordon, Ronnie and I spent a lot of good times together, but more importantly our times together allowed us to share feelings about changes in our lives as teen-agers in a world that is also changing fast and seems to be ever more dangerous. It allowed us to share secrets that will always be held confidential. It allowed us to talk about events, relationships and other people's actions that were important and beneficial to us, and ones that were difficult and hard for us to stomach.

Without condemning the community or anyone individually, for Gordon, hearing gossip that his dad had not died from being washed overboard off the ore carrier where worked, but instead jumped ship in some eastern city and abandoned him and the rest of his family caused him to become rebellious and anti-social.

This leads me to the main point of this speech. I would like all of us here to honor Gordon for being a war hero by being very careful of saying or spreading false statements or information about other people especially when you do not know if it is true or not. I believe many of you are Hank Williams fans, so heed the words from his song, "Be Careful of the Stones that You Throw." Not spreading these falsehoods is especially necessary when you are talking about people who are different from you, people who are of different nationalities, ethnic groups or of a different race. You should follow that old adage to not put down someone unless you have walked a mile in his shoes. If you do these things, you will honor Gordon.

Another way to honor Gordon is to be careful not to seek revenge. Revenge is most often more harmful to the one seeking it than the one being revenged. If you believe you have been harmed, make certain that the harm was real and was intentional. Then try to find out the reason for the other person's action and seek a resolution to the underlying cause of the dispute. If someone disagrees with you and demeans you, first make certain you were not wrong. Then talk to the other in a way that does not belittle them. If nothing else works, try forgiveness.

In the last letter Gordon wrote to me, only days before he made the decision to sacrifice his life to save his fellow soldiers, he told of how he was attacked by a Chinese soldier. The enemy apparently was out of ammunition and was trying to kill Gordon with his bayonet. Gordon turned quickly, and in the instant before he shot him, Gordon looked at the face of a boy younger than himself. He did not see any hate. The Chinese boy was his enemy, therefore he had to kill him. "But why was he my enemy?" Gordon had wondered.

As Jesus preached in The Sermon on the Mount, "Blessed are the peace-makers, for they shall be called the children of God. But I say unto you, that ye resist not evil but who shall smite thee on the right cheek, turn to him the other also. Ye heard that it hath been said thou shalt love thy neighbor and hate thine enemy. But I say unto you love your enemies, bless them that curse you, do good to them that hate you, and pray for them who despitefully use you and persecute you."

If you want to honor our war hero, seek to end violence in your heart, in your home, in your community, in your nation and in the world.

If you want to honor our war hero, work to achieve peace in your heart, in your home, in your community, in your nation and in the world.

If you want to honor our war hero, create love in your heart, in your home, in your community, in your nation and in the world.

Gordon, you have done your duty and given your life to save your comrades, but you have left a void in Ronnie's and my life.

I will always cherish the picture of the three of us in our high school yearbook where we were labeled as the Three Blind Mice. We may have been blind but we knew companionship and loyalty.

Larry tried hard to finish without crying but he failed. Through his tears, he ended "Gordon, I love you."

The audience was standing, some clapping but most crying. While everyone was watching Eleanor, her kids and Ronnie hugging Larry on the stage, no one noticed a woman with a pure Swedish look, long blonde hair, full blue eyes and a perfect model's body standing in the gymnasium doorway. She left quickly after Larry had finished his speech.

After the service a graveside ceremony was held with full military honors. As Larry walked up to the grave, he looked at the new gravestone for Tommy that Eleanor had recently bought at the insistence of her sons. The inscription read:

Thomas (Tommy) Haas
March 28, 1919 to October 27, 1946
Husband and Beloved Father

On the gravestone lay one single orchid.

Epilogue

Virgil Larsen's attorney and County Attorney Ryan agreed on a new plea bargain wherein he pled guilty to one count of perjury, which resulted in him serving 180 days in jail in addition to the time already served. However, Jay Nyquist, a close friend of Eddie Johansson, and the meanest and toughest dude in Isle, the last person someone would want to anger, put out the word that it wouldn't be safe for Virgil to live in Isle upon his release. "That son-of-a-bitch lied to save his own neck and almost caused Eddie to do hard time for life. He best not cross my path or he will be doing hard time for life in an intensive care unit," was the message Jay told a person who he knew would relay it to Virgil. Upon his release, Virgil, knowing Jay didn't make idle threats, moved to Redding, California. Two years later he was killed in a drug deal gone bad.

Eddie Johansson and Irving Moss both received a financial settlement for an undisclosed amount from Aitkin County after commencing a wrongful imprisonment lawsuit. Eddie used the money to start his own successful local construction company and Irving purchased a Mille Lacs Lake resort where he became one of the best fishing guides on the lake.

With Gordon's confession, the efforts by Steven Mitchell and the discovery of the inconsistency in his story, the FBI increased its efforts to obtain a confession from Roy Kelseltz that he intentionally knocked Tommy off the ship. He was interviewed nonstop at the FBI office in Duluth for 10 hours.

Roy didn't crack. However, he stopped frequently at different bars on his drive home to Buhl. Two miles from his house, on a flat dry road, he drove off the road at a high rate of speed and hit the largest tree in the area. He was killed instantly. Although he was very drunk, the highway patrol investigator believed it was suicide.

Ronnie, after losing Gordon to the war and Larry to new friends at the U, turned to the Lord. He became active in the local German Lutheran Church, took over the family farm which he expanded by buying several adjoining farms, and married Irene, with whom he had six children.

When Gordon's petition for being awarded the Congressional Medal of Honor was reviewed, his FBI file included his confession to the murder, so the petition was denied. He was awarded a Bronze Star.

Larry obtained his undergraduate degree in journalism from the University of Minnesota. His first job was with the *Wisconsin State Journal* in Madison. While working in Madison he obtained a Master's Degree from the University of Wisconsin. In addition to his other work, he wrote extensively about the primary election battle between Hubert Humphrey and John Kennedy. His articles won several journalism awards.

In 1963 he achieved his career goal when he was hired by the *New York Times*. From 1965 to 1973 he spent a considerable amount of time in Vietnam covering the war. His reporting of the inaccuracies in the government's reports on individual battles and the overall success of the war effort won him the disdain of President Johnson, a place on President Nixon's enemy list and a Pulitzer Prize.

It was 8:30 Sunday morning when Molly, cajoling Holly and Junior to get up and get dressed for church, heard the knock on the front door. Looking out the window she saw the Dakota County Sheriff's car, an Eagan Police car and two black sedans. She quickly picked up the phone and called the number she now knew by heart. A half-awake Steven answered the phone at the apartment he was living in since his divorce.

"I have a mob of police at my door," Molly said.

"Let them in but don't say anything to them. I'll be there within a half hour. After last night I'm a little tired, but I'll be there," Steven said.

"Mrs. Kelseltz, I don't know if you remember me? I'm Chief Rahn of the Eagan Police Department. I brought the news of your husband's death last year."

"I remember," Molly answered, coolly.

"This is Deputy Dahn of the Dakota County Sheriff's Department, and agents Woods and Eastman of the FBI." Chief Rahn motioned to the other three men who had pushed their way into the house past the chief.

"Mrs. Kelseltz, I have this search warrant issued by a judge which gives us the authority to search your house, car, and any other building or area on this property, as well as the right to obtain all your bank records for the last three years." Deputy Dahn handed a four-page document to Molly.

"I was going to church with my sister. I need to call her and tell her we are not going to be there." Molly took the warrant without looking at the document.

"We prefer you don't make any phone calls," Agent Eastman said. "While the other three officers are conducting the search, I would like to interview you. I have some questions we would like to clear up, both about the death of Thomas Haas and your deceased husband, Raymond."

Molly turned and said to Holly and Junior, "In the kitchen, kids. I'll make some breakfast." As she was shutting the kitchen door she said to Agent Eastman, "I have nothing to say."

Eastman conferred with the others and decided he would aid in the search. If something incriminating turned up, they would arrest Molly and take her downtown to the FBI offices for questioning. If nothing was found and she still refused to talk, they would take her downtown anyway.

As they were finishing their plans, Steven walked in with his law clerk. After talking to Molly for a few minutes and getting the warrant, he asked Chief Rahn, "Is Mrs. Kelseltz under arrest?"

The chief without any hesitation said, "No."

"Good, my law clerk will take her and the children to her sister's so they can go to church. I will stay here and observe the search. If you plan on taking property out of the house, please properly document what is being removed and provide me a copy of the documentation. I noted your request for the banking statements. I will have them delivered to whichever office you want by 11 o'clock, Tuesday morning. Chief Rahn, given you knew I was representing Mrs. Kelseltz, I'm surprised you needed to conduct this search at eight o'clock Sunday morning without giving me notice. I'll be in the kitchen working on some files if you have any questions for me." As Steven turned to walk away, he heard Agent Eastman quietly say, "Bastard." He didn't respond

When Steven left the room, his clerk took Holly and Junior to his car. Molly turned to Chief Rahn and asked, "Am I free to go?"

"Yes," Chief Rahn answered.

"One minute," Agent Eastman said. "Let me look in your purse."

He found nothing in the small purse Molly was carrying. No one noticed the purse Holly had carried out, which contained the letter Gordon had written to Molly.

The search didn't turn up any evidence linking Molly to Gordon's actions or otherwise connecting her to the murder. The review of the bank accounts didn't reveal any payments to Gordon except for a check in November of 1950 in the amount of $80.00. "Firewood" was written in the notation line. The bank account analysis did show payments to Steven Mitchell's law firm in a total amount of $4,298.00 for legal fees and costs. If the investigators could have had access to the law firm's banking records, which of course they didn't, they would have found a check to McNamara's Motorcycle Sales and Repair, Inc. in the amount of $1,298.00 marked "Costs - Thomas Haas Murder investigation."

Three months after the house search, the Dakota County Attorney's office notified Steven Mitchell that, barring discovery of additional evidence, Molly was no longer a subject of an investigation. Two months later Steven and Molly flew to Reno and got married.

Several months later, while the new couple relaxed in bed after a mutually satisfying love making session, Molly kissed Steven on the ear and whispered, "Oh, honey I am so happy. I never believed I would be this happy again after Tommy got killed and all the things that happened since. So, if ever you are not happy with me please tell me directly so I can deal with your unhappiness. Please don't cheat on me or feel you have to do things behind my back."

Steven sat up in bed, leaned on one elbow, looked Molly in her eyes with a mischievous grin on his face and said, "Don't worry sweetheart, knowing what I know, I would never, ever, do anything to cross you or cause you to be upset or angry with me."

ABOUT THE AUTHOR

Paul Simonson grew up on a small dairy farm six miles from Mille Lacs Lake, the youngest of twelve children. After graduating from McGrath High School in 1960, the University of Minnesota with an accounting degree, and William Mitchell College of Law, cum laude, he practiced as a business lawyer, CPA, and tax accountant. A lifelong interest in books and literary matter, including representing five used books sellers, led him to write *Murder on the Lake*, his first novel.